Aventurine
on the
Border

Also by Anne Britting Oleson

The Springs

Aventurine and the Reckoning
Aventurine on the Bailgate

Aventurine on the Border

AN AVENTURINE MORROW THRILLER

Anne Britting Oleson

Encircle Publications
Farmington, Maine U.S.A.

Encircle editor: Cynthia Brackett-Vincent

Cover and book design: Deirdre Wait

Author photo by Rosalie S. C. Bowman

Published by:

Encircle Publications, LLC
PO Box 187
Farmington, ME 04938

info@encirclepub.com
http://encirclepub.com

For Jim Pike:

A beloved man

who knew me for two-thirds of my life,

who witnessed all my idiocies in that time,

and who loved me anyway.

That is true friendship.

Part I:

The Kingdom of Hay

One

All the chairs on the back deck at the pub on Castle Street were stacked up against the rear fence; the tables were stripped of their umbrellas and stood around sadly in the sideways rain, waiting for custom that wouldn't come outside until the warmer months. Aventurine sighed and retraced her steps to the bar, where the boy—young enough to be her son, or her nephew, or something—knifed off the foam and set her pint on the mat.

"*Diolch*," she said.

"Something from the menu, then?" he asked. In English, because, as hard as she tried with her Welsh, her non-native-speaker status was obvious the moment she opened her mouth.

"I'm waiting for someone," she told him, smiling ruefully. He was really an endearing young person, reminding her very much of Lance. She tapped her card on the proffered machine.

"I'm here when you're ready." He shook his thick hair back from his brow.

Aventurine was drawn to the wood burner, and, ducking under a low beam with a notice that advised her to mind her head, chose a little two-top tucked in the corner next to it. She settled her pint on a coaster and slid into a chair beneath a still life. Absently, she picked up the second coaster and rolled it back and forth on its edge across the blond wood tabletop.

Micheline was late. She had chosen to sleep in rather than wander around the little shops in Back Fold. It was worrying. Micheline had never been one to experience a prolonged depression, but then again, neither had Paul, before the death of his father. Now Paul was off with Lance in Italy, but his burgeoning independence in dealing with his grief had removed the need for Mick to be his prop. Aventurine felt as though she were watching her sister collapse before her eyes. Sleeping late, sometimes into the afternoon: something Micheline had never done before.

Aventurine sighed and lowered her head into her hand. Mick needed to see someone, a counselor or therapist. She'd made sure Paul had talked to a professional, but had not, to Avi's knowledge, seen one herself. How hard should Aventurine push?

They'd just want me to take antidepressants. Avi could hear the protest in her sister's voice, just as she'd heard almost the same thing from Paul that afternoon in the summer on Westminster Bridge. It was the same protest she herself had made to her own therapist occasionally over the years. Well, depression did run in families, didn't it? Maybe it was finally showing up in theirs.

Fleetingly, Aventurine wondered how Nicola Hallsey felt about therapy and antidepressants. Then she bit her lip and shoved that thought away. She couldn't think about Nicola, their erstwhile half-sister, right now.

She downed half of the brown ale in one gulp.

When she opened her eyes, the door had swung back and Micheline entered from the street, throwing off the hood of her green rain jacket. She wiped her feet and looked around. Avi raised a hand, even though only one other table was occupied at this miserable noontime.

Mick nodded, conferred for a moment with the young barman, then came to the table bearing a pint similar to Avi's, and a menu. She shed her jacket and slipped into the opposite chair, her eyes lowered and with bruisy circles beneath them.

"Did you get some rest?" Aventurine asked.

"A little."

They both knew that was a lie.

"You haven't had breakfast. You must be starving."

Micheline made a deprecating face. "Not really." She moved her pint to the coaster Avi had rolled toward her, then pushed those aside to examine the menu. She frowned. Aventurine wondered what she was actually seeing on the card in front of her. Probably not much.

"Get some soup. I'm going to have the roasted vegetable salad."

"Order for me, will you?" Micheline rubbed her pale face with both hands. She seemed unable to settle, though her movements were sluggish. "I'm going to the ladies' room."

Aventurine watched her retreating back, feeling the twisting in her chest: what she would give to make things right for her twin sister. Because Mick's pain was her own; their feelings had been intertwined since birth. Before birth. She drained the rest of her pint, and took the empty glass up to the bar.

"*Ga i'r salad llysiau rhost? A peth dwr, plîs?*" she asked, stumbling over her pronunciation. "*A chawl y dydd i'm chwaer?*"

"Sure enough," said the barman. He winked.

"I heard from Paul after you left this morning," Micheline said. She hadn't touched her pint. She'd pushed the bowl of soup, nearly untouched, to the side. High color burned in her pale cheeks. She looked feverish.

Aventurine set her fork down. "How is he? What did he have to say?"

The young man came to check the fire in the burner next to them, and Micheline waited to answer until he'd shoved a log inside and gone away again.

"He's—okay. Italy seems to be good for him."

"Or Lance is."

Mick shrugged noncommittally. "Or Lance."

Aventurine let out a breath. "Mick, you need to give that boy a chance. He saved us. He genuinely cares for Paul. And if Paul reciprocates, Lance will be a fixture for a while." She didn't repeat Genevieve's words of the morning after that dreadful night on the York walls, that Lance and Paul would be connected for life now.

Again the shrug. "I know. Maybe if I have a chance to get to know him better. I didn't get to make a cross-country drive with Lance, not like you did. It would have been nice had they not immediately run off to Italy together; it would have been nice if they'd spent more time with me."

The wound was still, obviously, open. Aventurine knew that; the wound was still open for her as well. That Paul had found out about his parentage as he had, and that he had yet to forgive either of them for the secret they'd kept from him all his life.

"He couldn't. We—you—had to let him go off to work through his feelings in the best way he knew how."

"You sound like Genevieve when you talk like that," Micheline said impatiently. She took up a spoonful of soup and blew on it, though it was probably cool enough by now. Then she set the spoon down again. Her hands and wrists, Avi noticed, were startlingly bony.

"I wish." Aventurine speared a mushroom with her fork, and dragged it through a puddle of dressing. "So what did he have to say?" Paul had not called her. She tasted the bitterness of that at the back of her throat. She had heard nothing from him since the single picture he'd sent while she was in Lincoln. She put the mushroom in her mouth, trying to erase the taste of disappointment.

Another spoonful of soup, lifted, tasted, then the spoon returned to the bowl. "He's coming back here," Mick said. "With Lance. For Christmas."

"Here?"

There was a barely perceptible tightening of Micheline's jaw. "To the UK. To York. To Genevieve."

Not to either of them. Not to his mother, nor to his—mother. *His aunt*, she corrected herself sternly.

The bitterness had turned to bile. Aventurine fought it back, tinged as it was with guilt. She put a hand on her sister's arm. "I'm sorry, Mick."

That shrug. This time barely a lift of the shoulders, as though Mick was too tired to do any more. "It's okay. Genevieve to him is safe. She's in control."

That she was.

And there were all the things Genevieve wasn't telling Aventurine: another surprising source of bitterness. Paul and Lance had been issued an invitation for the holidays? And had apparently accepted? Not only was the old spy secretive, but she seemed to revel in her secrets.

"Has she found out anything more for you?" Aventurine asked. Suddenly the pumpkin and the seeds of the salad looked sad and unattractive. Her stomach rebelled at the thought of eating any more. The water glass was still half full, so she took it up and drank deeply. "About—Shep?"

Aventurine was treading as lightly as she knew how, but Micheline still looked stricken at the mention of her husband's name. Mick bit her lower lip and shook her head. When she met Avi's glance for the merest second before dropping her own, her eyes were damp.

"No," she whispered, as though strangling. "Nothing."

Still, what had Micheline hoped Genevieve would find out? That was something that puzzled Aventurine more each time she thought about it. The *Máquina*. The wreckage—flotsam near where the sailboat had last made contact. But no body. No Shep. And even though Micheline had mentioned making arrangements for a memorial service, it would seem that she had not quite extinguished the tiny flame of hope that burned deep inside her.

He's gone, Aventurine wanted to say to her. Almost wanted to shake her. *Shep's gone.*

She tightened her grip on her sister's arm. "I'm sorry, Mick," she repeated. Because there didn't really seem to be anything else to say.

Two

The rain had lessened from sideways sheets to a miserable drizzle by the time they'd finished lunch and returned to Castle Street. They turned toward the castle itself, the pavement uneven and slick under their feet. Aventurine left her hood down, and when she glanced sideways at her sister, noting the fine beading of rain on Mick's bangs, she knew her own hair would be netted in just the same way. The air was warm enough that it was only rain, however, not ice, and not snow. She looked off in the direction of the Black Mountains, hidden from view by the brick and stone buildings flanking the street: perhaps there would be snow on the peaks. She didn't really know what winter in the Border Country was like.

"Let's go look at the Honesty Bookshop," she suggested.

Micheline said nothing, but followed Aventurine along the street. Past the estate agent's, past the lower entrance to the Back Fold. While Avi glanced about curiously, Mick kept her head down. The streets were empty. On more pleasant days, Aventurine knew, the Back Fold would be crowded with shops strewing their wares nearly haphazardly onto the pavement: shelves of crystals, totes of teacups and saucers catching the eye. Today, winter approaching, everything in Hay-on-Wye was tucked under cover, buttoned up tightly against the atrocious weather. There was a loneliness to it: a town sullenly turning its back on them. Despite the rain, Avi slowed her pace, looking into secretive windows, reading signs; at her side, Micheline moved listlessly, uninterested in anything. Her hands were balled in her jacket pockets.

At the gateway in the stone wall, they turned into the motte of the castle, from which the stairs rose to the castle itself; these were new, not the rickety narrow ones Avi remembered from the last time she had visited. At the top, the great door was closed. To the left and right, the covered bookshelves stretched along the inside of the stone walls.

They were alone, no one else browsing in the Honesty Bookshop. Aventurine paused at the sign over the change box and was pleased to have no trouble decoding the instructions: *Llyfrau £1 yr un. Sganiwch yma dalu.* She was getting better at Welsh. She patted the pocket where she carried her pound coins, and was gratified to hear the dull clink.

Aventurine turned obsessively toward the non-fiction books, Micheline following behind almost robotically. Avi ran her index finger along the titles, shelved somewhat alphabetically, until she came to the middle of the alphabet. Sure enough, there were two books of hers: the one about Mobius, and the one about the Alaskan fisheries. She caressed them lovingly, as though they were old friends, or children. *May you go out into the world to be read and loved*, she wished them silently. Of course, at some point they had, she supposed, and chose not to further consider why they had been consigned to a charity sale. She drew the first one from the shelf, and digging the green pen she used for autographs from her purse, signed it on the title page; then she pulled out and signed the other. She resisted the urge to kiss them goodbye as she tucked them back into their shelves. Beside her, Mick still held her hands in her coat pockets, her eyes unfocused. The rain had increased again, and Avi closed her eyes for a moment, listening to it fall onto and drip off the roof of the shelter.

It wasn't really a conscious thought, but more of a gut instinct, that made Aventurine wander a bit further along, until she reached the place where the fiction resided. Again, she trailed a finger along the spines until she came to authors' names beginning with H. Yes, there was one book by N. B. Hallsey, and she allowed the feeling of vaguely resentful oneupmanship to fill up the back of her throat. *Beat you.* She couldn't help slipping it out of its place to look at the cover: *Sirens of Southampton.* A woman with black tresses flowing over her white shoulders and heaving bosom was leaning back against the bare chest of a Fabio wannabe, her eyes closed in what might have been passionate abandon. Avi flipped the book in her hand to look at the author photo on the back cover: Nicola, in that wide-brimmed hat, staring challengingly at the camera. Take off the hat, bob her hair, and the photo might have been of Avi or Mick. Ten years ago. Aventurine pressed her lips together and shoved the book back into its slot.

A sudden thought. She yanked it out again and flipped to the title page.

Nicola's signature was scrawled there in green ink.

She slapped the cover shut and jammed the book back into the shelf.

Still, she couldn't help herself: she wondered where Nicola was now, what she was doing. Back at work at the security firm, coming home of an evening to work on her bodice-rippers? Or would the company have foundered, its owner having met a tragic demise? That led her to wonder about the progress of the investigation into Magnus Etheridge's death, and whether the police had found a link between him and the woman in the garden of the Old Bishop's Palace. Whether the police had received the doctored digital recordings from the anonymous source, in which Magnus had admitted to his role in the theft of the Swynford Jewel, and the death at the Palace.

That led Aventurine's thoughts to Dominic Burroughs: the iciness of his gaze, the feel of his jaw against her hand, the shape of his mouth under hers.

Damn it.

Avi stepped away from the books and held her hand out into the rain, cupping her palm to allow a puddle to form. *Damn it all to hell.* Micheline had wandered away, and now a man with a very wet golden retriever stood between her and her sister. She hoped Mick was actually examining books, rather than just staring at them blindly. She hoped Mick was finding something to take herself out of herself. This depression was unlike her, and it filled Aventurine with a feeling of unease.

Unease. Dis-ease.

Aventurine turned her palm and let the rainwater run out. Then she wiped her hand down the leg of her jeans. She returned her attention to the books on the shelves before her. Perhaps there would be something she could read before bed.

At last, the clink of coinage in the payment box brought her attention around. Micheline had a couple of books under her arm, and before Aventurine could see the titles, Mick had shoved them into her bag. Almost surreptitiously.

"Ready to go?" she asked.

"What did you choose?"

Micheline shrugged and did not meet Aventurine's eyes. "Just a couple of light reads," she said evasively. As they passed through the stone gate into the street, she latched the flap of her bag closed.

Three

There was a roaring fire in the front room of Tŷ yn y Coed, the guest house they had chosen about a half-mile from the center of Hay. Micheline and Aventurine had shrugged out of their raincoats to the *tsk*-ing of the proprietress, who hung their wet things in the warming cupboard.

"In," she shooed. She herself was wearing a thick, multi-colored cardigan, obviously hand-made for warmth rather than style. "Take the chairs by the fire. Get yourself dried off and warmed up. I'll bring tea. Or would you rather have chocolate?"

If nothing else, the invitation to hot chocolate seemed to perk Mick up; that had always done the trick when they were kids, to get Micheline into good temper. Avi was grateful that Mick, at least, seemed to be trying to drag herself out of today's low place. Aventurine asked for tea; she'd long ago grown out of the habit of most sweet things. The proprietress hustled off toward the rear of the house. They heard a door close.

Micheline knelt on the hearth rug and took up the poker, adjusting the fire to lay another log atop it. Aventurine watched her sister in three-quarter profile, the fine nose, the determined forehead. She put a hand to the bridge of her own nose, and again thought fleetingly of Nicola.

"What is it?" she asked, pitching her voice low.

Mick shook her head.

"Is it catching up to you?" Aventurine pushed.

Again Mick shook her head. Her pale hair swung around her jawline. "No." There was a long pause, long enough for the hall clock outside the front room to ring the hour. A decidedly cheerful sound. At the other end of the room, the wind rattled the windows in their frames. "Yes," she said at last, her voice so low it was difficult to hear her over the rain and the crackling of the fire. "I'm so tired, Aventurine. So tired." She slumped back on her heels, but did not get up from the rug. "Sometimes I think if I could just sleep, for days and days, I could wake up and all of this would be a bad dream. Shep would be there, and Paul."

"I know, Mick. I know."

Micheline whirled. "No, you don't know. You can't know."

The words were like blows, so furious and full of pain were they. Aventurine shrank away from her twin's impotent fury.

"You can't possibly know." Micheline's face was white, her teeth bared. In the strange lighting, her skin was stretched tightly over her face, emphasizing the wings of her cheekbones.

There was the sound of a door again, and then a rattling of a tea tray. Hurriedly Micheline wiped her hands over her face, and resumed her seat in the chair by the fire. She did not look up when the proprietress wheeled in an old-fashioned tea cart.

"Here we are," the woman said cheerily. "It didn't take very long—I already had the kettle on for my own tea." She parked the cart at the table between the two library chairs, and transferred the cups and saucers. She poured first Micheline's hot chocolate, and then Aventurine's tea. "I'll let you two do your own cream and sugar, if that's all right with you? And I've brought along some scones and jam."

Despite not eating most of the roasted vegetables at lunch, Avi didn't feel the least bit peckish, but the smell of the scones—cranberry orange, from the scent—was enticing. "Thank you, Mrs. Davies."

"Sioned, please, Miss Morrow."

"Sioned, then." Aventurine smiled, though her face felt stiff. "I'm Aventurine. My sister is Micheline."

Mick nodded, her expression still brittle, her eyes glittering with useless unshed tears.

Sioned, to her credit, studied Micheline's face for the most fleeting of moments before smiling reassuringly and bustling off. No doubt back to the kitchen and her own tea. Curious she might have been, but she had the good sense not to be intrusive.

Aventurine's hand shook as she turned her teacup around in its saucer, the better to reach the handle. The cup and saucer rattled together as she moved it closer, checking the tea's strength. Dark, the way she liked it. Sioned had included a creamer and sugar; she had not yet learned that Avi took her tea black. *Black as her heart.* Those were Genevieve's words, and the clink of the teacup was loud in the room as she lifted it from the saucer and blew across the surface.

"Sorry," Micheline whispered. She picked up her own cup and stared down into its chocolate depths. "I'm sorry. For—lashing out."

Aventurine swallowed, her eyes prickling at her sister's distress. "I know. I just wish I could help."

Mick shook her head. "Nobody can."

Micheline didn't mention Genevieve. She didn't mention how Mick had asked the old spy for help. *She knows things. She knows people.* But the idea of Genevieve rooting around in this tragedy, pulling on the strands of her massive spider web of contacts and information, made Avi nervous. Anxious. There were times when she wished she'd never begun working with Genevieve on her biography. Had never acceded to the old woman's demand that she should be the one to write it. Because, when she leaned back in this chintz-covered chair, under the beamed ceiling, next to the blazing hearth, Aventurine realized that *that* was what it had been: an order. Hadn't Genevieve been the one to initiate contact? And now, as a direct result, here they were, Aventurine and Micheline, in a guesthouse on the Welsh Borders, at the end of a road on a figurative map that Genevieve had unfolded.

Avi blew on her tea and lifted the cup to her lips, staring into the fire, hyper-aware of her twin beside her, and the distress that seemed to ooze from her very pores. It was all Aventurine could do to refrain from crying in sympathy. From the painting above the mantelpiece, a bewhiskered old man in his pinks glared down at them; she glared back, feeling the urge to punch his self-satisfied face.

"I just—" Micheline took a long drink from her cup, and then set the hot chocolate aside, apparently thinking better of it. Her expression was nauseated, as though the drink upset her stomach. As though enjoying the drink made her sick. "I just want my husband back."

The despair in her voice. The anguish.

Aventurine set her own teacup aside.

Four

A message in the middle of the night.

Sorry so late. I wanted to wait until Paul was asleep.

It was the ping of Lance's incoming text that had awakened Aventurine from her doze in the darkened room. She knew she should have the phone on sleep, but she had gone back and forth on this since Shep's disappearance. Who knew who might need her in the middle of the night, or why?

Now she sat up slowly against the pillows and listened for sound in the room on the far side of the shared bath. Her nerves tautened and she held her breath. She thought she heard the springs of the old bed creak: Micheline rolling over. Awake? Asleep? Aventurine looked at the time: 1:22. Probably Mick was still awake. Quickly, she debated going to her sister and discarded the idea. Better to find out what Lance needed.

What's going on?

Weird thing.

What?

There was a long pause. Probably Lance was typing. Or thinking. Aventurine wished she could reach through the phone and grab Lance by the shoulders, give him a solid shake. Then she closed her eyes against the dark room to take a deep breath. Deep calming breath. Another. Lance was trying. She knew that. He was a good man, in an impossible situation. The text pinged, and she opened her eyes.

You're still in Wales?

Yes.

But I saw you. Here. This afternoon.

Sweet Mary and Joseph. Aventurine sucked in a breath.

Milan?

Yes. Micheline with you?

Yes.

Weird thing.

You'd better call me. Give me five minutes.

She ducked into the shared bath, and listened through the door: she heard Mick turn over again, and moments later, again. Slowly Avi backed out, put on her slippers, then crept out into the hallway and down the stairs to the front room, dark and cold now that the fire had been allowed to go out. She closed that door behind her and, her eyes adjusting, crossed to her chair of the afternoon. There she stared at the phone screen, touching it when it threatened to go dark, until the thing vibrated in her hand.

"Tell me," she ordered, her voice pitched low.

"We were at an outside table at the Café Dante. She walked by us, behind Paul. I thought she was you, but she never acknowledged us."

"He didn't see her?"

"Hell, I don't even know if *I* saw her. She was wearing oversized sunglasses and—"

"Don't tell me. A hat with a wide brim."

"No, why?"

Aventurine gripped the phone tighter. "No reason. Sorry. Go on."

"I mean, she had hair like yours. And your nose. I could have sworn it was you, or Paul's mother."

"Did you speak to her?"

There was an uncomfortable silence. Aventurine closed her eyes and imagined Lance, the swoop of curling dark hair over his dark eyes, the way he considered before he spoke, a tiny line forming between his brows.

"I didn't get a chance," he admitted at last. "I didn't even get a chance to point her out to Paul before she disappeared into a crowd of people heading toward the Castello Sforzesco." He coughed. "Afterwards, I wondered whether I hesitated just that moment too long, sort of intentionally."

Avi filed that one away for another moment. "And she made no motion, didn't look like she recognized you?"

"I don't know. The big glasses, you see?" Another cough, and his voice dropped slightly. "She certainly didn't pause on the way by or anything, as though she recognized us. And then—she was gone."

Aventurine released a long breath from her tight chest, the back of her neck prickling. "Well, we're here, both of us, in Hay. So it wasn't either of us. But—" Her voice trailed off. She hadn't told him about Nicola. What could she tell him? Either of them? *We think we have a half-sister we never knew about. And I don't quite trust her.*

Now Aventurine drew herself up sharply, examining her own thought. That was it, of course. Though she had not laid it out so clearly before. She didn't trust Nicola. There was something about her that made Avi flex her claws slightly, a defensive move.

"But?"

"Nothing. Nothing. Trying to think." She tried to even her tone, to sound nonchalant. "Of course, you're in Italy. It could be anyone. It could be some Neapolitan *contessa*."

"It could be." Lance didn't sound convinced.

Or it could be Nicola, keeping an eye on her newly-identified nephew, for reasons known only to herself.

"Listen," Aventurine said, suddenly feeling the weariness through her shoulders and along the back of her neck. The clock in the hallway chimed twice. "I need to talk more to you, but I can't get my head organized right now. Can I call you back tomorrow? At a normal hour?"

Lance chuckled, but the sound was forced. "Yeah. Sorry about that. I wanted to wait until Paul turned in, because I haven't told him about that woman. I didn't know what to tell him. I still don't."

"I wouldn't worry about it," Avi said quickly. "Coincidence. She's got nothing to do with any of us anyway." She hoped she sounded convincing.

"Yeah, you're probably right." Along the connection, she could hear him blowing out a breath. "All right. Ring me sometime tomorrow. Goodnight, Aventurine."

For a long time she sat on the edge of the chair, staring at the blank screen in her hand. *What the hell was Nicola doing?*

Because there was no doubt in her mind. None.

Five

The morning dawned bright and cold, and when Aventurine donned her winter coat and let herself out into the clear air, she saw her own breath billowing in clouds ahead of her. In the drive down to the road, the puddles shimmered with a skim of ice. She heard the raucous call of a crow off in the trees to her left, and she turned her head, but could make out no sheen of black in the barren trees.

"Hello, friend!"

The call was faint, and from the other side of the house, recognizably Sioned. The crow called again, and suddenly it swooped past Avi and disappeared toward the back garden. A small murder—three or four birds—lifted blackly from the shadowy trees into the pearlescent sky, to follow it. Avi jammed her gloved hands into her pockets and stepped off the porch.

When she reached the road, she turned to look back at the house, and her sister's room, the windows of which overlooked the drive. The curtains were still drawn. Whether Micheline was sleeping in, or merely staring upwards toward the shadowy ceiling, there was no way of knowing. Mick had mumbled something about how she wasn't hungry when Avi had tapped on the door and invited her to breakfast.

Aventurine turned to the left and headed uphill away from the village. There was no wind, and she was grateful; something told her that it would have been blowing into her face, making the upward trek more painful and arduous. The landscape around her—trees, some high fields—stretched away bleakly, closing in on midwinter. She would have to call Lance later, would have to feel him out about Paul and Christmas and the prospect of attempting to repair his relationship with his mother, and with her. And she had to find out more about Nicola—because there was no way that could be anyone else.

His mother.

Aventurine's thoughts circled back, and she felt the accustomed twinge.

She stopped in her tracks. The road was narrowing, becoming little more than a lane as it wound its way uphill; there should be a walking path veering off to the side here soon, if Google maps and Sioned were to be believed. Avi lifted her face to the sun, closing her eyes; the light played redly inside her eyelids, but there was no warmth. She blew out a long breath, imagining the clouds billowing and rolling back downhill the way she had come, rather than dissipating almost immediately, as they were wont to do. She wanted to imagine her breath causing ripples, causing shadows: she wanted to imagine the very act of her breathing leaving a mark on the world, as her actions had done, and were still doing. *How very little we actually think about that*, she mused, *how everything links to everything else.* Had she not said yes all those years ago to Micheline and Shep, would they have found themselves in this predicament? Had Shep not taken it upon himself to sail solo across the Atlantic as part of his midlife crisis? Had she never—and she felt the old pain and shame here, as though an echo—got involved with Neil in grad school?

When she opened her eyes again, one of the crows had lighted in a tree across the lane and now stared at her with one yellow eye, opening and closing its black beak soundlessly.

She brought out her phone to call Lance. There was no service.

Six

A venturine put her head down on the desk for a moment and breathed long and deeply, trying to slow the racing of her heart. In her head she could almost hear Genevieve urging her on.

Almost.

Because Genevieve didn't urge this time with words, but with that sardonic look, skewed sideways out of her hooded eyes, before she raised her brows and shrugged in a near-Gallic manner. Something she had learned from her French mother, all those years ago? No, more likely a mannerism of her very own, developed over time, as had been her persona.

Do it.

That voice was Aventurine's own.

Painfully she straightened, took one last look at the words on the screen, then clicked SEND.

She needed a drink.

Her knees creaked as she stood, and there was a decided kink in her lower back. How long had she sat here at the desk, polishing, revising, refitting, doing anything but submitting the piece to her agent? At some point—she couldn't quite remember when—she had heard Micheline leave her room and head downstairs. Had she returned? Aventurine didn't think so. This was a good sign: Mick moving, Mick doing something other than sinking into the morass of her own despair. Avi stretched her arms over her head, then bent to—almost—touch her toes, letting her shoulders and arms hang. Then she straightened again, shook herself, and headed downstairs.

Micheline was curled up on the sofa near the hearth, where once again the fire burned cheerfully. She wore a pair of rimless reading glasses, and turned a page in her book as Aventurine slowed in the doorway, as yet unnoticed. It should have been a relaxing scene, one that might have lifted the thin shawl of worry from her shoulders, had she not noticed Mick's tenseness, the intensity of her attention to the book in her hand—the fingers of which were white with the strength of her grip.

"What are you reading?"

Micheline jumped guiltily, and shoved the book down beside the cushion, almost as though she'd been caught reading a filthy magazine.

"Just—something I picked up at the Honesty Bookshop," she hedged. She lifted her glass from the coaster on the coffee table, and Avi noticed the slight shake of her hand. "I know it's a bit early, but I felt the urge for a whisky."

A clear invitation, and a clear dodge. Aventurine crossed to the drinks table and poured one finger of her own, all she really needed. She breathed in the heathery scent before taking the smallest of sips, and letting the whisky burn its way down her throat.

"Well?" Mick demanded. "The writing? Or should I not ask?"

As Aventurine approached to take one of the wing-backed chairs opposite, her sister swung her feet to the carpet, tucking the book further behind her. Avi pretended not to notice.

"I sent it."

"Oh, Avi!" Mick held out her glass. "Cheers!"

They toasted and drank.

"I know how hard this has been for you," Micheline said after a moment. She skittered a coaster from a little rack across the coffee table. "I know how hard this has been on you."

"And now I've sent a piece off."

"Tell me again which one. Not the article about Genevieve."

"No. I'm holding off on that until I get her OK."

They fell silent for a moment, listening to the crackling of the fire. With the way things had fallen out in York in the summer, it was highly unlikely Genevieve would OK the publication of anything that would link them together until she was dead. That thought sent a pang sharp as a dagger through Aventurine's gut: the idea of a world without Genevieve Smithson in it had become, in such a short time, untenable.

I'm an old woman.

She always said that, and she was right. She'd bypassed her Biblical three score and ten more than twenty years ago, and probably had never looked back.

"What are you thinking?" Micheline asked. "You suddenly looked stricken."

Aventurine met her sister's concerned green gaze, but couldn't hold it. She took another hurried drink, and the whisky burned. "About—writing Genevieve's story." She set her tumbler down, and stood to put another log on the fire. She could be as evasive as Mick. "This one was an article about Katherine Swynford."

"One of your Badass Bitches of Britain."

"One of them."

"And you've sent it off."

"The first thing I've sent off in ages."

"Oh, Avi, I'm so glad."

Aventurine was as well, not only for herself, but for the spark of emotion the news had elicited from her sister. She dropped back into her chair and raised the glass again.

"This is cause for celebration," Micheline continued. "Aventurine, what should we do? We should do something special." She raised her own glass. "And you should call Genevieve and let her know. She'll be so thrilled for you."

That made Aventurine laugh aloud. "*Thrilled* is not a word that I'd use to describe Genevieve. She doesn't do *thrilled*."

"Don't be stupid," Mick said, making a cross face. "You know she loves you."

"Genevieve doesn't do *love*, either."

But that thought gave Aventurine another pang in the gut. She took the last tiny drink of the scotch and turned her gaze to the fire.

When Mick excused herself to go upstairs for her genealogy, Aventurine waited a moment, listening, and then darted quickly to pull the book from behind the sofa cushion. *Nightmare Voyage* by Nicholas Black. Seafaring charts in red and black made up the cover art. "Ten men set out, but only one returned," the blurb read. Aventurine, glancing over her shoulder, pulled out her phone and took a picture. Then she hurriedly tucked the book back down into its hiding place as she heard her sister's return.

Seven

A t the Smithy tonight. Bring your sisters.

Aventurine glared at the text message. She clicked the screen closed, and then just as quickly opened it again.

Gio. The bastard.

Over afternoon tea and cake supplied by Sioned, she showed the message to Micheline.

"Sioned," Mick called toward the kitchen, "do you know where the Smithy is?"

The proprietress came back into the dining room, wiping her hands on a dish towel. This afternoon she had pulled her curly hair away from her forehead with a multicolored headband. "The Smithy? You mean the music place?" She brushed the back of her hand over her flushed brow. "Over in Brecon. Someone good on, then?"

"Gio Constantine," Micheline said. "Tonight, I gather."

Outside the small-paned window, flakes of snow were falling somewhat indecisively.

"The singer? I like some of his stuff." Sioned laughed. "My husband used to call him a soulful singer-songwriter, especially when he was being snarky."

A grin tugged at Mick's lips, and she cast her eyes down to her lemon drizzle cake. Avi laughed outright. Maybe a little meanly. *Take that, Gio.*

"Are you two fans, then?"

"By way of being friends," Micheline corrected. Aventurine snorted into her teacup. "Stop it, Avi."

Sioned looked appalled. "And I said that. Oh, I'm sorry."

Aventurine waved her apology away. "I've heard him say the same thing about himself." She smiled reassuringly. "It's not too far away, then?"

"About fifteen miles? Half an hour?"

"Thanks. You wouldn't care to come along with us?"

But Sioned threw up her hands and laughed. "Ah, no, but thanks. My husband would haunt me forever if I did that." Still laughing, she disappeared back into the kitchen.

Now Micheline laughed, the first time in a while Aventurine had heard the sound.

"What?"

"You're surely not thinking of going?" Mick demanded. "This is not at all what I meant by *celebrating* your submission."

"I'm thinking of it, and thinking of bringing my sister." Aventurine glared. Then she stopped, drawing the phone back toward her, touching the screen into life again.

Micheline had gone still, seemingly having had the same thought.

Bring your sisters.

"Oh," Micheline said.

"Now we *have* to go."

They were in the rental car. The snow had stopped, but the lane was still narrow, the road gleaming blackly in the yellow of the headlights. As the evening had worn on, it had become increasingly difficult to keep Micheline focused on the evening before them.

"This is stupid," Micheline had said, tugging on her gloves against the weak heater, and adjusting her seatbelt. "After the way he behaved in Lincoln. After the way he treated you."

"*Sisters.* He wrote *sisters.* Plural."

"It's probably a typo." Micheline sighed. "You're dragging me fifteen miles out in the dead of winter, in the dead of night, for a typo." Now she was rooting in her purse, and Aventurine knew she was looking for her cigarettes. Not that Mick would smoke in the car—she knew better than that; it was just that she needed to touch the pack for some weird sort of reassurance.

"You know you don't think so. And neither do I. He thinks Nicola is here with us. Having a cute little bonding vacation or something."

"Did you invite her?"

Aventurine slowed as they entered the village, hitting the blinker for the turn. "Of course, I didn't." She could feel her lips pursing together, and tried to relax her face before she got those pinched old-lady lines around her mouth. "I don't know about you, Micheline, but something just doesn't sit right with me about her."

"You're being melodramatic."

"I'm being cautious."

Micheline sighed again and set her purse on the floor between her feet. "You are the one who brought us her father."

"If he *is* her father." They both spoke the words at the same time, and then they both laughed nervously. They both wanted to know, but they both dreaded finding out.

"Poor Henry," Avi said at last. "I wish I knew what to do about him. I guess part of my worry is that I don't think Nicola is being entirely straight with him, either. She knows more than she's told him. Hell, she knows more than she's told us."

"Can't it just be as much of a shock to her as it is to us?"

"I don't know," Aventurine groaned. That was it, wasn't it? Nicola had done the DNA test for some reason, and having found those echoes of her own existence mixed in with Nicola's at her house, Avi couldn't shake the feeling that Nicola had known—something. She drove out of Hay toward the southwest, following the directions of the in-dash SatNav. The headlights cut through the darkness, leading them onward. Otherwise, the road seemed to be deserted. She hoped the traffic picked up the closer they got to Brecon, or else Gio's audience was going to be somewhat stunted. Perhaps that's why he'd invited them. Avi and her *sisters*. She tried to formulate her thoughts aloud. "Remember: she did the DNA testing before you did. And I'm the one whose life she's been busily mirroring—not you. So if I'm feeling less than enthusiastic about Nicola, I guess you're just going to have to put up with it. Because there it is."

Micheline touched her arm lightly, then withdrew. It was all the reassurance Aventurine needed.

"If it means anything—"

It would always mean something.

"—I'm not quite comfortable about Nicola, either."

Slowing at a corner, Aventurine smiled gently in the darkness. "You're just nicer about it, that's all."

She found a parking spot on Ship Street and slotted the car in. They then made their way to Bell Street and the venue.

"Very industrial," Mick said, hands in pockets. The glow from the streetlights carved her features sharply, shadowed her eyes in their sockets.

"Very."

They pushed the door open into a wave of noise, which did not subside in the least. Mick went in search of a table, while Aventurine went to the bar for drinks: their established routine. When Avi finally moved into the dim interior, glasses in hand, she found her sister at a table in the front, slightly to the left, just beyond the sound board; she wondered fleetingly whom Mick had to mug to get the seats. She slid one of the pints across the scarred tabletop, and, shedding her coat, fell into the chair Micheline kicked out for her. It wobbled, as though with uneven legs.

"Do you think the front's a good idea?" she asked, leaning in close and shouting to be heard above the din.

"He wants to see us, let's make sure he sees us."

"Unless you're a typo."

"Shut up."

Aventurine picked up the cider and sipped. It was quite tart, with bubbles that snapped against the roof of her mouth. She could see how people might not realize just how lethal this stuff was. A fun drink. But one that would hammer the uninitiated before she turned around. This would be her only, thank you very much.

"I'm sincerely hoping he has something to tell us other than how he slept on the couch," Aventurine said bitterly.

"About what?"

"Nicola, for one. He obviously expects her to be here. He obviously knows more about her than we do."

"You don't know that."

"I've known him a long time, Mick."

"Biblically speaking."

"Shut up."

But it felt good, the wordplay with Micheline. It felt as though it had been years since her twin had teased. Aventurine had missed it. She leaned over to rest her head on Mick's shoulder. Just for a moment. Just for an acknowledgment.

The lights dimmed, and up on the stage, Gio appeared before the double doors of the loading bay, picking up one of the acoustic guitars arranged on stands behind the metal stool. He waved cheerfully at the darkened venue, then plugged in with the cord left draped over the mic stand. Aventurine recognized every movement—every step of his, onstage, was choreographed; every bit of between-songs chatter rehearsed. Gio, she knew, never left a single thing to chance in his gigs. His set lists had been written out ages in advance, the songs shifting between cuts from his many albums, organized to elicit very particular responses from his audiences. He had it down to a science.

He should, after all this time.

That was a mean thought, Aventurine chided herself. She, a writer who wrote, revised, revised again, organizing her words—sentences—chapters to elicit very particular responses from her readers. All to make it look easy, if not spontaneous, on the receiving end.

Still, she couldn't help herself. She just felt mean about Gio. She knew, looking up at his handsome chiseled face, that Micheline had been right when calling her a dog in a manger. Mick was always right. She didn't want Gio—not entirely; not with the baggage the both of them carried—but she didn't want anyone else to have him, either.

Especially not Nicola.

Who might be her sister. Who probably was her sister.

The whole thing just made her feel dirty.

She picked up her pint and looked at the spotlight through it, admiring the color. Then she took another sip. Gio took that opportunity to turn toward their table and wink. A few arpeggio tuning runs, and he eased into "No Ghosts," his cover of the Colin Moore song.

"I think I'm going to be sick," Aventurine said to Micheline.

She wasn't, though. *Don't let him do this*, Mick had muttered in her ear, sternly. Mick hadn't said *I told you so*, though she would have been perfectly justified in doing so. *Suck it up, sister.* So, Aventurine had made her face an expressionless mask each time Gio had turned in their direction. He had the good sense not to call them out from the stage, though he did call out a couple near the back, who apparently were celebrating an anniversary of some sort. Once his set was done, Aventurine and Micheline stared stonily at their drinks while he chatted up people at the merch table, signing autographs and posing for the odd selfie.

"Buy you a drink, ladies?" he asked at last, sidling up to the table.

"I'm fine," Avi said.

He grinned that engaging smile. "Ah, yes. You're a lightweight, my darling girl. I always forget."

"I'm not." Micheline held out her empty pint glass pointedly.

Gio looked momentarily taken aback, but then took her glass to the bar.

"Bitch," Avi said.

"Hey, it's a free drink. And I'm not driving."

She had a point.

When Gio returned, he slid into the chair opposite them, dealing the drinks as though dealing a hand of poker. He slid a glass of tonic to Avi with a grin.

"Only two of you?"

Aventurine shot Micheline a knowing look.

"What were you expecting?"

Gio smiled disarmingly. "I was hoping to see all three of you."

"Three?" Mick asked, widening her eyes innocently.

Avi snorted. "We're twins, Gio. Not triplets. Unless you need your eyes checked."

He shifted in his chair, taking a long time to sip his pint. "I thought you might have brought Nicola along."

"Nicola. Nicola Hallsey?"

Gio's usual confidence seemed to be ebbing away. "Come on, Aventurine. You know she told me about that DNA test." He half-laughed. "As though I wouldn't have been able to tell anyway."

A woman in a black leather jacket adorned with silver spikes appeared at his shoulder. "Mr. Constantine," she interrupted. "Gio." She held out a CD, the cellophane removed already. "Could I get you to autograph this?"

Immediately the smoothness was back, Gio's smile slipping over his features like a mask. "Of course." He took the proffered pen and scribbled that all-too-familiar swirling autograph across the bottom of the CD cover.

"And a picture with me, maybe?" the woman pressed. She drew out her cell phone and handed it to Micheline. "Maybe you could take it for us?" She leaned down and pressed her face close to Gio's, one red-nailed hand on his shoulder. Damned good thing she hadn't asked Avi, who would have found some way to destroy it. Beside her, Mick clicked away cheerily.

"Thanks," the woman cooed, taking back the phone and looking at the photos. "These your friends, Gio?"

"We're not friends," Avi said.

"We're his dates," Mick added. Her smile was mean. Aventurine hadn't known her sister had it in her. Gio laughed. The woman in leather eased off and allowed herself to be swept away toward the bar.

"My dates?" He quirked an eyebrow.

"Or not," Aventurine shot back. "I guess you were looking for Nicola, but—" and she looked around vaguely— "she seems to have stood you up."

Micheline had slugged back almost half of this new pint. She leveled her gaze at Gio over the rim of her glass. "What made you think she was with us?"

He shrugged. "She said she was going to be."

Aventurine froze. Micheline sloshed her drink onto the table, and quickly grabbed a napkin to attempt to stanch the puddle.

"*She said what?*"

Gio seemed puzzled by their reactions. "She said she was coming out here to spend some time with you two. She had some days off, and you all had things you needed to talk about. Family things."

Aventurine exchanged a look with Micheline. "First I've heard of it."

"Or I," Mick agreed.

"Maybe I got it wrong." Gio was trying to play it cool, that much was obvious, but those tiny tell-tale annoyance lines had appeared around his mouth.

"When did she tell you this?" Aventurine pressed, leaning in. The sound of the crowd was building; more people were coming in from the street, and it would soon be time for Gio's second set.

"I called her a week or so ago—after you two left Lincoln. When you wouldn't answer my calls, Avi." He sounded petulant.

Did he actually blame her for not picking up when she saw his number? He was lucky he'd texted this time, and that she was distracted, looking for Lance to return her own call.

"And you haven't talked to her since."

"She hasn't answered my calls."

Micheline laughed and pushed her now-empty glass toward Gio. "Your round, I think. Again." She turned to Avi. "See? You two must be sisters. You have so much in common."

Gio threw up his hands, but gathered the glasses and headed up to the bar.

"You're getting drunk," Aventurine said. "If you're not already."

Micheline waved the warning away. "At least I'll sleep."

"After you have the bed-spins for a while." Aventurine sighed and leaned in again. Mick's moods were so changeable. "I need you sober. I need you to pay attention to this."

Another dismissive wave. Gio returned and handed round the glasses. "I got more tonic for you," he said, sliding the sweating glass toward Avi. "Didn't want you to feel left out while the rest of us got pie-eyed."

He showed no sign of inebriation; but of course, as he'd told Aventurine time and again over the years, he was the consummate professional, or the professional consumer. Whichever. Avi glared at him. But she took the tonic water anyway; as Micheline had pointed out, it was a free drink.

"We were talking about Nicola," she reminded him.

"And how she's not with us," Micheline said. Her voice sounded vaguely off, the words almost—but not quite—slurring.

Again Gio threw up his hands. "Listen, I don't know, do I? She's one of you lot, and I've learned that I have no idea what any of you are up to."

"Nor I you," Avi shot back.

He ignored her. "She told me she was coming to talk to you. That's the last I heard. I've been left on read since then—by all of you—"

"Not by me," Mick cut in cheerily.

Gio ignored her, too. "I just thought maybe we could get together, since I was in the area, and we might just let bygones be bygones, and all that. I didn't know it was going to cause an international incident."

"Well, we are foreign nationals," Mick reminded him, and giggled.

She took a drink, and only spilled a little when she aimed her glass at the coaster again.

"Your sister's drunk," Gio said.

"And you have to go play another set."

He downed the last of his cider and pushed away from the table, acknowledging a wave from a man on the stage. "Will you be here when I get done?"

"Probably not."

Eight

A venturine half-carried her sister up the stairs, making it just in time to the bathroom. She held back Micheline's hair and tried not to breathe in the stink of vomit. When Mick had finally emptied her stomach, she sobbed quietly, her head on her arm. Avi sat her on the edge of the tub, stripped off her coat, and patted her face gently with a dampened towel.

"I'm such a mess, Avi," Mick murmured. Her eye makeup was running; Aventurine rinsed the towel in the sink, and wiped at the streaks gingerly.

"You are. It's a good thing I love you."

"I'm sorry. I just wanted to drink, and forget, and sleep."

"I know."

"And now I'll have the bed-spins, just like you said."

"Yep. Is this the part where I say 'I told you so'? Well, I told you so."

"Bitch." But Mick's heart wasn't in it.

"Not just any bitch. I'm a badass bitch, and don't you forget it."

Micheline hiccupped and got to her feet unsteadily. Aventurine tucked the damp towel under her elbow, and took Mick's arm.

"I wish I were more like you," Mick said sadly.

"Oh, honey." Avi nudged open the door, and then piloted them into Mick's room. With her free hand she slapped at the light switch on the wall. "There's nobody more like me than you, in the whole entire world."

Not even Nicola. No matter how hard she tried.

Mick fell asleep almost as soon as Avi had got her changed and tucked under the duvet. Aventurine kissed her on the forehead.

On the way out of the room, she spotted *Nightmare Voyage* on the dresser, and surreptitiously snatched it up to bring with her. She tossed her coat and bag aside in her own room, flicked on the light, and sank to the bed, feeling guilty before she even slid open the cover. Mick had hidden the book from her, slipping it into her bag at the Honesty Bookshop, tucking it down behind the cushion in the front room downstairs. For some reason, her sister did not want her to see the book, to know the title or perhaps the subject matter.

The reason why was fairly obvious: a book about men sailing solo around the world, just as Shep had been sailing solo across the Atlantic. This book had caught Mick's eye, and she had been compelled to buy it—and she knew how Aventurine would feel about the compulsion. *Oh, Mick.*

Aventurine let out a sigh. She hadn't broken trust with her sister: even when she'd had Shep's letter in her possession, she had not opened it, as it hadn't been meant for her. But how could she help Micheline, if Micheline wouldn't allow it? If Micheline kept secrets? She took a deep breath, pressing her lips together, and flipped back the cover.

Micheline's name was written on the front page, above the blurbs. *Micheline M. Genthner.*

She looked again. That wasn't Mick's handwriting.

And Mick didn't write in green ink.

Aventurine couldn't sleep. She lay in the center of the bed, arms by her sides, and stared up into the darkness.

Micheline had found a book in the Honesty Bookshop with her own name in it. No matter how Avi turned the idea over in her mind, no matter from which angle she examined it, it made no sense.

If Mick had owned this book, and donated it or discarded it, she would have done it in Connecticut. How, then, would it have ended up on a shelf in Hay-on-Wye?

If Mick had owned this book, how had her name appeared, written in a hand not hers, in ink the color of which she didn't use?

Yet if Mick hadn't owned this book, why was her name inside the cover?

And how much of a coincidence was it that she had, out of all the thousands of used books in the Honesty Bookshop, found this one? Perhaps the title had caught her eye, with Shep constantly at the front of her mind. *But it had her name in it.* It was almost as though someone had planted it for her to find—but how on earth could anyone have known she would?

Abruptly, Aventurine sat up again and pulled the chain on the bedside lamp. The book stared up at her: mocked her. She picked it up gingerly, as one might a mousetrap, wary of it snapping closed on her. She opened the cover and looked at the name again. Not Paul's handwriting, and certainly not Shep's sharp, incisive letters. Green ink: Aventurine herself wrote in green ink, as a sort of branding, when she signed her books. And—Nicola did, as well. N. B. Hallsey. Avi could see the swirling autograph in her mind's eye. Might this be Nicola's handwriting?

But why would Nicola do this? It seemed cruel.

Aventurine flipped the pages back and forth in her hands, trying to understand. Trying to find the message the book had for her. No, for her sister. Someone—Nicola?—had written Mick's name, left the book for her to find, then...what?

That's when her eye caught the underline.

She'd lost the page again. Slowly Aventurine started from the beginning, running her gaze down each page. What had she seen?

There it was. Underlined in pencil: a single sentence.

From its beginning to its mysterious end, the voyage was chaos.

Aventurine slumped back. It sure was.

Then she scrabbled for her phone, on its charger, and took a picture.

What was this supposed to tell Micheline? Obviously it had something to do with Shep. It couldn't not, could it? A book about sailing. Mick's name. Chaos. With Shep's death, everything had gone to hell for Micheline.

Aventurine flipped the page. And on 135, again underlined in that pencil, this time half a sentence: *No matter what happened, he couldn't bring himself to turn back.*

Holding her breath, she flipped to the next page, and there, a third underline, again, only part of a sentence: *he disappeared over the darkened horizon.*

Feeling dizzy and frightened, she paged through the remainder of the book slowly, but found no other marks. No other underlining. Nothing else. Aventurine took pictures of the pages, and then, in a moment of caution, uploaded the three photos to the cloud for safe keeping.

What did it mean? What was the message? What was her sister supposed to understand from this?

Aventurine would have to ask her. But Aventurine couldn't ask her, not without giving away the violation of privacy, the breaking of trust.

She had to help her twin. She had to help. Aventurine squeezed her head between her hands, quailing. Because the only way to help was to hurt first, and she didn't know if she had the stomach for that.

Nine

In the morning, Aventurine called Lance and got his voicemail.

"Call me when you can," she said, trying and failing to keep the urgency from her voice.

Then she dialed Genevieve, who picked up at the first ring, as though expecting her call.

"I think," the old woman said without preamble, "that the answer might just lie in Southampton."

As always, Aventurine found herself reeling at the opening gambit. "The answer? The answer to what? What's the question?" There were, after all, so many.

This would be the point when anyone else would laugh, having got one up on Avi with her level of intelligence. *I know more than you do.* But of course, Genevieve knowing more than Aventurine did was not unusual; it was, in fact, to be expected. And Genevieve did not laugh.

"I've been just thinking things through."

"Things. Shep things?"

"Shep things, as you so inelegantly put it."

"Southampton." The mention of the city roiled Aventurine's stomach. Instinctively she held out her hand to examine her palm, but the scrapes from the bricked pavement had long since healed. That didn't mean she couldn't see them in her mind's eye: the gravel, the blood. The rest of her suddenly flamed into remembered pain as well, but she tamped it down. She wouldn't think of that. She wouldn't think of *the thing* which Neil had done.

"You might have to go back there," Genevieve said. Her voice was surprisingly gentle. "Or at least Micheline might have to, if she wants to understand."

Perhaps it was the residual fear and loathing and anger that welled up to overpower her. "Understand what?" she demanded, her voice sharper than she intended. She closed her eyes and now images of Neil were replaced by a field of flotsam, somewhere in the Atlantic: coolers, scraps of wood, life jackets. "Shep's dead, Genevieve. *Dead*. He was lost at sea, and giving my sister hope like this is not just wrong, it's heartless."

Her voice was rising. Her hands were shaking. Furiously, Aventurine stood and crossed to the window, pulling back the curtain to look down into the damp and gloomy front garden. It wasn't raining this noontime, but neither had the sun managed to struggle out from behind the dingy grey cloud cover. The grass below was brown and dead, leaves and branches and other debris raked into a pile at the bottom of the garden. As she watched, a crow lighted on a bare branch to the left, opening and closing its beak, calling to her though she could not hear. Perhaps the same one from the other day. Aventurine leaned her forehead against the wavy glass, welcoming the coldness against her skin. *Hello, friend.*

"Shep's dead, Genevieve," she repeated. Dully.

"Shep Genthner is in limbo," the old woman said. "He is Shrödinger's proverbial cat. He is neither dead nor alive."

"You're being deliberately cruel. You're leading Micheline on, and she's vulnerable."

A long breath of impatience. "There is no proof either way. Your sister understands this at a visceral level. And until she finds some proof, pointing in either direction, she can't move on, Aventurine. Thus Micheline is in limbo as well."

"But—lost at sea, Genevieve." Aventurine pressed her eyes closed against an incipient headache—so unfair, as she had had only that one pint of cider last night—and when she opened them again, the crow still fixed her with its beady eye. Even from this distance, when it opened its gleaming black beak, she was certain she could see its tongue, mocking her. Friend, indeed. "The very nature of *lost at sea* means that there isn't proof either way, as you point out. Means that there may never be any proof either way."

"That's true."

"And that's why encouraging Mick like this is cruel."

There was a surprisingly long pause. Then, "Do you think I'm cruel, Aventurine?"

The question was not what Avi expected. It smacked of self-questioning, of a slight falling off of self-confidence. And Genevieve was nothing if not self-confident. The footing beneath Aventurine shifted slightly.

"I—I hadn't thought so."

A sigh, reaching to her from York. "I'm practical, Aventurine. I'm careful. I consider the options, and I go with the one that will take me closer to the objective. If people are hurt, I can't help that. But please remember one thing: I have never, in all my life, intentionally done anything with the primary goal of hurting someone, except as an act of war. I am not willfully cruel, Aventurine. If you think about everything you've ever learned from me, you'll realize that that's true." The old woman paused, as though surprised at her own loquaciousness. "Now. That's enough in that vein."

"But—"

"Aventurine." The firmness in Genevieve's voice brought Avi up short. "Stop. I'm not encouraging your sister one way or another. If anything, I'm supporting her. She asked for help finding information. I have contacts. She knows that. It doesn't hurt for me to pull a few strings, call in a few favors—I've got so little time left to be doing that, God knows—and find out if there's any further noise out there she hasn't heard."

"And if you find—definitive evidence—that Shep is dead—" Avi didn't say *body*; she couldn't bring herself to even think the word.

"Then I lay that before Micheline, and you comfort her as best you can."

Suddenly the crow leapt upward into the late November air with a shiver of black wing, startled. Below and to the right, Micheline herself appeared, stepping down from the front stoop into the garden. Aventurine had never heard her sister leave the room on the other side of the bath and head downstairs. She watched her now, foreshortened, huddled into her coat with her shoulders slumped, as she scuffed through the dead leaves. Her movements seemed haphazard, without design; her head was bowed, her eyes on the ground. Suddenly she veered off toward a little trellis at the end of the garden, bare now, under which was placed a small stone bench. Micheline reached down to wipe some brown leaves away, and then sat. Collapsed was perhaps a better word, Avi thought; Mick looked as though the few yards from the house to the bench had taken all her stores of energy.

For some moments, Micheline stared sightlessly at the fallowing flower beds, which in the summer would no doubt be Sioned's pride and joy, but which now seemed to mirror her own listlessness. Then she pulled her hands from her pockets, and, fisted in one, was a crumpled envelope. This she opened slowly, and drew out a single sheet; she unfolded it carefully as if mindful of its delicate nature. Aventurine watched her sister bend her head to read. It didn't take long. Then Micheline dropped her head into her hands, her shoulders shaking.

Aventurine felt the tears in her own eyes fall, felt them tracing their way down her own cheeks. She felt like a voyeur, secretly watching this very private distress. The envelope—the paper—no doubt Shep's last letter, the one he'd left for Micheline in the locked box at the Southampton boatyard.

"Aventurine?"

Genevieve's voice was so low, and so far away, that Avi wasn't certain whether she had imagined it.

"I don't know if I can," she whispered. "I don't know if there's any comfort for her."

Ten

She hurriedly told Genevieve about the book, and with an *I need to think about this*, the old spy rang off. Aventurine remained at the window, looking down helplessly at her sobbing twin, who was pressing the letter to her mouth.

Avi had never read the letter.

Micheline had never shown it to her, once they had recovered it, unopened, from Neil's things; Avi had never asked. It was one of the very few things they had never shared. In fact, from the moment in Genevieve's front hallway when she had handed it to her sister, to this, Aventurine had not even laid eyes on the letter.

Now it would seem like Micheline kept it with her, took it out sometimes to reread it, or just to touch it, rather like a talisman. Shep's last words to her. In Shep's handwriting.

It had been well over a year. Well over. Since Micheline had called Aventurine in the middle of the night with the news of the wreck of the *Máquina*. There had been no further news. The authorities had long since stopped looking for survivors—survivor—and had closed the case, leaving Micheline to go to court to have Shep declared dead. Something, Aventurine knew, her sister had not yet had the heart to do.

It went deeper than that, Avi realized now. Somewhere deep inside her, so deep that she did not admit it even to the person who had known her longest, known her since before birth, Micheline refused to accept the idea that her husband was dead. Thus Genevieve's involvement. Thus a sobbing Micheline, wandering this winter-soaked garden in the border country, clutching Shep's last words to her.

But.

If Shep had not gone down with the *Máquina*, then what?

Where had he been all this time?

Aventurine gazed down into the grey-scale world, Micheline long since having got up and wandered further into the rain and out of her sight.

If Shep were still alive, he had made no attempt to contact the one person who loved him more than any other. Perhaps loved him beyond all reason.

If Shep was still alive, he had forced his wife and his son into despair—for what?

Aventurine realized her hands were clenched in fists by her sides.

If Shep was still alive, she'd kill him. *Bastard.*

Aventurine, in turmoil, turned to the writing, which was going, it felt, somewhat haphazardly.

Her notes on the table to the left, her coffee on the right, she typed a sentence, deleted it, typed another, revised it back to the first. None of it made any sense; none of it connected in any way to anything else. Outside the window the wind had picked up, until it was howling like a mad thing around Tŷ yn y Coed. Micheline had returned a while back, her slow steps echoing their way up the stairs and along the hallway; after a bit, Avi had heard the sound of the squeaky bed springs as Mick had sunk down into the mattress, and presumably her despair.

Avi found herself grateful that Shep was not alive and there with them, what with the noisiness of the old beds; but then she sat back, with a realization like a punch to the solar plexus, that if Shep were alive, Micheline would probably not be in the room next door. The pair of them would either be safely ensconced at home, or at some warm beach on the Mediterranean.

Damn you, Shep.

She poured another cup of coffee from the carafe Sioned had provided.

An entire paragraph, anyway.

She missed the days when she could dash off a couple of pages in a sitting. If this was writer's block, she hated it. *Fallowing*, Genevieve would correct her sternly. The old woman insisted that *something* was working in the back of Aventurine's brain, even as she found nothing coming out as a product. Fallowing, like overwintering. Roots underground, storing energy to send shoots sunward when the time was right. She closed her eyes. The wind rattled the windows again, and when Avi opened her eyes, she saw the glass so streaked with rain that the outside world might have been a late painting by Monet, so indistinct was everything.

The phone buzzed on the charger on the bedside table. An incoming text.

For half a moment, Aventurine thought to ignore it. *Go to hell, Gio.*

Then she thought: *Paul. Or Lance.*

Aventurine cursed. She'd meant to try Lance again, but had forgotten, she's been so engrossed with wrestling the words.

But when she pushed away from the table in the corner to grab the phone, she found it was neither.

It was Henry Hallsey.

Is Nicola with you?

Aventurine still had the photograph of Nicola on her phone. She texted it to Lance.

Is this her?

Then she had another thought. She dug out the paperback she had stolen from Nicola's flat, the one with the author photo on the back cover of Nicola smiling up from under the wide-brimmed hat.

Here's another one.

Would she have been wearing the hat in winter in Italy? It was a sunhat. No, Lance said the woman he'd seen hadn't been wearing a hat at all. Oh, what the hell did it matter, anyway?

Henry thought Nicola was with her and Mick.

Gio thought Nicola was with her and Mick.

Obviously they both got that idea from somewhere. And the common denominator was, of course, Nicola herself.

The room, charming in pale golds and greens, was beginning to feel claustrophobic.

She hurriedly replied to Henry. No, she isn't. What's wrong? Then she gathered up the carafe, now empty, and went downstairs to Sioned's kitchen.

Eleven

Several days they'd been staying, and so concerned was she with Micheline's demeanor that she hadn't really studied their hostess at all. No wonder she couldn't write a damned thing—her powers of observation were all off kilter. Now Aventurine leaned her head on her hand and watched as Sioned ran the water for the electric kettle, and flicked on the switch, which cast a blue glow on the shining granite countertop.

"Have a seat," the other woman invited. At the far end of the kitchen, warmed as it was by the deep blue Aga, two high-backed chintz armchairs kept cozy company. Over the rolled arm of one a book lay open, its cover multi-colored. *London: the Biography*. Peter Ackroyd. Somewhere back in her little apartment on the Back Bay, Aventurine had her own copy of the book.

"How are you liking the Ackroyd?" she asked.

When Sioned Davies smiled, the skin around her eyes crinkled, and a dimple formed in each cheek. "Oh, that book. It's a good friend." The kettle snicked off, and she swished some hot water in the teapot, poured it out, measured in the tea leaves and filled it again. A tea tray was already laid out, as though she expected company, or perhaps wouldn't dream of finding herself unprepared should some happen along. She opened a canister and set some ginger biscuits on a plate. "I don't think I've ever read the entirety after the first time, but every once in a while I delve in if I need reminding."

"Reminding?" There was something attractive about the way Sioned spoke about the book, about the reading of it. As though they were friends. Maybe Sioned could be friends with her books?

Sioned brought the tray over and set it on the tiled table between the chairs. She settled opposite Aventurine, and took the book up to close it gently. "I used to live in London, ages ago, when my husband and I were first married."

She wasn't married now, this much Aventurine knew. A widow. Though she still wore her wedding ring, a plain narrow band which seemed loose on the finger of her left hand.

"Celyn never liked it there though, and when he retired, we came back here." She smiled gently, and held up the delicate milk jug, an offering. Aventurine shook her head. Sioned wrinkled her nose cheerfully, and poured out the black tea for her. Sioned took her own tea with both milk and sugar.

"Celyn grew up here?"

"Down along in Cusop Dingle. His brother still lives in the house they were born in." She sighed. "Poor Dafydd. His wife up and left him a few years back." Sioned shook her head. "But you don't want to hear about that."

Aventurine blew across the surface of her tea, which was steaming gently, the scent filling her nose. She *did* want to hear about Dafydd Davies, though, but she could hardly say so. Other people's stories. Other people's problems. One never knew, listening carefully, where the thread of narrative would weave in and out, until one heard it. One never knew where inspiration would appear, until it did.

"And what about you?" Avi asked. "Before you decided to run a bed and breakfast hotel. What did you do?"

Sioned smiled. "I was a nurse. I started in the OR, moved to A & E, and then went into elder care." She seemed to be gazing inward, or backward. "That was the part I liked best, but at the same time, it was the most difficult."

"Why was that?"

"People died in all my work fields, but in elder care, you know it's coming, but you come to know your patients, and that makes it hardest." She lifted her teacup to her lips, still curved upwards in that gentle smile. Then she set her cup and saucer on the low table and tilted her head. "You ask questions like a reporter. Are you?"

"A reporter?" Aventurine laughed, but there was a bitter edge to the laughter. "No. I used to be. But I haven't been for years."

"Why did you stop?"

Well, Neil. Well, hell. Aventurine didn't say that, of course. And was it really true? He'd made her life hell for a while, but then she'd been able to reinvent herself. Right? Her own smile felt as though it had turned grim. "Now I just write books." Obviously not ones that Sioned had read, and there was a bit of a pang of disappointment in that for her.

"Oh." The other woman's hand fluttered down onto the cover of the Ackroyd book. "Oh. I'm sorry. Should I know you? Am I being dreadfully ignorant here?"

This time Aventurine's laugh was genuine. "Don't worry about it. I've done well with a bunch of books—and I even found a couple of mine down in the Honesty Bookshop."

"Then you've made it big then," Sioned said, with a wink. She topped up both their tea cups, added a bit more milk and sugar to her own. "I'll look you up next time I'm down in the village. Or I'll check in the library."

A gust of wind rattled the kitchen windows, but the room was warm. A bookcase took up the wall to Sioned's right; it was stuffed full, books tucked in atop the serried rows. A reader, obviously. It was impossible to tell where *London* made its home among those companions. Avi half-smiled, thinking of her own bookcases in the apartment—how they appeared to have no order, though if called upon she could pluck any of her books out at any time. The ease of familiarity.

"And your sister? Mrs. Genthner?"

Aventurine sighed, her glance shifting to the rain-streaked window and back again. "Micheline used to work as an arts administrator.

She took an early retirement when she lost her husband."

"Oh, that's a shame," Sioned said.

"I kind of wish she'd kept on," Avi mused; the words formed from a nebulous thought she'd carried for a while now. "I wish she'd kept something in her life to keep her occupied."

"She does seem sad." Then Sioned clicked her tongue. "Listen to me. Going on like I know anything about anybody else's situation. But—when Celyn died, I would have been absolutely lost without this place. Doing for guests, changing beds, making breakfast. Like you said: something to keep myself occupied." A fleeting sadness crossed her face and was gone. "Sometimes it's hard to go forward, when you've devoted your life to someone." She patted Aventurine's arm, much as though commiserating with her, rather than with her sister. Then she got to her feet. "I'm just going to hot this tea up a bit."

Aventurine watched her straight back, her strong shoulders. Every movement, as Sioned rinsed and refilled the kettle, rinsed the pot and re-measured the tea, was purposeful.

"Did you and Celyn have any children?"

Again that fleeting sadness, there and gone. "No, it never happened for us. Do you have any? Does Mrs. Genthner?"

"None for me—I've never married. And it's too late now." Aventurine was proud of herself for not hesitating, not stumbling over the words. She took a deep breath. "Micheline has a son, Paul. He's twenty-three. Nearly twenty-four."

"How has he done with his father's death?" The tea hotted up, Sioned returned to her seat in the warm corner. "Tell me if I'm being too nosy. It really isn't any of my business."

Aventurine shrugged. "It's all right. But yes, he's been having a hard time. You see, Shep—his father—was lost at sea."

Sioned stopped midway in pouring the tea, and set the teapot down again. It clinked on the metal tray. She pressed a hand to her mouth. "Oh, Aventurine, that's terrible." The hand was trembling. "Just terrible, for both of them. For all of you."

Avi nodded. "Yeah. They're both struggling with it."

A sudden gust of wind rattled the windows again, and Sioned looked up sharply. "This storm," she murmured, as though it were a personal insult. "I hope we don't have a power cut. I hope trees don't come down on the road." She chuckled grimly. "With no trees close to the house, we don't have much of a windbreak up here. But by the same token, no trees will fall onto the roof, either."

"Small mercies." Aventurine sipped from her cup.

The other woman nodded. "Small mercies."

With a creak, the door from the hall swung open, and Micheline appeared. Her face looked wan from sleep, and her hair was slightly mussed, as though she could not find a comb and could not be bothered about it.

"I'd wondered where you'd gone," she said. Her eyes took in the cozy corner of the kitchen, the tea things. "Am I interrupting?"

Aventurine felt a pang of embarrassment—she'd almost been caught out, talking about her sister—though she had said nothing that wasn't apparent, nothing that wasn't common knowledge. Still, Mick probably wouldn't be comfortable knowing others were talking about her. "No," she said quickly. "Not at all."

"Come on in," Sioned invited. "Let me get another cup."

Avi stood to get a third chair from the table. "Take that one," she said, pointing to the armchair. "I warmed it up for you."

Despite her feeble protestations, Micheline slumped into the comfortable chair. Sioned poured, then handed her a cup and saucer.

"We were just wondering whether there'd be a power cut," their hostess said, throwing a glance over her shoulder toward the window. "We don't often have them, but that wind is certainly howling."

Micheline nodded, looking over the cup she held in both hands. "It kept me from sleeping."

"I was just going to ask how your nap was," Aventurine said, taking a sip from her own tea. Still black as her heart, still hot and delicious. "I guess it didn't go well, then."

Mick made a sour face.

"Have you tried melatonin?" Sioned suggested. "I don't usually go for things like that, but after Celyn died, the doctor prescribed Xanax for me, and it made me sleepwalk into walls." She smiled ruefully. "But I've found melatonin helps, and if I've been sleepwalking, I don't know anything about it."

Sioned sounded so cheerful that Aventurine couldn't help but grin a little. She slewed a glance toward Micheline, to see her response. Especially her response to Sioned's mention of her husband's death. Sometimes, Avi had come to realize, attempts at sympathy—attempts at empathy—simply closed her sister down.

Now it looked as though Micheline was making an extra effort to remain engaged. "I haven't tried it." She looked toward the storm outside the window and frowned. "But I don't think I'll be going out in search of it today."

"Never fear. I've some you can try tonight if you're interested." Sioned now cupped her tea in both hands as Mick had done. "I'll bring it up to your room later." Again she laughed. "Listen to me. I sound like some pusher of herbal remedies and essential oils. Fine thing from a nurse."

"Retired," Avi pointed out.

"Retired," Sioned agreed.

Another gust of wind shook the windows, and the lights flickered and finally went out, leaving them in semi-darkness.

Twelve

They all retired early after vegetable omelettes Sioned had whipped up on the Aga. "Conventional gas flue," she had said cheerfully. "The only ones worth having when there's no electric on." She had lifted her head to listen to the storm raging around Tŷ yn y Coed. "It'll blow itself out by the morning. I'll have to walk down to my brother-in-law's for more eggs, early, if either of you feel up to it."

When she awoke, electricity restored, Aventurine found herself on a footpath through the copse, heading toward Cusop at sunrise the next morning. The world seemed muted, a kind of watercolor, the browns and greens and greys washing one into another, textureless. The sky was lightening, though under the trees was still filmy dimness, but Sioned marched along briskly in her Wellies, sure of the path, no doubt having made the trek innumerable times over the years. Avi had borrowed a pair of high waterproof boots, which she suspected had belonged to Celyn Davies, and squelched along beside her.

"I hope you don't think I was too forward last night," Sioned tossed over her shoulder. She wore a black beanie with a jaunty white pompom atop; her cheeks were reddened in the cold, as no doubt Aventurine's were as well. "Asking about you and your sister. Twin sister, I expect, from the look of the pair of you—though stranger things have happened."

It was almost a question.

Stranger things did indeed happen.

"Yes. Twins." The path was rough and uneven, the wet leaves slick underfoot, and Aventurine found herself wishing for one of Genevieve's blackthorn sticks. She made a mental note to stop into James Smith & Sons in New Oxford Street for one, the next time she was in London. Then she caught herself and changed her mind. Meanwhile, she kept her gaze on the damp ground before her.

Overhead, a sharp demanding bird call. Sioned drew up and lifted her eyes, scanning the bony tree branches overhead.

"Crow," she said, and pointed.

The black bird was silhouetted on a black limb.

"Hello, friend," Sioned called. There was a pause, and then the bird called back. Sioned smiled and marched on. "Most of them know me. Almost there, Aventurine."

Up ahead the path turned a corner. Avi thought she could see movement through the trees.

"Someone's coming. Did you tell Dafydd we'd be along this morning?"

But something didn't feel right. There was a sudden stillness in the air, and then a flutter as the crow lifted off. Avi looked around quickly. No one appeared on the path before them.

"That was—odd," she said, to break the uncomfortable silence.

They rounded the corner.

A man sat on a stump, leaning against the trunk of the tree behind him. His chin was sunk upon his chest, as though he were in deep thought. Or sleeping.

"Dafydd?" Sioned called. Then suddenly more urgent. "*Dafydd?*"

The figure made no move.

Sioned broke into a stumbling run. Aventurine fumbled in her pocket for her cell phone.

Despite Sioned and Aventurine's best joint efforts at CPR, there was no sign of life in Dafydd Davies when the paramedics loaded him into the ambulance and sped away, siren wailing.

"A lift to the hospital?" the constable asked, leaning in solicitously toward Sioned, who held a trembling hand to her white face.

She lifted stricken eyes. "He's gone, isn't he, Glyn?" she asked, her voice higher than normal. "Dafydd. They won't bring him back."

For a moment the policeman hesitated, but then shook his head. "No. More than likely not." Neither from the hospital, nor from the bourne from whence no traveler returned. There was a crackle from his radio, and he made an apologetic face. "Need to take this, then." He stepped a few feet away, along the path toward the farmhouse, the way the paramedics had gone.

The sun had fully risen now, and with it the dawn chorus resumed. Aventurine tucked her hands into her pockets; she hadn't noticed while they had been kneeling in the mud, alternately breathing for Dafydd's lungs and beating for his heart, but she was cold. Very cold. The adrenaline rush was seeping away, and all that was left was the shock. The birds, though—they made her irrationally angry, with their chattering reminder that for everyone else, life went on. *Damned birds.* She scuffed the toe of her too-big boots into the mud.

"Don't," Sioned said quickly. She laid a hand on Aventurine's arm, and dropped it just as quickly.

"Don't what?"

Sioned dropped her gaze to the muddied ground, where a tangled mess of footprints told a frenzied story. "Don't make it any worse," she said. She breathed in deeply. "Glyn's going to have to tape this place off."

"Tape it off?"

Sioned shrugged helplessly. "It was an unattended death, Aventurine. Until the autopsy—" she took another deep breath before trying again. "Until the autopsy is done, the police have to treat this as suspicious."

Thirteen

Aventurine returned to Tŷ yn y Coed with a cat carrier, containing perhaps the calmest feline she'd ever come across. She took the carrier into the kitchen as Sioned—gone down to the hospital with Glyn—had instructed, then closed the door into the rest of the house before letting the cat out.

Billie, Sioned had said, and for the first time had looked as though she might cry. *After Billie Holliday.* The cat was small, a dark calico with a smattering of grey around her nose and mouth. *She's ten or eleven. I don't even remember.*

"What are you doing?" Micheline had appeared in the doorway.

"Close the door again. We don't know how Billie's going to adjust."

"Billie?"

"The cat."

Micheline pulled the door shut behind her again. "Whose cat?"

"Dafydd Davies's cat. Sioned's brother-in-law." Aventurine bit her lip, picturing the way Dafydd had slumped hard as Sioned had attempted to lay him flat on the muddy ground for CPR. She opened a packet of cat food—Sioned had handed her several from Dafydd's kitchen, and she'd shoved them into her coat pockets—and found a dish to slop the unappetizing goop in. This she set on the floor by the sink. "We went down to get eggs. And we—found him." She dropped into one of the high-backed chairs and glanced up at the clock over the Aga. Not even eleven. She was exhausted.

"Found him?" Micheline began opening and closing cupboards, until she found the coffee grounds for the press. Then she set the kettle on and began measuring. "You look like you need a stiff drink, not coffee."

"It's way too early." Aventurine's head was pounding. "He'd had a heart attack or something. Sioned and I did CPR until the paramedics came, just in case, but I think he was already dead before we started."

"Oh, Aventurine," Mick breathed in sympathy, coming to sit next to her. She put a hand on Avi's arm. "Oh, honey."

The sympathy made the backs of Aventurine's eyes prickle, the unshed tears threatening. She dropped her face into her hands. Micheline rubbed her shoulder gently, murmuring endearments.

It was the cat, Billie, threading between her ankles and chirping lightly, that made her sit up at last. She dropped a hand to stroke the black and orange fur. When she straightened, Billie jumped up onto her knees and began to knead.

"No claws," she ordered, automatically. Billie did what Billie did.

"Where's Sioned?" Micheline asked after a moment.

Avi's nose was running, and she patted her pockets for a Kleenex, finding only more packets of cat food. "She rode into the hospital with the police constable to—take care of the formalities. And then she was going to stop into the station and give a statement about— finding her brother-in-law."

The coffee ready, Micheline poured, and then retook the other armchair. She was chewing her lower lip, looking down into her coffee cup as though for a message. A clue. An idea.

"What?" Aventurine prodded.

When Micheline looked up, her shadowed eyes were troubled. "Just—the police."

Aventurine ran a hand through her hair. "I know."

"Another body, Aventurine."

The word made Avi wince. "I know."

"We've got to get out of here." Micheline had only taken one sip of her coffee, and now she set the cup aside with such hurry that it spilled onto the table. "We can't stay here any longer." She stood, looked around almost as though trapped; her agitation was palpable, escalating.

"Micheline—"

Now her eyes blazed. "Don't be stupid, Aventurine. We can't be involved with the police here. We need to protect Paul." Her voice was climbing toward hysteria.

"Nobody knows about Paul," Aventurine reminded her. "And we're going to end up looking pretty suspicious if we disappear the moment Dafydd Davies turns up dead."

"But—"

"Micheline, sit down." Aventurine reached out a hand to tug on her arm. "Sit down. We need to stay put until the authorities do the examination, where they'll more than likely discover he'd had a heart attack. Just a heart attack."

Slowly, with the movements of an elderly person, Micheline lowered herself again into her chair, then cradled her chin in her hands.

"Mick, breathe," Avi urged.

But Micheline shook her head, sudden tears flying from her cheeks. "I'm afraid for him. So afraid."

"I know." The words seemed useless, pointless. "I know." The same fear, gnawing and omnipresent, lived inside Avi's own ribcage.

Micheline scrubbed at her face, but the tears continued to fall. "I just don't know what to do," she sobbed, breaking down as quickly as she had wound herself up. "I don't know how to help him. I don't know how to find out about Shep. My whole family is going to hell, and I can't do anything for them. Not a damned thing."

Fourteen

Micheline had gone out, refusing company, leaving Aventurine by the fire with her notebook, jotting down notes for further research into Katherine Swynford. Her thoughts kept straying, though, and she kept pulling up the pictures on her phone of the underlined passages from *Nightmare Voyage*. What did they mean? Why these words? And why did the book have Mick's name in it, in a hand not hers?

She should have discussed it further with Genevieve, when she had called. She had intended to. But the old woman had made her so angry that she'd quite forgotten her purpose.

Aventurine flipped the page and copied the three lines from her phone screen.

From its beginning to its mysterious end, the voyage was chaos.
No matter what happened, he couldn't bring himself to turn back.
He disappeared over the darkened horizon.

Now she stared at them. Three lines. That might or might not be linked.

Well, they were linked, at their lowest common denominator, she chided herself, being from the same book. She skimmed the pages on which the underlined words resided: they all seemed to be about a sailor called Donald Crowhurst. She set the notebook aside and looked up the name on her phone: an inept and overambitious sailer who had participated in a solo around-the-world competition, but who, it transpired, had never left the Atlantic, and who finally leapt from his own boat, *Teignmouth Electron*, when that became obvious to the sailing world.

Aventurine sat back in the library chair, and stuck her feet out toward the hearth, thinking. Someone had obviously left that book for Micheline. *Micheline M. Genthner.* She flipped to the first page and examined the handwriting: no one's she recognized. But someone had known Mick was going to be there; someone had placed the book in such a way that Mick had found it, had paid her one pound for it. Someone who knew about Mick, and about Shep's disappearance. Someone here, in Hay-on-Wye. Someone who knew way too much about Micheline, and by corollary, about Aventurine.

She quickly dialed Genevieve's number. The phone rang and rang at the other end, until the voicemail message, unchanged from the default impersonal voice, answered. But at that moment, there was a determined knock at the front door. She clicked out of the call without leaving a message.

"Why are you here?" Aventurine demanded.

Dominic Burroughs wore a black raincoat, but no hat. The drizzle had matted his dark hair and streaked down his face. His hands were jammed into his pockets. He stood back away from the door, a curtain of runoff falling between them from the roof overhang.

"The fortuneteller sent me." Burroughs took a hand from his pocket to wipe his face. It had little effect.

"What the hell is that supposed to mean?"

He held out the hand, palm toward her, as though deflecting her words, her annoyance. "Look, do you want to let me in? I walked up from the village. It's pretty wet out here. Not fit for man nor beast, as they say."

Aventurine wondered which he was. She stepped back, wary. When she closed the door behind him, she found him shrugging off the dripping raincoat. His shoes had left wet footprints on the hardwood floor.

"For God's sake, take your shoes off," she ordered. "I've got the fire in the front room. You can try to dry them off, and your coat, too, but I sure don't want you tracking all over the house. You'll tick off the landlady."

She led him into the front room. He set his shoes on the hearthrug, close to the fire irons; Aventurine took his coat and hung it over a chair nearby. When he settled into the seat she indicated—usually inhabited by Mick—and stuck his feet out toward the fire, she noted that his socks were mismatched: one blue, one brown. Was he colorblind? Or had he just dressed this morning in a hurry? It didn't seem the sort of question one just asked, so she pretended she hadn't noticed.

"Tea? Something stronger?"

He half-smiled at her attempt at the unflappable hostess. "Scotch, if you have it."

Aventurine poured him a finger from Sioned's drinks cart, and placed the glass on the low table between the high-backed chairs. There was no way in hell that she was going to hand it to him, and risk touching his skin: she'd probably drop the damned glass on the carpet.

Burroughs seemed to be making himself comfortable. He leaned his head back, his glass cradled in his hands, his eyes closed. He obviously had learned this conversational technique from the same school Genevieve had learned hers. *Don't say anything. Make them talk. People will, just to fill the silence.*

And Aventurine fell for it. "I haven't the slightest idea why you're here. Don't you have a job?" Burroughs's presence alone exacerbated her anxiety, and the anxiety made her snarky.

He cast her a sideways look over his whisky. "I'm allowed days off."

Aventurine met his glance with a slicing one of her own. "So you just came to Hay on your day off. That's all. A distance of a couple hundred miles."

"I read books."

His evasiveness annoyed her; his half-smile annoyed her more.

"This is not a bookshop. Try Richard Booth's." Aventurine glared at him. Her eye fell on her open notebook, which she tried surreptitiously to close. "I'm beginning to feel like you're a bit stalker-ish."

"Ish."

Avi crossed her arms and leaned back in her high-backed chair, mirroring him, waiting. A challenge. For what it was worth, she was on what counted as home turf. *Ish.* She could wait all day. Or until Micheline, or Sioned, who had gone down to her brother-in-law's farmhouse again, returned. *She* didn't have to drive a couple hundred miles back to Lincoln.

For a long time, Burroughs also said nothing, just sipped his whisky while considering the crackling fire. His upper lip glistened slightly with his drink; his black hair was still damp with rain, and Avi wondered how it would feel to run her hands through it.

She found herself gripping the arms of her chair tightly. *Stop it, Aventurine.* She felt the blood rush up into her face and was grateful for the dim lighting.

Burroughs's mouth was turned up at the corner. Too late, she realized he could see her plainly in the mirror to the left of the mantelpiece. She wished she hadn't opted out of the drink now.

"You'd better just tell me what you're up to. Before I go upstairs and lock myself in my room, and leave you down here to explain your presence to the landlady."

"Oh, you'll stick around," Burroughs said comfortably, without looking in her direction. "Because you're curious. I pique your curiosity." He smiled to himself.

"And you're smug. Presumptuous." Aventurine climbed to her feet.

She made it all the way to the door before he spoke. Dryly. Musingly. "I wonder. About Hay Castle."

Aventurine paused, despite herself. But she said nothing.

"It's such a high place."

She did not turn. The doorknob was cold under her hand.

"You seem to be drawn to high places. All the time. City walls. Cathedral roofs. Now ruinous castles."

Still she said nothing. But she could feel her shoulders tighten, as though racked to a band of steel.

"It's just curious, isn't it?" he continued blandly. "How people keep tumbling to their deaths from those high places."

She heard the click as he set his whisky glass on the low table once again.

Say nothing.

Genevieve's voice.

Still, Aventurine could not keep herself from turning slowly and making her way back to her chair. She lowered herself into it much as any ninety-year-old woman, other than Genevieve, would: wincing, then leaning back, clasping her hands in her lap.

Burroughs had finished his whisky, and now he stood to pad his way, in his stockinged feet, to the drinks cart, where he rattled about in the bottles, then poured himself another tot.

"I hope your landlady doesn't mind," he said, lifting an empty glass in her direction, an invitation to join him; Aventurine shook her head, so he recapped the bottle. Her knuckles had begun to ache, and she loosened her fingers. When Burroughs regained the chair beside her, he stuck his feet out before him once again, toward the fire.

"Drinking on duty." Avi attempted a light, mocking tone, but was unsure of her success.

Slowly he turned his hooded eyes on her. "I'm not on duty."

This time it was Joe Friday's gravelly voice in her head, warning her that anything she said could be used against her in a court of law. Did they Mirandize people in the U.K.? She would have to look it up.

"So. Day off, in one of the rainiest Novembers in Hay history, and you come here to look at books." Did she sound skeptical enough?

"I told you. I like books."

"And cat and mouse games." The iron bar she fancied she'd been carrying across her shoulders for ages now seemed to be growing heavier. She touched the notebook, aligning it with the edge of the table. The notebook with the book quotes in it. *Someone else liked* books. *And cat and mouse games.* Unless—but the thought was fleeting, and disappeared.

"Only with you, Aventurine."

She turned to him, feeling her eyes grow wide in her face.

That corner of his mouth turned up again. He held out his glass and turned it in his elegant fingers, in the light of the fire. "Though I've never been certain whether I'm the cat, or the mouse."

Oh. He was certain.

Aventurine wished again for a fortifying drink; why had she turned down his offer? Stupid. She wished for the wily presence of Genevieve, while she was wishing. Or even that the sitting room door would open and Micheline would breeze in—though Mick had hardly been *breezing* anywhere lately. Anything to draw his mocking attention away from her. Avi glanced around the darkening room, where the shadows cast by the flickering fire menaced rather than comforted. There seemed to be no help forthcoming from any quarter.

"I've changed my mind about that drink. Can I top you off?" It hurt to stand, it hurt to walk, she was so tense. The bottle clinked against the edge of her glass, and she bit her lip, holding the whisky up in his direction. When he covered his glass with his hand, she said, "Well, then. Maybe you'd throw another log on that fire." The longcase clock in the hall rang the hour, the sound muted by the closed door; the colors outside the bow window had become dull, faded. Night and winter were drawing in.

Aventurine debated turning on a light. She didn't like the idea of his watching her from the shadows like some sort of predator. She liked even less the idea of giving up the cover the dimness the afternoon gave her. It was like chess, this game they were playing, and she was forced, inexorably, into a defensive position. She had to think two—three—four steps ahead; and conditional thinking always gave her a headache. Commander Smith would no doubt have found her useless. God knows Genevieve would have had her own reservations. *Take control of her own life, indeed.*

The fire blazed up under Burroughs's expert ministration, and the shadows ebbed around them. He set the poker aside and checked his shoes before dusting off his hands and climbing to his feet from the hearth rug. "Suit you?" he asked. His eyes were shadowed, but his voice was still mocking.

Avi tipped a healthy slug of whisky down her throat and returned to her seat. The drink burned, and she immediately began to cough. She set her glass beside his on the table and tried to regain control. Her eyes were streaming. Her face in her hands, Aventurine sensed rather than saw Burroughs lower himself into a crouch before her. He reached a hand to thump her back.

"Easy, tiger," he murmured, close to her ear.

"I'm okay," she gasped, attempting to pull away from his encircling arm. "I'm okay."

Burroughs laughed. When she opened her eyes, he rocked away on his heels and held out a handkerchief for her watering eyes.

"Stop it," she ordered. She pushed his hand away. "I told you I'm fine."

"All right." He tucked his handkerchief away again in his back pocket. Still close. Too close. He seemed to be reveling in her discomfort, though he made no move to come any closer.

Genevieve's warning sounded very far away. Aventurine tried to pull back, but she was trapped in her chair. She glared at him, trying to convey a distaste she could not really feel. *Think of Paul*, she reminded herself, panicking. *Protect Paul.*

And just like that, he straightened and returned to his chair.

Aventurine fell back in her own seat. "Holy Mary, mother of God."

"Not hardly." His teeth showed white when he grinned, and she fought an overwhelming urge to punch them down his throat. Kiss the bastard, or kill him: there seemed no middle ground. "Remember that night at the cathedral, Aventurine?" he continued. "Bonfire Night. In more ways than one."

Remember? It had been just a few weeks ago. She kept silent. Anything she said could be used against her, in a court of law or otherwise. All of this added to her anxiety. She clenched her hands. Unclenched them. Her knuckles hurt.

Burroughs seemed not to notice. "I've been thinking about that for ages."

That. Aventurine didn't need to ask what he meant by *that.* She couldn't help but wonder what it would be like to do *that* again. Stupid girl. She tried to shut out Genevieve's warning voice altogether. But the old woman had become her conscience. *Stay away from that policeman. Stay away from that policeman.*

Now she added *don't sleep with that policeman.*

Burroughs appeared not to notice—or at least not to care about— her befuddlement. He lifted his half-empty drink and kept on.

"I couldn't stop thinking about that, you know, Aventurine." He sighed, tipping back his glass, and then once again holding it up to peer through it at the fire. "How you acted drunk, how you tasted drunk, and how I can't get past this feeling that you weren't even close to drunk."

"If it looks like a duck—"

He cut her off. "Oh no, Aventurine. You're no duck. And I'm no fool."

"I never said you were—"

Again he spoke over her. "Unless I'm very much a fool." His glass empty, Burroughs set it on the table and got to his feet. He crossed to the fire, prodded the coals with the poker, then set that aside against the carved fireplace surround. "You see, I very much wanted to kiss a woman who either makes a habit of being in the absolute wrong place at the wrong time, or who is a cold-blooded killer." Slowly he turned to face her, his profile illuminated from below, all sharp angles and shadows. "Which is it, Aventurine?"

Dumbfounded, she could only stare up at him.

He thought she was a killer.

She wanted to defend herself, but how could she possibly explain any of it to him, without beginning at the beginning, and implicating Paul? Who had only been defending Genevieve, but who had swung that fatal blow at Neil. And how all of them became accessories after the fact, in attempting to delay discovery of Neil's death. She'd have to admit her own role. Micheline's. Lance's. And later, Nicola's and Henry's. No. They were all implicated, all in too deep, and there was no safe way to explain anything.

"Don't look at me like that," Burroughs said, his voice raw.

She had no words.

"Don't, Aventurine." He turned—almost flung—himself away, leaning heavily against the mantelpiece, his head on one hand. He muttered something, something she couldn't quite hear, but which sounded like *I hate this*. She looked at his back, the still-damp shoulders of his pale blue shirt.

The impossible moment stretched.

"Well, if this isn't a turn-up for the books."

Aventurine sprang up at the sound of Micheline's dry voice, awash in—what? Embarrassment? Shame? Relief? *She hadn't done anything. She hadn't said anything.* But she felt disappointment at that: definitely disappointment, as her hands remembered the feel of his shoulders, his chest, as she had kissed him on Bonfire Night.

Micheline advanced into the room, stooping to turn on a table lamp as she passed. She swept a hand toward the glassware on the table. "I see you've started early." Her fine eyebrows rose over her sunken eyes. Her voice, to Aventurine, sounded barely controlled, and there was anger in the look she cast Avi. "Or possibly several things." She held out a formal hand to Burroughs. "I'm Micheline Genthner. I don't believe we've met."

Slowly Burroughs took her hand. "Dominic Burroughs, Mrs. Genthner," he said easily. Avi had to admire his aplomb, though she resented it a great deal.

"Detective Chief Inspector Burroughs," Aventurine pointed out, keeping her voice flat. "From Lincoln."

Micheline's mouth tightened.

Burroughs's eyes roved between the two of them. Mick, as always, looked far more put-together, though her eyes were sunken and shadowed, more pronounced in her pale face by the low lighting. No stranger would see the anger, but to Aventurine it was plain. She knew her own face would be flushed, and she caught herself putting a hand to her hair and finding it mussed.

"My twin sister," Aventurine clarified, as though it would be necessary. Under Mick's calculating eye, she resisted the urge to touch her fingers to her lips. Her voice, too—it sounded breathless, as though she'd been running. "Most people can't tell us apart. She's younger, by eight minutes." Babbling. She was babbling. She snapped her mouth closed.

"And how much younger is Nicola Hallsey?" Burroughs asked mildly. Just a question in passing.

"We don't—" Micheline broke off, started again. "I don't know what you're talking about."

We. I. Pronoun confusion. A common occurrence. No doubt Burroughs picked up on it.

"My mistake," he said. "You'll have to forgive me. I get so confused."

Aventurine doubted it. Mick looked like she did, too.

"To what do we owe the pleasure?" Micheline made it sound as though it wasn't a pleasure at all, but rather an interrogation. Complete with implements of torture.

Burroughs smiled at Mick, but Avi knew the smile was directed toward her. "I thought, as I was passing through to look at the books—I like books—I'd stop in to say hello to Aventurine. To Ms. Morrow." If anything, his smile grew broader, more wolfish. "And now that my shoes have dried, I'll put them back on and be on my way."

Aventurine saw Micheline's glance take in his stockinged feet as he seated himself to pull on his shoes—which didn't appear dry at all, and which made squelching noises as he tied them. Slowly Mick turned back to Avi. *What the hell?* she mouthed.

Aventurine made a tiny gesture with the fingers of her left hand. *Wait.* She took his coat from the back of the chair near the fender and shook it out. Still damp, but at least raindrops didn't go flying everywhere. Satisfied with his shoes, he shrugged his way into the coat.

"Thank you," he said, bowing slightly. "And thank your landlady for the whisky. I'll see myself out."

Avi and Mick glanced quickly at each other, then turned their gazes to his retreating back. Avi was holding her breath, and she rather thought her sister was, too.

Burroughs had his hand on the doorknob when he turned to cast them one last look. His eyes flickered from one to the other. A couple of quick steps brought him back to Aventurine, where he grasped her upper arms and kissed her, brief but hard.

"I can tell the difference," he said against her mouth, before turning away.

This time Aventurine couldn't help but put a shaking hand to her lips.

"Your socks don't match," Micheline called after him.

They only heard his laugh until the closing front door cut it off.

Fifteen

"What the hell was that all about?" Micheline demanded. She tore off her raincoat impatiently, threw it aside, and then poured herself a drink, which she then set on the mantelpiece before whirling away. "That policeman. He's the one from Lincoln. *That* Chief Inspector Dominic Burroughs."

"Yes." Slowly Aventurine moved to sink into her chair, her fingers still at her lips. "DCI Burroughs."

"Rather a formal way to refer to a man you were kissing like that."

"Dominic. His name is Dominic. And *he* was kissing *me*." She had come that close, Aventurine realized, *that* close. She looked up at the pale, unhappy oval of her sister's face. "Thank God you came back. I would have done it otherwise, Mick. I would have taken him upstairs. I would have taken him to bed."

"Are you insane, Aventurine?"

"I know."

"What were you thinking?"

"I know."

"And risk everything?"

"Micheline, *I know.*"

Side by side now in their accustomed high-backed chairs, the sisters sat back. The waves of anger, tinged by fear, that rolled off of Micheline were almost palpable. She had left her drink up on the mantelpiece, and seemed to have forgotten it. She glared fiercely into the fire. Aventurine dropped her own gaze to the two empty glasses on the table, which might have looked companionable, but she knew better.

"Aventurine," Micheline whispered after a moment, "I trusted you."

"I didn't tell him anything."

"You let him kiss you."

"I didn't *let* him do *anything*. You stood right there. You saw it all."

"You could have avoided him."

"How? Tell me how." Avi took a deep breath. "I didn't invite him here, Mick. I don't even know how he knew we were here. He just showed up."

"You could have—"

"Run him off?" Aventurine laughed bitterly. "I don't see how I could have, without arousing his suspicions. Arousing his suspicions *more*."

"But Paul—"

Aventurine threw herself to her feet, impatiently. "Come on, Micheline. Paul is everything I think about. All the time. Every damned moment. How to protect him. How to keep him safe."

"Talking to a policeman—kissing a policeman—is going to keep him *safe*?"

"Behaving suspiciously around a policeman is going to keep Paul safe?" Avi countered. "Be smart about this, Mick."

Micheline looked away, her lips pressed tightly together. "Why?" she demanded. She was as close to being on screech as it was possible for anyone to be. "Why was he even here?"

"Looking at books."

"Aventurine, so help me God—"

Avi threw up her hands. "That's what he said—that's all I know."

"And you believe him?"

"Of course I don't believe him. What kind of an idiot do you think I am?"

There was a discreet knock at the door, and Sioned peered around at them. "I'm sorry. Am I interrupting? I just got back from Dafydd's. I thought you might like tea?" Indeed, even with the distance between them, her exhausted face was in evidence.

Aventurine quickly put up a hand. "We're fine, Sioned. Please don't go to any trouble."

But Sioned only shook her head. "I've already started the water. It's no trouble." She looked down at her hands, frowning. "It's better if I keep busy."

They acquiesced, and she disappeared again.

Micheline sighed and ran a hand over her tired face. Her skin looked grey from exhaustion, just as Sioned's had. "I'm sorry. *I'm sorry.* I don't think you're an idiot at all." She, like Burroughs before her, stuck her stockinged feet out toward the fire, where the log fell and sparked up the chimney.

Aventurine, too, deflated. "I've been hanging out with Genevieve enough over the past several months to never take anyone at face value again." Mick looked stricken, and Avi put a hand out to touch her arm. "Except you, of course." They both had the same face, after all.

And so did Nicola.

She thrust the thought away.

"I don't think he really cared whether I believed him or not. After all, even if he knew we were in Hay, he surely didn't know *where* in Hay. And Tŷ yn y Coed isn't exactly on the main drag, so his finding us here can't be coincidental. He had to realize I'd know he was up to something."

"And he said nothing else?"

Aventurine snorted. "Didn't have much chance, did he?"

"Brazen." Mick was trying.

"Hey, I'm just practicing being a Bad-Ass Bitch of Britain."

"Well, yeah, there's that."

Avi had begun to feel the iron easing out of her shoulders; it was a relief, too, to find the tiniest spark of Mick's sense of humor showing through. As much as Avi had enjoyed the taste and the feel of Dominic Burroughs, it was not healthy to be in a constant state of vague panic. "He did actually say something—odd—before—"

"Something more odd than mentioning Nicola?"

"Before that."

"Do we need to wait for the tea for this?"

With perfect timing, Sioned appeared again at the door, pushing the trolley. This afternoon she had included scones. She positioned the cart, straightened, and brushed her hands off on her apron. Those hands, Aventurine noticed, had a slight tremor.

"Sit with us?" Avi asked. "Have a cup of tea?"

But Sioned waved the suggestion away. "Thank you, no. Too much to do here. Dafydd—" her voice trailed away.

Aventurine nodded. "Of course. If you change your mind, we're here."

Aventurine watched Sioned's retreating back, then turned to her sister. Was exhaustion contagious? She felt a weakness creeping up inside herself, and was grateful when Mick, making short work of pouring out the tea, handed her a cup, steaming and black.

"Go on, then," Micheline prodded.

The tea burned in her mouth. Avi grimaced. "He said he didn't know whether I was a person in the wrong place at the wrong time, or—"

"Or?"

"Or a cold-blooded killer."

"Shit."

"Shit is correct."

Micheline added more milk to her tea, and took a long drink. Then she poured more from the teapot into her cup. "Shit, Aventurine. What did you tell him?"

"I didn't answer. Because, again, I don't think my answer would really matter to him."

Mick's ironic laugh strangled into a hiccup. "No. No." She set her cup aside; her hand, too, was visibly shaking. "No, a person who needs to ask that question has already decided upon the answer."

She leaned back, her eyes on the mirror beside the mantel. "But then again, if he's made up his mind about you, then—" her voice trailed off, and she shifted her glance to Avi, and back to the mirror again—" then he's not looking at Paul."

"So I should sacrifice myself for Paul?"

Micheline turned the full power of her burning gaze upon Aventurine.

"Yes."

Sixteen

A text, while Avi was putting another log on the fire. She drew the phone from her pocket and read it quickly.

I need to talk to you. Make sure you're alone.

She straightened so abruptly that she knocked her head on the mantelpiece.

"Careful," Mick said automatically.

Aventurine put her hand to her hairline. "Am I bleeding? I think I'm bleeding."

"You're a drama queen."

"I've got to check."

Leaving her sister in the dimness of the front room, Aventurine dodged up the stairs and into her room.

What is it?

The cell phone vibrated. She answered. "What is it?"

"Are you alone?"

"I left Mick downstairs."

"Good. That's the best way to help your sister."

"For what?"

"You need to find that letter. We need to know what's in it. She's hiding something from us. Or at least, she's not giving us the entire story. And we can't help her unless we know everything."

"I can't—"

"You can." The connection was cut.

Damn it.

Aventurine glanced guiltily over her shoulder, feeling the prickles of sweat at her hairline. She peered into the mirror over the sink—she was *not* bleeding, though there was a reddened patch of skin where she had knocked herself, and she might have a bruise by morning. In her palm, the brass knob to Micheline's door was cold, but turned easily; she was disappointed, having wanted it to be locked, so that she would be forced to return to her own room, call Genevieve back, and give her a helpless *oh, well*. But that wish, too, was stupid: she could see, in her mind's eye, the hardening of the old spy's expression, could hear her sardonic voice ordering her to *find the key*, or perhaps to *use a credit card*.

I don't have Mary Wentworth's bank card, she heard herself protest.

Avi strained to hear any sounds of movement in the house that would help her place the other women. Micheline was still at her tea, awaiting Aventurine's return; Sioned was probably still in the kitchen. Still, she couldn't be too long in her sister's room. She couldn't be caught going through her sister's things. That was a violation of trust, and she knew it; it was simply not done. Except— it had to be done. Genevieve had—mostly—convinced her.

She's hiding something from us.

There was nothing Aventurine wanted more than to help her sister, and by extension, her nephew. *Damn you, Shep.* She turned the knob slowly and slipped into the bedroom, then she closed her eyes and leaned against the door, trying to regulate her breathing. On the bedside table she saw the book, *Nightmare Voyage*, where she'd left it. She picked it up. If Mick reappeared, Avi would tell her she was just returning the book. She'd say she found it downstairs, that Mick must have left it there—and hopefully she wouldn't question.

Aventurine scanned the room. Where would Micheline keep the

letter, so important to her that she kept it near all the time, and had since she had first received it? Avi bit her lip. The entire effort would be moot if Mick had that envelope in her pocket downstairs. But there was nothing for it: Aventurine was in, and she had to look.

The phone buzzed again.

Don't waste time reading it. Take a picture and get out.

Nothing atop the dresser. Hurriedly Aventurine opened the drawers and ran her hands between T-shirts and folded jeans. She loathed herself as she sifted through the drawer with socks and underwear. Nothing.

Aventurine paused again and listened to the house. She could hear no one stirring. Mick and Sioned were staying put in their respective rooms.

There was another book on the far nightstand. Avi reached for it, then stopped, her hand in midair, her mouth suddenly dry. *Three Months Lost at Sea.* There was a familiar yellow and orange train ticket tucked between the pages as a bookmark. Again she was struck by her position, violating her twin's privacy. She glanced furtively over her shoulder again, but the door to the hallway remained closed, the house quiet. She was still the only person moving. That didn't make any of this less distasteful.

She picked up the book and opened it first to the flyleaf: *Micheline M. Genthner.* Not in her sister's handwriting. A quick picture, and then she opened further to the train ticket. Was this the place Mick had most recently left off reading? Or was there something on this page that struck her enough to need to mark it? She scanned until she found the underline: *Disaster at sea can happen in a flash. Without warning. It can happen after a stretch of anticipation and anxiety. It does not always come in storms, but may arise when the ocean is calm and flat.*

Her stomach dropped. She hurriedly snapped a picture of this page as well. As she turned to slip her phone back into her pocket, the book fell from the bed with a thud. She glanced around quickly, listening to see if there was any reaction to the noise. Nothing. So far so good. She stooped to the book, and found, penciled in at the bottom of the page, a light note.

Tylwyth teg

More Welsh.

Aventurine really wasn't that good. Not even close to fluent. However, she was getting better at decoding, as her vocabulary increased. This had her stumped—she had never come across these words in her attempts at learning the language. She supposed she could look it up, but there really wasn't time right now. She set the book back on the coverlet and retrieved her phone, Genevieve's instructions in her head. She took one picture, and then a second just to be sure.

There was no time. On the off-chance there was something else, she sifted through the remainder of the pages. No other scraps of paper marked other places. She found no other writing with this cursory examination.

But still no letter.

Then, a thought.

Setting *Adrift* back on the nightstand, she slid a hand beneath the plumped-up pillows on the bed.

And there it was. Another book. Of course.

Mick and Avi had always shared the habit of tucking their present read beneath their pillows when they began to doze off. As children, they had both kept flashlights under their pillows as well, for clandestine reading. Even though she was an adult, Avi still retained that habit, because one never knew when the power would go out, or when she'd need a means of self-defense.

God, she was beginning to think like Genevieve. *Self-defense.* That was disconcerting.

This one was *Foxglove Summer*, from the Rivers of London series. Good old Ben Aaronovitch. Slowly Aventurine lay the book on the coverlet, in the impression the other had left, and flipped through it with a cautious finger. Sandwiched between the pages was the letter. She stared at it for a horrified moment, then glanced around guiltily.

We can't help her unless we know.

The envelope was much grimier than Aventurine remembered, probably from Micheline's constant handling: it was more creased, but her sister's name—*Micheline*—was still clear, incised as it was in Shep's forceful handwriting. Avi took a quick photo of where the envelope was *in situ*. Then she eased it from its place and slid her finger under the flap.

A noise in the lower hall—the front door? Front room door? Door to the kitchen? Most likely Micheline, wondering what was keeping her. Hurriedly, Aventurine pulled the single sheet from the envelope and flattened it out on the coverlet. She snatched up her phone yet again, and, holding the paper with her free hand, snapped a burst of pictures. Then she stuffed the letter back into its envelope, the envelope back into *Foxglove Summer*, and replaced the book under the pillow.

Steps approaching up the stairway. Hastily Aventurine slipped into the bathroom and closed the door. At the moment she heard the creak of Mick's bedroom door's hinges, she flushed the toilet.

Washing her hands under the faucet did nothing to alleviate her feelings of guilt, however. She suspected, should she look up into the mirror over the sink, that she would see not herself, but Lady Macbeth at her most haunted and deranged. "*Out, out, damned spot,*" she found herself muttering.

"Is that you, Avi?" Micheline called.

For a moment, Aventurine opened her mouth and nothing came out. She had violated her sister's privacy, her sister's trust. She pressed her cold wet hands to her face. "Who else?" she managed at last; her voice sounded strangled to her own ears. She grabbed the hand towel and scrubbed her cheeks with it. Then she opened the bathroom door to her sister, for all the world as though she had not just availed herself of what was arguably Micheline's most private possession.

She hadn't read it.

The thought appeared like a lifeline.

Looking into her sister's wan face as Micheline flicked on the bedside light, Aventurine tried to comfort herself by reminding herself she hadn't read the contents of the letter yet, and could still delete the photos without reading the last words Shep had sent to his wife.

Still, that would not erase the fact that she had searched her sister's belongings for that letter, had opened that letter, had taken photos of that letter—all without Micheline's permission.

She was damned either way.

Micheline now seated herself on the bed, her coat thrown over the back of the nearby desk chair. She looked up as Aventurine stepped further into the bedroom.

"Are you okay?" Mick frowned. "You look—odd."

Aventurine felt odd. She shook her head. "Not feeling quite—right—this afternoon." That much, at any rate, was true. She found it difficult to meet her twin's eyes, and rubbed at her own with her balled fists.

"Was it the phone call?"

The pause was only a fraction of a moment, and Avi hoped Mick hadn't noticed; she'd quite forgotten her excuse to leave the front room and come upstairs. "No. No, that's all right." She licked her lips. "It was my agent." She took a deep breath.

"Do you need something?" Mick got to her feet slowly, as though she knew how she ought to respond, but was finding it hard. "Panadol? Antacids? More tea?"

But Aventurine only held up a hand. "Darkness, I think," she said, a kind of dodge. "Quiet. I think I'll just pull the curtains and have a lie-down." She peered again at her sister, pale, wan, sluggish. "I suggest you do the same."

Seventeen

Aventurine finally sat up on the bed where she had tried, with no success, to nap. There was no sound from the room beyond the bath. She pulled on her jacket and went downstairs and outside, where the rain had ended, albeit reluctantly. It was cold, but without wind; in the garden, where the sky glowed eerily to the west where the sun was setting, and more eerily to the east where the moon rose, she found Sioned, who straightened at her appearance. The other woman put one hand to the small of her back; in the other she held a pair of secateurs. She wore no gardening gloves. At her feet lay bits of dead branches she'd cut and thrown to the ground. Her round face was reddened and damp, though whether from the misty November air or from tears, it was impossible to tell.

A rusty wheelbarrow stood half-full nearby. Wordlessly Aventurine made her way down the steps to gather the dead branches and toss them in with the others.

"Do you need any more help?" It was the only kind of sympathy Avi knew how to offer. "It's going to be too dark to work in a few minutes."

Sioned shrugged, pulling her shoulders back into a stretch. Up close, her greying hair was benetted with tiny beads of moisture. "Not really. There's no hurry with all this." She waved a vague hand around at a garden disordered by wind and rain. "I just didn't know what to do with myself." She looked down at the secateurs in her hand as though seeing them for the first time and not recognizing them at all.

A crow called from a tree at the end of the garden, another answering from behind the house and over the road. The sky overhead was sullen.

"Hello, friend," they both called at the same time, and then both laughed uneasily.

"I leave them things," Sioned said, looking in the direction of the trees, that might have been inching ever closer in the strange and subdued light. "Unmatched earrings. Bottle tops. Five P coins." Her smile seemed to be directed more inward then out, somehow. "They like shiny things. *Arian*." Another helpless shrug. "Dafydd did that, and it's a habit I picked up from him. I was nervous about crows—big black things, you know, the Morrigan—before he taught me that they had different personalities. Now they're friends."

"You'll miss him."

"Yes. He was a good man, Dafydd." Suddenly, she slapped a hand to her forehead. "Oh. His ex-wife."

Aventurine wiped at her face, now feeling as damp as Sioned's looked. She glanced up toward the windows, and picked out the one behind which was Micheline's room. Was that a hand at the curtain? "Ex-wife?" Sioned had mentioned her before.

"She left him—a couple of years ago. He really hadn't been right since. But I don't know where she's gone. Surely she'd want to know that he's—died." Sioned scuffed the toe of her work boots into the wet ground. "I don't even know why I'm out here. It's too wet, too cold." She glanced sideways, her mouth twisted. "Come inside and have a hot drink with me. This gardening isn't going to solve anything." She took a step toward the full wheelbarrow, and then waved it off impatiently. "I'll get that later. Or not."

Aventurine followed her toward the kitchen door, shoving her own cold hands into the pockets of her jacket.

The kitchen smelled warm and inviting; Aventurine was able to trace the scent to the big pot on the back of the Aga, warming gently. Stew of some sort, meaty and rich. A round loaf on the sideboard was covered with a cloth. Dinner, she thought, for the grieving and otherwise troubled.

"I hope you and your sister will stay in and have a bit of supper with me," Sioned said as she shed her raincoat and lined her boots up on the rack beside the door. When she glanced up, there appeared to be more lines around her eyes and mouth, and her expression was tired. "It's not a nice evening to walk down into the village, and quite frankly—" her half-smile was rueful— "I don't much fancy being alone in this old house tonight."

Dafydd, of course. Aventurine nodded. "Yes. I understand."

The tea appeared quickly, and Sioned indicated the chairs in the corner. Avi took one after kicking off her own muddy shoes.

"*Rhag ofn i'w ysbryd gerdded*," she said, wiping a hand across her brow. She glanced over and chuckled mirthlessly. "Something my mother-in-law used to say. Then she'd cross herself, though she wasn't Catholic."

Avi frowned. *Ysbryd.* She knew that one.

Sioned slipped into her chair. "In case his spirit walks," she translated. "Though I don't think Dafydd will." Her eyes swam in unshed tears, and she turned a quick look on Avi. "You're right. I'll miss him. He was a—strange—man, Dafydd, but kind. Kept more to himself once his wife left, but the kindness never left him."

Aventurine nodded and sipped her tea.

Sioned sighed and set her cup aside; from a wide basket on the other side of her chair, she withdrew a length of knitting, a soft grey, but as yet unidentifiable. Narrow, and round: a sock? But Sioned crushed it in her hands, and dropped her hands to her lap.

The slightest of pressure around her ankles: Avi looked down to the cat Billie, twining around her legs. She patted her lap, an invitation, and Billie leapt up without hesitation.

"No claws," Aventurine instructed out of habit. The cat gave her a slow blink. Acquiescence, or disdain? One could never tell with cats. Cautiously she ran her hand down the tortie fur.

Outside the window, the day had fully surrendered to night. In the moonlight, the back garden shimmered, otherworldly. Billie washed her face gently with a delicate paw, and then curled into a ball on Avi's lap.

"You're a Welsh speaker," she said.

Sioned shrugged. "Enough to get by." That rueful half-smile again. "I've picked up some over the years—can't be helped, marrying into this family, and then returning here when Celyn retired."

"But—you have a Welsh name?"

This time the smile was full. "Parental vagaries. Perhaps mine wanted me to be Welsh, or perhaps recognize the Welsh blood in our family. Perhaps they were just manifesting my destiny for me." She looked down at her knitting, but did not lift it from her lap.

Billie was still, wound into a cat-bagel shape. Avi petted her roundness again, and the cat began to purr gently. Outside, the silveriness had gone, the moon perhaps swallowed by clouds. "Can you tell me what *tylwyth teg* means?"

"*Tylwyth teg*?" Sioned echoed, picking up her teacup again. "Whatever would you need to know that for?"

Aventurine frowned. When she stopped stroking Billie, the cat opened her eyes and did a slow yellow blink. Avi began again, and the purring resumed. "Humor me for a second. I'm not sure where this is going." Well, she did know, but she felt the urge to play this one close to the chest.

Sioned shrugged. "All right. The *tylwyth teg* are fairies. The fair family, literally."

"Fairies."

"There are several branches. Most bear no resemblance to Tinkerbell, however, no matter what J. M. Barrie might have you believe."

"Mischievous? Or evil?" No one bore any resemblance to Tinkerbell anywhere other than in Neverland, but that was beside the point.

Aventurine reached to her pocket for her phone, but did not draw it out, unwilling to look at the pictures she'd snapped earlier, unwilling to let Sioned—anyone—see what she had found.

"Mostly mischievous. Welsh fairies sometimes work in mines, which is rather to be expected. Sometimes they deal in changelings."

Aventurine's chest constricted. Billie flexed her claws, and Avi felt them in her leg. She shifted, and the cat, disturbed and disgusted, leapt down and sashayed away. "Changelings?" she managed.

"Children. The *tylwyth teg* steal them in the night, replace them with look-alikes."

Look-alikes.

Aventurine drew in a sharp breath.

Sioned glanced up from her knitting. "Are you all right, Aventurine? You've suddenly got a strange look about you."

Quickly, Aventurine pulled herself together, managing a tight laugh. "I'm fine. Just—Billie and her claws."

Billie had gone to her cat bed near the sink, and turned her back on both of them.

"I'm so sorry—"

"It's nothing." Aventurine waved a hand. "Changelings?"

Again the shrug. Sioned peered out the window into the again-shimmering darkness and shrugged. "You know. Changing one baby for another in the night. Magic might be necessary to return the stolen child to its true home, its true family."

Stolen child.

A poem by William Butler Yeats. Aventurine knew that one. And she knew the song the Waterboys had made of it. She had not read the poem nor listened to the song in years, unable to think of babies changing hands without equating it to her own situation. Her twin sister's situation. Paul's situation.

But there had been no magic involved there. Just love. And secrecy.

"Can I ask you why you're suddenly interested in the *tylwyth teg*?" Sioned glanced over, then away again. She lifted the teapot. Avi's tea was gone now; her stomach was roiling, and she didn't think she could bear to drink anymore. "Or is it some writing thing, and I'm intruding? Don't be afraid to tell me, if that's the case. I won't mind at all."

"I ran across it in a book," Aventurine said. Which was true, and seemed to satisfy the other woman.

They fell silent. At last, Sioned retrieved her knitting and now frowned gently down at the rows, running a hand along the needle and counting to herself. Aventurine turned back to the window, but barely registered the otherworldly evening outside. She pressed a hand to her leg, where Billie's clawing still hurt, wondering, again, about the words. Fairies. Written in the margin in what was not her sister's handwriting. The page had been marked, though, no doubt by Micheline. What was Micheline thinking about that? What was she supposed to know?

And why was she keeping it secret?

On the way to her room—"*it's only stew; we can eat whenever you like*"—Aventurine paused a moment at her sister's door. She lifted a hand to knock, but thought she heard a muffled sob.

"Mick?" she called softly.

There was an audible click, and the thin sliver of light on the floor of the hallway at her feet disappeared.

But not before she'd seen the book on the low shelf between their two doors, pale, where it had been shelved backwards. A collected Yeats. Aventurine pulled it out and, tucking it under her arm, continued to her own room, heartsick.

Eighteen

In her hand, Aventurine held her phone, glowing eerily in the darkness of her midnight bedroom. It was open to the photo Lance had sent from the evening street outside the Teatro alla Scala. Avi chewed her lip and threw her head back on the pillow, looking out the window at the moon without really seeing it.

What could it mean?

Nicola. In Italy. In Milan.

Crossing and recrossing Paul and Lance's path.

After Henry had texted the other evening to ask whether she was in Hay with Aventurine and Micheline. No. She was in Milan with—and not with—Paul and Lance.

The moon looked a sliver less than full: was it before or after the full moon? She hadn't looked at a calendar, checked dates, in a while. She knew hardly anything about the heavens in any case, and once again cursed her lack of knowledge. Shep would know, having had to teach himself to navigate by the stars. Shep, whose knowledge of celestial navigation had done him no good at all. Shep, who had been lost at sea.

Aventurine breathed in the cold air, which felt brittle in her lungs. She closed her eyes and listened to the sounds of the night in Tŷ yn y Coed. The old house creaked and groaned as it settled for sleep. From Mick's room beyond the adjoining bath—she'd left the door cracked—she heard the creak of bedsprings, and then nothing else.

Mick turning over in her sleep; at least she wasn't sobbing, at least she might be getting some rest. In her mind's eye she imagined her sister sleeping fitfully, clutching Shep's letter to her breast, the letter Micheline had no doubt by now memorized, but the handwriting of which she gazed at hungrily every day. The letter she, Aventurine, had opened and had taken a photograph of. The photo in her phone's app right now.

She clenched her eyes shut against the wave of revulsion at what she had done.

She hadn't read it.

Aventurine clutched at that scrap, the only thing that allowed her any self-respect at all. There was still a chance at redemption: there was still time to delete the photograph without looking. Without reading those very precious, very private words.

It was an edge. A cliff upon which she was precariously balanced. If she read those words, that was something from which there would be no going back.

Aventurine took a deep breath.

She dropped the phone onto the coverlet, where it gave off its eerie accusing glow. Way back in the summer, Paul, fueled by Neil's poisonous insinuations, had accused her of sleeping with Shep, of having an affair with her twin sister's husband. Aventurine choked back the bile, which rose into her throat at the thought. Shep had been Micheline's from the moment he had set eyes on her; Shep would never have—had never—looked in Aventurine's direction. Shep could definitely tell them apart. And there was no way in hell that Aventurine would ever have betrayed her twin's trust like that.

How much difference was there between that, and this photographing of Shep's last message to Micheline?

But she hadn't read it yet.

She could just—not.

For the longest of moments, Aventurine closed her eyes and imagined herself free of the weight of her own actions. Of her own betrayal. Knowing, all the while, in the roiling pit of her stomach, that it didn't matter. She had searched her sister's room. She had found and photographed the letter. She had lied. She had violated Micheline's trust.

The phone buzzed again, another text.

Who is this?

Aventurine stared at the photograph of Nicola, seated in the gloaming on one of the stone benches of the semi-circle before the Teatro alla Scala. She had her phone out, and did not seem to be aware of Lance's furtive photo. Even with her head bowed to her own screen, her features were obvious.

Nicola Hallsey, she texted back.

Grandmother, cousin, half-sister.

The stolen child. The words came unbidden. Aventurine had thought of them in the context of Paul, earlier. But they could apply just as easily to Nicola. *The changeling.*

Unless she and Micheline were the changelings.

She stared at the face, the hair. So like her own. So like her sister's. Either way, possibly Paul's aunt.

Be careful of her, she texted hurriedly. **She could be dangerous.**

Part II:

Puzzle Pieces

Nineteen

This is where it begins.

Or ends. Aventurine had a sense of doom—of meeting her fate as she sank down on the edge of the bed in Micheline's room. Micheline's *former* room. Avi glanced around helplessly. Nothing of Mick's was left: the wardrobe stood empty, a door hanging ajar. The hairbrush and makeup paraphernalia were gone from the top of the dresser. No book lay on the bedside table; when she slid her hand under the pillow—which still bore the impression of her sister's head—Avi found the Aaronovitch book gone as well. Through the door to the bathroom, she could see Mick's toothbrush still in the glass at the back of the sink. Mick had cleared out and forgotten her toothbrush—or had left it there, trying not to disturb Aventurine in her sleep. Somehow both options left Avi feeling incredibly bereft.

Micheline must have gone in the night; she had to have moved swiftly and silently to keep Aventurine from hearing her in her flight. Feeling numb, Avi stood again and stumbled to the window. The rental car was gone. Mick had taken it, had disappeared silently into the darkness, and Aventurine, in sleep, had noticed nothing.

Avi leaned her forehead against the cold glass and closed her eyes against the frosty grey November morning. Under her hand, the curtain felt rough, and she clenched the material in her fingers, trying somehow to find the thing she could hold onto.

Not even a note. Her sister—her *twin* sister—Micheline had not even left a note for her saying where she had gone or why.

For a long time, Aventurine stood frozen, her hands twined in the curtains. In the distance, she heard Sioned moving about downstairs: opening and closing a door, then running the vacuum cleaner. Normal sounds. Everyday sounds. And still Micheline was gone.

Everything so neat. So planned. No sign of struggle, no sign of haste, no sign of indecision. Simple planning. As though Micheline had known she was going. And she had said nothing to Aventurine.

When the early morning sun had crept upwards over the hills into the garden, Avi finally looked up again. She needed to talk to someone. Paul, perhaps? He might know where his mother had gone. She might have gone to meet him. That made sense, didn't it? Except for their estrangement—Paul had not wanted anything to do with either of them for months, since Neil had given him the photograph, had twisted the story of his birth into something ugly.

She drew her phone from the pocket of her robe.

"Mick's gone," she gasped out.

"Calm down," Genevieve ordered. Her voice was sharp and incisive, even through the phone line. Aventurine reeled back as though she had been slapped. She took a deep breath, then another. For a long moment neither of them spoke, but it was enough, knowing that the words—the thing—had been thrown out there into the world. "I was afraid of that." This time, Genevieve's words were so low that Aventurine had trouble hearing them. Perhaps she had imagined them.

"I don't know where to go. I don't know where to look for her." Avi's own voice was rising in fear and frustration. She turned about frantically, to look at the emptied room.

"Listen to me, Aventurine. Just *listen*."

Aventurine dropped her face into her hand and, steady breathing no longer a possibility, gulped for air. Her chest ached with the effort.

Her head spun.

"Do nothing."

"But—"

"Just *listen*, Aventurine. You have no idea where your sister has gone. None."

"No." The admission itself was painful. The sister with whom she shared everything—keeping this secret from her, whatever it was.

"Then it makes no sense whatsoever for you to go haring off in a direction that might be entirely wrong. You need to stay put until we gather some more information."

"I can't just sit here in Hay—"

"You *can* just sit there in Hay. And more than that, you have to. At least until we can put out some feelers and get some responses."

Tears. They were hot against her skin. Anguished. Avi imagined the old woman, a spider unmoving in the center of her web, waiting for a motion from one of the many strands radiating outward. The thought was not comforting, but rather repulsive and intimidating.

"But what can I do?" Aventurine hiccuped. "I have to do something."

"Call Paul." The answer was prompt. "He's your best lead. His mother might have let something slip to him—if she hasn't told him outright what she's up to."

Aventurine recoiled. What if Micheline *hadn't* told him what she was up to? That would make, for him, two parents missing. "He'll be terrified." And he was far away, physically and emotionally: Avi wouldn't be able to help.

"He's an adult. He'll need to learn how to face unpleasantness at some point in his life. You can't coddle him forever."

The coldness in Genevieve's voice was shocking.

"Meanwhile, I will see what I can find out, if anything, from my friends." *Friends?* "I'll be in touch, and pass that information on."

"But—"

A monumental sigh. "Call Paul. See what he knows. Stay put. And remember—" Genevieve's voice had become stern, the tone of

Commander Smith echoing down the decades— "Remember that information flows both ways."

The call ended.

"He's in the shower," Lance said. "What's wrong?"

Aventurine didn't know whether she was disappointed or relieved to have reached Lance instead of Paul. "Look, Lance," she said uncertainly, "I don't want to frighten him—"

"What's wrong?" There was movement, the sound of a door opening and shutting. Lance's voice had dropped slightly, as though he were trying to be sure Paul didn't overhear.

"Micheline's taken off in the night." It was difficult to keep her own voice steady.

Lance's voice was even quieter, nearly a whisper. "What do you mean, taken off? I don't understand."

"She packed all her stuff, took the rental car, and left Tŷ yn y Coed."

"What do you mean?" he demanded again. "Did you argue? Did she leave a note?"

"Of course we didn't argue." Avi couldn't keep the defensiveness from her words. She and her sister didn't argue, had never argued. They'd disagreed on things, sure, but disagreements had never degenerated to argument. They had understood each other far too well. But now—did Aventurine understand Micheline at all?

"I'm sorry." Lance was quick to backtrack.

"And no note. I looked everywhere—under pillows, under the bed. If she'd left one and she'd wanted me to know where she was going, she'd have left it on the pillow, or on the dresser—somewhere I'd be sure to find it." Aventurine didn't bother to say that, had she wanted Avi to know what she was doing and where she was going, Micheline could have just come through the adjoining bathroom and told her. Could have mentioned it before they'd both, ostensibly, gone to bed.

Could have just said something.

But Micheline had said nothing. Micheline had been quiet—had she been secretive?—for days. Aventurine had attributed the lethargy to her ongoing distress about Shep, and about Paul. But what if there had been something else, something she'd missed?

But she hadn't missed it, had she?

The books. The names on each flyleaf. The underlining.

So caught up in her own feelings of guilt, she had not even thought to put the puzzle pieces together. Books about sailing the Atlantic, solo. Books about people dying at sea, becoming lost at sea. Books hinting at stolen children.

They had been placed for Micheline to find them. They had been clues that hinted at information about Shep.

Lance's voice cut through her thoughts, interrupting before she could follow them, or even connect them. "I don't know if Paul's heard from her in the past couple of days," Lance was saying, slowly, as though thinking aloud. "He usually says something. You know, like 'my mother just called,' something like that."

"I'm just afraid to ask him directly," Aventurine admitted. "I mean, what if she didn't say anything to him? That would be two parents gone missing. But if she *did* say something, I need to know what it was. I need to figure out what she's doing."

"Why?"

The question threw her. *Why?*

"I'm afraid, Lance," she managed at last. Her voice sounded weak. "She's been acting strangely. Not like my sister at all. She's more depressed than ever—she isn't getting better about dealing with Shep's death—"

"Disappearance."

Aventurine took a deep breath. Lance was going down that murky path, too, it would seem, following Paul. "But she isn't dealing with it, Lance. If anything, she's getting worse. And she's my twin sister. I need to help her."

I need her.

And there was more, of course, but she hadn't figured out what the books meant, and could hardly attempt to explain it to him.

Down the line, Lance let out a long slow breath. "Listen, Aventurine. I have to go. But I'll try to find out if Paul's heard from his mother. I'll go carefully, I promise. And I'll let you know what Paul says. If you hear anything at all from Micheline, text me. I mean—" and he tried to sound cheerful— "she'll probably call you today and let you know what she's doing."

Aventurine tried to be reassured by his words. "Probably," she agreed. She wished, however, that she believed it.

Micheline had taken the car.

Avi stood now at her own window, staring down blankly at the space in the driveway where the little Renault had been parked when she'd gone to bed the previous evening. The empty space, now puddled and muddy.

With shaking hands, she drew her phone from her pocket once again and hit her sister's speed dial.

The call went straight to voicemail.

"Where the hell are you?" she demanded. There didn't seem to be anything else to say in her panicked state, so she slammed her finger into the red button and cut the connection. Whirling away from the window, she threw the phone down on the bed.

She had left both bathroom doors open, and now she steadied herself against the frame, staring through to Mick's room. Her eyes flitted over the neatly-made bed, the empty closet. All traces of her sister, save the lonely toothbrush, had been erased. It was as though she had never taken up residence in the adjoining room. As though Aventurine had never had a twin sister.

She inhaled unsteadily, and then blew out the breath again. Slowly she crossed the rug to her own unmade bed and sank down on the rumpled coverlet, her hands pressed together uselessly in her lap. She couldn't think. Her mind was blank. Micheline was gone. Micheline had packed up in the night and left, taking the car, without saying a word.

She had taken the car.

But Aventurine had had the keys. She looked around the room, confused. The keys had been in her purse. Right? She tried to remember the last time she had felt the ridged metal under her fingers. Yes, she had dropped the keys into her purse, and had not thought of them again, as nearly everything around Hay was within walking distance of Tŷ yn y Coed.

Her purse. She got to her feet, stumbled to the wardrobe, and wrenched open the heavy door. Her purse was hanging from the hook inside. She dumped the contents out quickly on the dresser and rifled through them, even though it was obvious. The keys were not there. At some point, Micheline had come into her room and taken the keys from her bag. Which meant premeditation.

Micheline had planned her flight. This proved it. It was no spur-of-the-moment thing.

Aventurine pressed both hands to the dresser top and leaned into them, trying to steady herself; her knees felt weak, her legs rubbery. She closed her eyes, breathed deeply.

Micheline had planned to leave.

Aventurine felt the betrayal deep in her gut.

When she fell back onto her own bed, the slow tears turned to full sobs, which wracked her.

Twenty

My darling Micheline,

If you are reading this, then the worst has happened. The Máquina *has foundered—perhaps the wreckage has been discovered. I've tried to protect both of you from the worst of it all.*

Whatever you hear, do not believe it all. Do not ever blame yourself for any of this. Know that my need to sail the Atlantic was never a choice, but a compulsion. Beyond that, know that I love you—and Paul—without measure. I truly believe that you and I will be together again someday.

Holding on to you. Can you feel it?

All my love,
Shep

Twenty-one

Sioned had left breakfast under a warming dome in the dining room, and plates for two; she obviously didn't know about Micheline's flight. Aventurine had never felt less like eating in her life; the shower she'd forced herself to take did not make her feel less dirty. She pushed open the door to the kitchen, and found it empty save the cat, who looked up from her bed and did a slow blink at her. Sioned's coat, normally on the peg beside the back door, was gone; probably she'd gone off on her morning walk, to collect the post, or pick up some milk, or any one of the other things she did to keep moving.

Aventurine brought her plate into the kitchen, and, plucking up a piece of cold toast, left the rest for Billie, to choose what of it she wanted. Then Avi dashed back upstairs to get her own coat and bag before heading out and down the long lane toward town. Perhaps Sioned had the right idea. Keep moving. No ideas at all had come to her while she remained inside.

Except to follow Micheline. But how? Without any idea of her sister's destination; without any means of transport?

The sky this morning was mostly grey and foreboding, but over in Herefordshire, there was a break in the clouds, as though the blue were fighting to get out. *Enough blue to make a Dutchman's britches*, her mother would have said cheerfully, and Aventurine skidded to a stop on the bridge and leaned against the parapet for a moment, looking along the rushing Wye without really seeing it. *Her mother.*

It had been more than twenty years since the deaths of their parents. Over time, her mother's voice had faded, like the lonely whistle of a far-off train. But now Aventurine heard the words so clearly her mother might have been standing beside her, gazing up at the troubled sky with—perhaps unwarranted—optimism. The optimism, Aventurine knew, that had made her mother so attractive to her father. Avi glanced to the other side, half-expecting to see her mother, or her mother's shadow, but there was nothing save for morning traffic rattling over the bridge. Why, then, was she suddenly being haunted by this memory?

She didn't believe in ghosts, not really. Sighing, Aventurine pushed off again. If she did believe, she might ask their mother—and their father, too, for good measure—to watch over Micheline, wherever she had gone, on whatever mad errand drew her. As it was, the idea of her sister off and alone, doing something she couldn't share with her, nor with Paul, nor even Genevieve: it made her chest hurt. Micheline had to be feeling so alone, carrying that *something* that had made her go off, secretly.

Blindly, Aventurine turned onto Broad Street and climbed the gentle hill on the rough pavement, crossing over at the clock tower, and heading up Lion Street. A turn onto Castle Street, and there was the cafe; she didn't feel as cozy as this place looked, and she still didn't feel like eating anything, but a caffeine headache was beginning to niggle behind her eyes. She passed along the side of the building until she came to the carry-out window, where she stood, her hands jammed into her pockets, a tunneling breeze lifting her hair away from her brow.

The menu on the wall to her left spun. Too many choices. It was hard to think. "*Ga i goffi gwyn fflat, plîs?*"

"Coming right up!" the barista said cheerily. She placed two large china mugs on the sill, then leaned out to shout into the street. "Kevin! *Kevin!*"

A man emerged from the shop next door and came to collect his mugs.

Sadly, Aventurine's coffee did not come in a mug, but in a plain old paper cup. By now, the rain was splattering the narrow street; the benches along the side of the coffee shop were unsheltered, so Avi dodged around the corner and up the steps to take cover in the Buttermarket. She was not alone; at the far end, a group of young people huddled over a phone, and she thought she could hear the buzz of shared music. She chose a folding chair, left over from some event she'd obviously missed.

"Dutchman's britches my eye, Mum," she muttered to herself. The coffee was too hot to drink, so she leaned forward, elbows on her knees, both hands wrapped around the cup, and watched the narrow street. The rain was picking up. Another handful of people hustled into the shelter of the Buttermarket; one of them was Dominic Burroughs. Aventurine shrank away, but it was too late as, spotting her, he grinned and brought another chair over to sit next to her.

"I'm surprised to find you here," he said. "I thought I saw your rental car heading out of town early this morning. I guess I was wrong." He peered more closely at her. "You look like hell."

"Thanks." He didn't, and Aventurine resented it. She turned the coffee cup in her hands, willing herself to drink it and failing miserably. "I feel like hell."

Burroughs, too, had a cup of coffee, and a palmier in a napkin. He broke a piece off and held it out.

Wordlessly—and gratefully—she took it and ate it. Side by side, they gazed out through the pillars and into the rain.

"Why?" he asked at last. He leaned forward, mirroring her. "What's wrong?"

All the voices inside her head—Genevieve's, Micheline's—began their immediate clamoring of warnings, and she squeezed her eyes shut, trying to silence them. "Mick's missing," she said at last, tossing aside all caution. "She left sometime before I awoke."

Maybe it was the stricken note in her voice that gave him pause. Instead of speaking right away, Burroughs looked down at the remaining bit of pastry in his hands, then held out the napkin to her.

"Thus the rental car," he said.

Her stomach still felt as though it were churning, but Aventurine felt the vague lightheadedness coming on, and knew she'd be unable to think, unable to function, if she didn't eat. She took the remains of the palmier.

"Did you have an argument?" he asked at last, sipping from his coffee.

Burroughs, too. Aventurine chewed over the last bit of pastry before answering. "Micheline's my twin. We don't argue. We don't always agree, but we don't argue."

He let out a noise, which might have been a chuckle. "All right, then. What did you disagree about?"

But that wasn't it, either. They had been uncomfortable with each other; Mick had been secretive, hadn't she? And Aventurine felt guilty. Of course, there had been the tense discussion about the presence of Dominic Burroughs himself—but she couldn't tell him that without going into the reasons why, and that was information it was best to keep to herself.

"She's unhappy. About her husband Shep."

"Shep Genthner. Who is dead."

Aventurine snapped her gaze to his face.

Burroughs shrugged. "I'm a cop. I looked it up." He took another drink from his cup. "Go on."

The internal voices were screaming now, but Aventurine wanted—needed—someone to talk to about this.

"I don't think—" she paused, took a deep breath, began again. "I don't think Micheline believes it. That he's dead."

"And you?"

Aventurine threw up her free hand in despair. "I don't know anymore. I don't know what I believe."

There was a call on her cellphone. Aventurine snatched it out of her pocket, hoping against hope for Micheline.

"Aventurine, it's Sioned."

Avi felt her shoulders fall. "Sioned. Hi. What's up?"

"Mrs. Genthner's room?" Sioned sounded confused. "I went to

bring clean towels, and her room's empty. Totally empty—"

"Sioned, she's decided to leave." Aventurine handed the coffee to Burroughs and pressed a hand to her forehead. "A—family emergency."

"Oh. Oh, Aventurine, how dreadful. And you? Will you be going? You two still have several nights paid up."

"I don't know. I'm waiting on word. I'll—let you know as soon as I hear something."

The other woman sounded anxious. "Oh, but that's not quite right. She left a book. Mrs. Genthner. In the wardrobe. I put it in your room. I hope that's all right. She might want it back."

Aventurine froze. She felt Burroughs's eyes on her, but could not move. "What book?"

"*December* by Phil Rickman. I left it on your bedside table."

"Yes, yes, that's fine." Aventurine's lips felt numb. She thanked Sioned and rang off, then sat staring at the home screen of her phone.

"What is it?" Burroughs said, prying her fingers open and returning her coffee cup. "Drink that. You look like you need it."

She spun to face him. "Have you ever read a book called *December*, by Phil Rickman?"

He nodded. "Yes. That's the one that takes place in a fictionalized version of Llanthony. Not too far from here, really."

She didn't even feel herself making the decision. "Can you take me there?"

Twenty-two

"This is a leap of faith for me," Burroughs said as they pulled up in front of Tŷ yn y Coed in his car.

Her phone rang. Aventurine cast him a glance and climbed out of his car, walking a few feet away. Lance.

"What did he say?" she asked quickly.

"Paul hasn't heard from her." Lance drew in a breath. "Listen, Aventurine. I'm trying to keep cool about this and not get his wind up, but it's hard. Paul's suspicious. Have you heard from her?"

"No, but I have a lead." Quickly, she told him about the book. "I think she might have gone to this Llanthony place."

"Why? And why take all her things?"

"I don't know. I won't know until I go look."

"But—you said she took the car."

Aventurine cast a glance over her shoulder to where Burroughs was leaning against the driver's side door, looking over the front of the bed and breakfast.

"I've got a friend who's going to take me. Says it's not far."

"Look, I've got to go." Lance sounded unhappy. "Aventurine, I don't know what's going on, but please be careful."

"I'd like to come up and look at your sister's room," Burroughs said as he followed her into the front hall.

"Why?" Aventurine turned with a hand on the newel post. "She went willingly. And even if I had any suspicions otherwise—which I don't—Sioned's already been in to do the room."

He shrugged. "Fresh pair of eyes, that's all. And if the landlady's already done the room, it's not as though I'd be invading her privacy." His eyes were piercing as he looked into her face.

Invading her privacy. Aventurine gulped. He couldn't do any worse than she herself had already done. "Come on, then."

She felt him behind her all the way up the staircase and along the hall to her room. She unlocked the door. "You can get in through our shared bath," she directed, pointing to the closed door. He nodded and moved away.

Aventurine sat on the bed and picked up the copy of *December* from the nightstand. Instinct took her to the flyleaf first, where she expected to find her sister's name, written in that unfamiliar hand.

Aventurine D. Morrow.

She dropped the book.

"You okay?" Burroughs called from the other bedroom. When she didn't answer straight away, he stuck his head back in to look at her. "Are you okay?"

Avi looked up at him. "This is not my book."

"The landlady said she found it in here," He gestured over his shoulder.

Aventurine shook her head. "Then it should have Micheline's name in it. But it doesn't. It has my name in it."

Burroughs approached, stooped, and retrieved the book. He flipped to the first page. "Yep. Aventurine D. Morrow."

"But it's not my book. And it's not my handwriting. And I never use my middle initial for anything." He sat next to her, slowly, a few inches away, still looking at the flyleaf. "All the other books had Mick's name in them."

"She wrote your name instead?"

"That's not her handwriting, either."

Half a moment, while Burroughs gazed down at the name. Then,

"*All* the other books?"

"There were others. Left for us. No, left for Mick." Hurriedly, her words tumbling one over another, Aventurine explained about the other books Micheline had had in her possession, books apparently left for her to find at the Honesty Bookshop.

"Who would do this?"

"I don't know. That's it, don't you see? Someone knows about Shep: the first books were about sailing solo across the Atlantic, and that's how Shep was lost."

"Left where your sister would find them. With her name written inside, so she'd know they were meant for her."

"Yes."

"What did she tell you about them?"

Aventurine shook her head, the shame washing up over her again; she'd never be free of it. "She didn't tell me anything about them. I— came upon them by accident."

"Accident?"

"She'd hidden them."

Aventurine looked away from what she knew would be Burroughs's judgment.

Book still in hand, Burroughs stood to pull aside the curtain and look out on the front garden.

"So, someone was sending your sister messages. Using these books as a means." He narrowed his eyes. From outside she heard the cawing of the crows, and wondered whether Sioned was communing with them. "Do you still have the books?"

Aventurine shook her head. "No. I put them back where I found them. I didn't want Micheline to know that I—"

"That you were going through her things."

"Yes." The word was louder than she intended. She licked her lips and lowered her voice. "It was obvious that something was going on with her. She wouldn't tell me. I had to do something." She sniffed. "I was frightened for her. She's been so—sad—since Shep... since he—"

"Died. Disappeared."

"Yes. Since then." She wiped a hand across her brow. "So, no. I don't have the books. I put them back." Then she looked up. "But I took pictures."

Burroughs dropped the curtain back into place. "Then you'd better show me."

Each photo deepened the frown lines between his eyes. He did not speak as she showed him each one: cover, flyleaf, underlinings. When at last he'd considered each, he opened *December* and looked again at her name.

"Aventurine," he said, "whoever is doing this is evil."

She didn't have time to reel from the shock of the word before her phone rang again. This time, Paul. Her heart leaped.

He cut straight to the chase. "Aventurine, we're coming back. We have a flight out this afternoon. We'll be at Gatwick at eight."

"I'll be there."

He cut the call. She was left, once again, staring at the screen. She had no idea how she would get there, but she'd meet Paul and Lance. She couldn't not.

"Be where? When?"

"Gatwick. This evening. Eight."

He nodded. "I'll take you. Get your things together and tell the landlady."

Twenty-three

E^{*vil.*} Aventurine stared straight ahead, where the rain streaked the windshield. The road out of Hay had begun to climb, away from the river valley and into wild open hilly country. There were sheep, who looked drowned and miserable. Is this the way Micheline had gone, then? And she'd had how many hours of a head start? It was all guesswork; there was no real way to know until they got to Llanthony. And if Mick hadn't, what then? What if all of this was some sort of wild goose chase? What if Micheline had gone somewhere else entirely, and the person leaving the book clues was simply trying to throw them off?

Micheline could have gone anywhere.

There was nothing, even, to say that she was still in the country. She might have been enticed—compelled—to go anywhere in the world.

Except... the book. For the hundredth time, Aventurine turned it over in her hands. *December.* She'd thumbed through it frantically for underlines, and found none. It was enough, apparently, that someone wanted her to go to the Priory, and trusted that she'd be clever enough to figure that out.

"Llanthony Priory is pretty far out of the way," Burroughs said, turning the defroster on high. The road was narrowing. Somewhere down in the valley behind them, below the filmy clouds, was Hay. "I haven't even got a clue what we'd be looking for."

"Somebody wants me to go there. The book has my name in it."

"But not your sister's. And your sister didn't leave this clue?"

"It's not her handwriting. I told you. And she would never include my middle initial."

"So, we'll know what we're supposed to find when we see it?"

Aventurine didn't know. She wiped the condensation from her side window and looked outside at the passing moody hills. "I was just worrying that it might be a wild goose chase. That this—person—" and she shook the book— "might be sending us this way after sending Mick in the opposite direction."

"And we won't know that until we get there."

"If we know it then at all."

"But we've got to try, I think. You do, too." The rain was coming down harder now, and Burroughs didn't look at her, kept his eyes steadily on the road. He was a policeman, after all, she told herself; they probably had all sorts of training for things like this. "I meant what I said. The person doing this to your sister is evil. Cruel."

Aventurine nodded. "That's what I said to Genevieve."

"Genevieve?"

Damn it. "A friend," she said quickly.

The briefest of glances, easily read, and then his eyes were back on the road. He didn't trust her, had already admitted that he had no idea of what she was capable. He might, as far as he knew, find himself dead somewhere on Hoffa's Dike, with a crazed serial killer driving off in his car. Aventurine wanted to laugh at this point, or perhaps she wanted to cry. Everything, it seemed, had gone somehow so badly wrong. Micheline missing. Shep dead. Paul—and Lance— making their terrified way back to England. Nicola—where? And the overwhelming weight of police suspicion, dressed up like Dominic Burroughs. She cast a quick sideways glance at him as he negotiated the crest of a hill, where some sheep seemed to find the view enticing.

"Welcome to the Brecons," he said.

He really shouldn't have sounded so nervous. Aventurine glanced at him again, surreptitiously. If she truly was a hardened killer, he looked as though he was fit enough to handle the situation, and her—something else he probably trained in at the police academy. Unless she had a gun? She could lure him deep into the hills—the road to Llanthony was narrowing to little more than a winding lane, and as they came down from the barren hills, hedgerows grew up beside them—and shoot him. But no one had a gun in this country, least of all a writer.

Still, she mused, her list of alleged victims? Mostly dead through falls. Perhaps he was wary of going too deep into the Brecon Beacons, where she might trip him, or push him? Again she looked at his arms, his shoulders. No, he'd probably wrestle her to the ground in the best-case scenario, drag her over the edge with him in the worst, like Holmes and Moriarty.

"What are you smirking about?" he asked.

"I'm trying to imagine myself as a cold-blooded killer."

The road had turned to dirt. Every now and again they passed a pull-off, where cars could press up against the hedges to let oncoming traffic pass. No more sheep watched them suspiciously as they passed.

"Oh, it's not that hard," he said casually, as though talking about walking, or boiling water.

Again she turned to wipe at the window and peer out into the gloom, surprised at how much his words stung.

"After all, you're so hard and determined." He slowed into a turnout to let two oncoming cars by. "And so secretive." He sighed, and then pulled out again into the lane, dripping from the branches reaching toward each other from either side. "Who knows? Maybe someday you'll trust me enough to tell me *all* your secrets."

Aventurine doubted it, and that thought stung as well.

"What is this place?" Avi knew, from reading the Rickman book, but being here was somehow something different.

The question could have been one of many levels. Burroughs

turned the car down the side lane, driving past the great barn and the church, then turning into the unpaved car park on the right. Only two other cars were there; a black and white cat meandered between the puddles, unconcerned. The rain had nearly stopped now.

"Former priory," Burroughs said, backing the car into a slot. He looked through the windshield at the ragged trees, which hid much of the view of the remains of Llanthony.

Against the foul grey November sky—a bad-tempered color Aventurine resented—some of the grey stonework stood like jagged teeth. She shivered. Instinctively, she put her hand to her bag, where she had tucked the battered copy of *December*. She zipped the pocket closed, against any more rain. "Let me guess." She undid her seatbelt and shoved the door open. "Torn down by Henry VIII during the Reformation."

"I don't know." Burroughs also climbed out of the car. "You're the researcher."

She glared at him over the roof. "It's *your* country."

Burroughs held up his hands, mock defensively. "I'm not Welsh."

Aventurine slammed the car door and spun on her heel to head the few yards back along the car park to the entranceway. She heard the snick of the lock behind her—why anyone would need to lock a car out here, she didn't know, unless, perhaps, one was a policeman and had that sort of behavior ingrained: that training again. When she heard no footsteps, she stopped to glance over her shoulder, and saw Burroughs stooping to scratch the cat behind its ears. She turned away at this demonstration of humanity.

What is this place?

She skirted the puddles and made her way through the broken walls. Across the swathe of browned grass rose the arches that, at some point, might have marked the nave, or the cloisters, a long curtain of stone cut through with archways for windows; on the grey-green hills above and beyond that, she could see the white clouds of sheep grazing. To the left, the toilets and tea room; in the far corner, the square tower that she reminded herself, from skimming the Phil

111

Rickman in the car, had once upon a time housed a recording studio. Like Rockfield, but spookier.

What had Micheline wanted here? Why had she come? Why had she left the Rickman novel in the wardrobe, when she'd taken all the others? *If* she had been the one to leave it. But who else? Sioned? That didn't even make sense.

Of course—she might not even have come here. But Burroughs had seen the rental car heading out of town this morning, he'd said. He'd also said he could have made a mistake.

She turned again to look at him, approaching from the car park, his business with the black and white cat apparently concluded successfully. He held her gaze steadily. No, she didn't think he had been mistaken. Even in the grey light of predawn, he would have noted the car's make and model, would probably have recognized the number plate. He had seen Micheline. He had been surprised to find Avi in the Buttermarket because he had thought, in the early hours, that the driver was Aventurine.

What he had been doing walking the streets of Hay at dawn was another question entirely; she tucked it away for another time.

"What are we looking for?"

Aventurine threw her hands wide. "I wish I could tell you. Something. Anything."

He had drawn abreast. His shoes were caked with mud. Avi wondered fleetingly if his socks matched.

"And if you saw it, would you recognize it?"

She shrugged helplessly. "We've hashed through this already. I don't know. I've never been here before. Have you?"

"Only read about it. If there was something out of the ordinary, I wouldn't know."

Aventurine looked around at the winter-dead grass, the broken stones, the soaring hills, the sullen sky. The absolute hopelessness of this journey, the wild-goose-chase nature of it, gripped her. She bit her lip.

Burroughs had his hands in his pockets and was gazing up at the sky. He probably thought she was an idiot. He probably knew this entire drive had been pointless, or at least, he had figured that out by now. Her gaze skidded away in embarrassment, but then slowly returned to his face. He was, she realized, here. Whether he put any credence in her fears or not—he had come here with her. When he dropped his eyes, she looked away again quickly, as she felt her face warm.

"Let's have a look around, then," he suggested. A gust of wind lifted the black wing of hair from his forehead, and he buttoned up the front of his coat. "Something might strike us."

But nothing did, though they explored the priory ruins, and read the historical signage. The cat joined them for a while, but then got bored and wandered off toward the tea room.

"It seems a good idea," Burroughs suggested, waving at the erect tail.

He held the door for her, and she slipped inside. It seemed to be an undercroft of some sort, vaults curving overhead, and the bar at one end.

"Oh! You're back!" exclaimed the woman behind the counter. She pushed a pair of reading glasses up into her silver hair. "Did you find what you needed?"

Aventurine felt Burroughs's hand on her arm. Steadying her, or warning?

"Oh," she said quickly. "You must have seen my sister—my twin?"

"She came on ahead of us," Burroughs said. "Car trouble, you know. We said we'd catch up."

The woman leaned forward, frowning. "Ah, I see it now. She looked tired, your sister, more tired than you. Have you found her then?"

Aventurine ordered coffee for them both. "No, she doesn't seem to have waited. How long ago was she in here?"

The clock to the side read a bit past one. As she clinked the cups together, the woman frowned. "Not long after we opened. Eleven, maybe? She didn't want lunch. Coffee, the loo."

"Was she alone?" Avi asked.

"She was, though she seemed to be looking for someone."

"Probably us. It took longer to change the tire than we thought." Burroughs tapped his bank card on the reader. "Thanks. I'm sure she's just gone ahead to the hotel."

They turned to find a seat in the empty room.

"She wasn't half so talkative as she was the last time she was here," the woman continued.

Aventurine spilled her coffee.

"The last time?" Burroughs asked.

"Oh, two weeks ago. A Saturday again. She didn't tell you?"

Avi met Burroughs's eyes. "We were together. Not here." Her voice was nearly a whisper.

After a moment he snapped his fingers and reached into his inside pocket. "Oh, no, it wasn't her," he said. "Probably it was my wife's younger sister."

Wife? Aventurine felt her eyes widen.

The woman had brought a cloth to wipe Aventurine's spill. She paused, cocked her head. "Younger sister?"

The photo Burroughs set on the table before her was a copy of the one Henry Hallsey had given the police in Lincoln. Nicola. Aventurine nearly spilled her coffee again.

"May I?" The woman took the picture, pulled her readers back down onto her nose, and squinted. Then she looked over the glasses at Aventurine and back. "You're right, I think. It was this woman two weeks ago. Your younger sister? That's amazing. You three have some really strong genes."

"That's what I've always told them," Burroughs said mildly. Aventurine resisted the urge to kick him under the table.

"Is she meeting you later, too? That ought to make a nice family party."

"It ought to, oughtn't it?"

This time Avi did kick him.

When they made their way back to the car park, the black and white cat, seeing them, crouched low to the ground, then backed away slowly, hissing, before dodging into the underbrush.

"I guess he doesn't like you anymore, either," Aventurine said tartly. "And I'm not your wife."

"Thank God."

Twenty-four

"Why are you here?"

Llanthony and its mysteries behind them, they were heading toward Newport and, eventually, the motorway.

Aventurine laughed nervously. "That's such an existential question."

"I'm an existential guy." But Burroughs waited as he drove, clearly expecting an answer. Clearly willing to wait for it. He was persistent, she had to give him that much.

Still, she hesitated. "You have to be clearer than that. What do you mean by *here*? Here in this car? In this country? In the world? Are you being physical here, or philosophical?"

Out of the corner of her eye, she saw the side of his mouth turn up, and she felt her face flush. He recognized a dodge when he heard it.

"Let's start *here* here. In the UK in general. We can narrow it down later."

Aventurine waved a hand over her shoulder. "I was in Hay to hole up and get some actual writing done. I'm with you now because I'm on the trail of my missing sister. *Hopefully* on the trail of my missing sister."

"And Lincoln?" he pressed. "How'd you end up on my patch?"

Aventurine refused to look at him. "Writing. It's what I do."

"Then there's York."

Once again the hackles rose on her neck. *Paul.* What did Burroughs know? Probably nothing. Probably he was just fishing. He was always just fishing.

116

"Researching," she said shortly. She wished he'd stop talking so she could think: about Micheline, and now, about Nicola. She wished he'd stop asking the questions that made her feel defensive, as though she were being interrogated. Well, she was being interrogated, wasn't she? He was playing, simultaneously, good cop/bad cop: professing to help her look for Micheline, while still investigating the business in Lincoln. She pressed her lips together. She'd better not let on to Genevieve that she was driving about the countryside with Dominic Burroughs. Detective Chief Inspector Dominic Burroughs. *I warned you*, Genevieve would say, and of course she'd be right. Aventurine should never have turned to him for help, should never have climbed into that passenger seat. Dominic Burroughs could be dangerous. For all of them.

"You just research people to death, don't you?" he mused.

She bit her lip. She spun the bracelets on her left arm, running her fingers over each stone, trying to channel Genevieve. How would the old woman respond now?

Stay where you are, she had ordered back in Hay. *Wait. Do nothing.*

That seemed particularly ironic, particularly unfair.

Despite the old spy's words echoing now inside her head, she knew. Genevieve would be doing something. She would not be sitting around, waiting for something to happen so she could react. She would be ahead of the game, staying one step in front of her adversary; she would be forcing her adversary's hand.

But who was the adversary here?

Aventurine had no clue. She had no idea what she was up against. On the one hand, Burroughs, of course. On the other, who? Who was leading them on into the metaphorical deep wood, dropping annotated books for clues along the path? She had no idea what was going on. Only that Micheline was missing.

"What is it?"

Avi snapped back to the present, her fingers momentarily tightening on the bracelets, then loosening again. "What is what?"

Burroughs met her eyes momentarily, and then returned his

attention to the road. "You just looked so—quizzical. For just a moment. That's all."

Quizzical.

The word caught Aventurine by surprise and she caught her breath. Because it suddenly occurred to her that, for as long as she could remember, no one had really looked at her face. *Looked.*

She squeezed her eyes shut. Probably it was the worry, and the exhaustion, but she felt the prickle of tears behind her eyelids, and angrily forced them back. She was not a cryer. She wasn't.

"I don't know what you mean," she said.

"Okay." But he sounded somehow disappointed.

Aventurine dozed briefly, and when she started awake again, she had a hazy recollection of a visit she and Micheline had made to an esoteric bookshop in Seven Dials. *A diversion*, she had suggested to Mick. Clutching at straws. Trying to find something—anything—to help Mick climb out of the deep hole Shep's death had dug in her life.

"What is it?" Burroughs asked again. They were approaching a village, but the road was narrow, and he was forced to pull the car into another layby to allow an oncoming tractor to pass. Aventurine found herself studying his elegant hands on the steering wheel. A police detective had no business having such elegant hands.

"Seven Dials," she said.

"You're not saying we have to go there now."

"Micheline and I went to a bookshop there," she said, ignoring him as she attempted to disentangle memory from dream. "The kind of place that sells not just books but crystals and divining rods and incense and tarot cards. There was a tarot card reader in a little room in the back."

The tractor passed, the driver lifting a hand in a wave. Burroughs pulled out and started along the road again. An elderly woman walking a small dog stopped to stare at them; Burroughs waved. "And what does this have to do with anything?"

"There was a small crystal ball on a black wooden base, on one of the shelves." Aventurine cupped her hands to indicate the size. "You could see all the cracks and fissures and imperfections in it. The shop assistant told me that whoever bought that would have to work on clearing it with intent, every day, before that person would be able to divine with it."

"You have to make a crystal ball clear before you can use it?" Even with his eyes on the road, Burroughs's brow lowered skeptically.

"Apparently." Aventurine sighed and dropped her head back against the headrest. "I mean, I stared into it, and all I saw were cracks and fissures and imperfections." She snorted. "But maybe that really is my future." She pressed her lips together to keep them from quivering. How had things gotten to this state?

Burroughs said nothing. Aventurine appreciated his forbearance.

"I wanted Mick to look into it and tell me what she saw, but she wanted to get her cards read."

"She believes in that sort of thing?" Burroughs obviously did not.

Aventurine shrugged helplessly. "She's never expressed belief, in all our lives together. She was always a big one for scoffing at horoscopes and all those other things."

"So you two went in. What did you find out?"

Now Aventurine pressed the balls of her hands to her eyes. "Correction. Micheline went in. I stayed out."

"Weren't you curious at all?"

"She didn't want me to come with her."

Aventurine paused, picking over her own words. She had thought that, not really knowing anything about a tarot card reading, maybe it wouldn't work if too many people were there: maybe it would disturb the atmosphere or something. Work, she snorted now. When Micheline had suggested she go to the brasserie just down the road to wait, Avi had assumed that Mick would tell her all about it once she appeared.

And she hadn't. That was the thing, wasn't it? How had Mick seemed when she'd dropped her bag on the chair at the brasserie's

119

high top? No, wait. She had taken out a paper bag, and had handed it across to Aventurine, who had pulled out a bracelet of small irregular green stones.

Put it on, Micheline had urged. *It's aventurine. The stone of opportunity.*

It was one of the two Aventurine wore now, along with the blue one Genevieve had given her for her birthday. She turned them both about on her left wrist. It had been a distraction, hadn't it? Mick had handed her the bracelet, and they'd argued desultorily about whether stones really had powers until the espresso martinis had arrived, rich and dark with coffee beans floating on the top. They had never returned to the topic of the tarot reading at all.

"Do you think she might have heard something in the reading that upset her?" Burroughs asked, his voice cutting through her thoughts. "Your sister?"

"Tarot readings are right up there with horoscopes," Aventurine said, holding up her hands. "They're all bull."

He flicked the indicator and slowed, coming up to an intersection. "That's as may be. But we're not talking about you and what you believe. We're talking about your sister who apparently believes in a reading enough to pay money to have one."

Aventurine dipped her head. He was right, of course. Despite her talk about the worthlessness of the esoteric, Mick had always been more superstitious than she—though never to this extent. "I've been trying to remember. Was she upset? She really didn't show it. Was she secretive? I'm beginning to realize that she probably was, because she did work at deflecting my attention. I didn't press." She wiped a hand across her face. "I really didn't ask the questions I should have."

His touch on her arm was quick, reassuring. "But you didn't know she was going to do this now. You didn't know she was going to do a bunk."

"But I should have known," she protested. "I should have known. She's my sister. My twin."

They were coasting down a long hill. The hedgerows rose up on either side of the car, though straight ahead, the countryside, grey and brooding and somehow beautiful despite it—or perhaps because of it—spread out, crossed and crossed again with the hedges dividing the fields, which in turn climbed their way into the far mountains.

There was a shrill beep.

"Shit," Burroughs hissed.

"What is it?"

The car began wobbling, and Burroughs's knuckles were white on the wheel.

"Tire light's on." His face had hardened. "Hold on, Aventurine. We've blown a tire."

Twenty-five

The car was an automatic; Burroughs shifted into 'L' and the engine raced even as it worked to slow them down. He pumped the brakes. Aventurine grabbed the door handle convulsively. They'd be all right, she told herself, as long as there was no oncoming traffic.

Which suddenly there was. A white box truck was laboring uphill toward them.

Burroughs laid on the horn. He had his foot on the brake pedal, but the car still careened back and forth between the hedgerows.

"Shit," he hissed again.

Midway down the hill was a layby carved into the hedge, on their side.

"Hold on!"

He yanked the handbrake as he pulled the wheel to the left. The scraping and bumping seemed to go on forever, and when the car finally came to a stop, Aventurine found herself leaning to her right, her face turned into Burroughs's shoulder. He slumped back in his seat. The hood of the car was buried in the hedge.

With a slightly shaking hand, Burroughs reached to kill the engine. "You all right?

Carefully, Aventurine sat up and did a quick inventory. Her shoulder felt sore with the seatbelt whiplash, and she realized she was still holding her breath. The contents of her bag were strewn over the floor at her feet. "I'm okay," she said slowly. "You?"

122

"Right as rain," he said sardonically. "I should have paid more attention in my DTU."

Shouting, a knock on the driver's side window. The engine turned off, the window button wouldn't work; Burroughs opened the door and undid his seatbelt instead.

"You guys okay? What the hell happened?" The lorry driver's face, above his beard, was pale, but as Burroughs pulled himself from the car, the man's panic turned the corner into anger. "What the hell are you playing at?"

Burroughs leaned back inside and extended a hand to Aventurine. "Can you climb over the console?" he asked.

She was scrabbling around on the floor, shoving things—card case, phone, pens, notebook, recorder, *December*—back into her bag. "Just let me get my stuff."

Burroughs turned back to the angry driver. "Tire blew. The layby seemed a better option than your front grill."

Aventurine, all her belongings—she hoped—gathered, clambered over the gearshift and the driver's seat, then allowed Burroughs to help her out onto the lane. Shading her eyes with her hand, she looked first up the hill from whence they'd come, then down past the lorry, and at last, at Burroughs's car. She wouldn't have been able to get out of the passenger side; had the day been warmer and her window open, she'd have got a branch in the eye at the very least.

Casting them both a look, which said plainly that he took them for idiots who didn't know how to drive on narrow country lanes, the driver examined the tires. The front driver's side was flat, the rim nearly cutting through the rubber. He bent to run his hand over it, then grunted. He indicated a spot.

"See that?"

Burroughs and Aventurine leaned forward.

"Did we pick up something? Nail, sharp rock?" Aventurine asked.

The driver shook his head. "Sidewall." He ran his fingers over a spot. "There. And the hole's straight and thin."

"I don't know what that means."

The lorry driver straightened and stroked his red beard with a hand. "It means intent." His pale eyes flickered to Burroughs. "You didn't feel it?"

"Came on up there." Burroughs jerked his chin toward the long hill behind them. "Rather sudden." He raised an eyebrow in Avi's direction where she leaned against the car, her arms wrapped around herself protectively. She had begun to feel cold: probably a delayed reaction. "You're sure you're all right?"

"Shaken," she said. "Not stirred."

"I'd better call it in."

They watched the flatbed wrecker make its way up the hill, the lights giving off an ironic, even mocking glow in the growing mist. Aventurine rubbed her arms against the chill; beside her, Burroughs crossed his arms, and rocked back on his heels.

"Those tires," he said slowly, "were new. Couple of weeks. The air pressure was fine when we left Hay this morning."

"You checked?"

He slew her a sharp glance. "I always check."

"You're a strange man."

Burroughs only shrugged.

A strange policeman. A suspicious policeman.

"So, what are you telling me?"

For a moment he said nothing, just rocked back and stared up at the unfriendly cloudy sky. Then, "I thought the road was getting bad. It's a dirt road. Rutted."

Aventurine waited.

"But it was the tire, wasn't it? The entire time." His face grew hard. "It was a slow leak. In the sidewall. Straight and narrow. And then it gave."

"What are you saying?" Aventurine was beginning to feel the alarm at the back of her mind. She turned to face him. His profile was like granite, and his eyes glinted.

"If there hadn't been a layby, or if I hadn't been able to slow the car and run it into the hedge there, we would have ended up as roadway fatalities."

Now she gripped his arm. "*What are you saying?*"

Burroughs turned slowly and put his hands on both her shoulders. "I need you to think carefully, Aventurine," he said. "Who wants you dead?"

Twenty-six

The other front tire was flat as well, another tell-tale slice in the sidewall. "Might not have gone down for hours," the flatbed driver said laconically. "But once one did, it put stress on the other." He looked them over speculatively as he winched Burroughs's car onto his truck. "Bit of bad luck, that."

Understatement of the year. They rode into town in the truck in silence, made much easier as Aventurine elected to sit in the jumpseat in the back. Up front, Burroughs sat stonily, and the driver, who had at first been inclined to chattiness, had fallen silent as well.

Who wanted her dead?

Slicing tires and causing slow leaks was an iffy way to choose, if that in fact had been the intent; of all the ways to kill a person, cutting tires seemed rather a haphazard way to go about it. All the things that could go wrong—or right, if she wanted to think about it that way— flats, for example, at the wrong time, when it would have been easier just to pull over. And it wasn't even her car—how could anyone know she'd asked Burroughs for a lift to Llanthony this morning?

"Two things," she said, clambering down from the cab at the garage where they'd get two new tires. "One: how do we know that wasn't just a warning? And two: how do we know that it wasn't meant for you?"

Burroughs waited until the driver had disappeared into the garage, headed toward a long high rack of tires at the rear.

126

"Because," he said. "I'm a law-abiding citizen."

They were back on the road in an hour; though the front and passenger side were scratched up from their rude meeting with the hedgerow, there was, the mechanic told them as he wiped his hands on a red rag, no further damage.

Their silence stretched once they hit the motorway and crossed the Severn Bridge. They stopped at the motorway services outside Hungerford for a break and food, but their conversation was desultory. Aventurine had a headache, perhaps from thinking about all the disparate pieces of this puzzle, none of which seemed to fit together. Or perhaps it was from lack of caffeine; the coffee machine at the garage had looked like it might be plague-inducing, and she'd dared not risk it.

"Look," she said finally, as the signs for Gatwick began appearing on the M25. "You don't have to come any further with me. You can drop me off at arrivals, and be on your way. We can rent a car from there."

Burroughs didn't look up from the roadway. The traffic had been sporadic, but now was becoming heavier; tail lights shone ahead of them in the encroaching darkness as the afternoon eased into evening.

The silence fell again, and it was not comfortable.

"I don't have to," he said eventually. He flicked on the directional, glanced over his shoulder, changed lanes.

But Aventurine suddenly needed him to leave her. To go. She needed him to let her out, and to drive off to—wherever he'd drive off to. She needed him to stay away from Paul and Lance. Especially Paul.

He doesn't know anything.

Not for certain, anyway.

Burroughs suspected. Something. His sharp comments made that obvious. And she couldn't risk Paul, in a fit of temper, or through carelessness, giving the detective any more fodder for his suspicions. Lance—she frowned, and then remembered to smooth the expression from her face—Lance could probably hold his own. Paul was the fragile one, the wildcard. Aventurine needed to keep Burroughs and Paul far away from one another. She needed to see Dominic Burroughs's tail lights disappearing in the distance. As much as she didn't want him to leave.

She cursed herself. McDonald's flashed past, and she glared at it as though it were the root of all evil.

"I don't have to go any further," he repeated. "But I will." He turned into the carpark. Luck was with them, and he slid the car into a spot just as a panel van pulled away from it. He turned the engine off and undid his seatbelt.

Aventurine stared straight forward, past the parked cars to the traffic on the access road. "Why?" she asked at last. "I don't understand what it is you want."

He pocketed the keys and nudged open the door. Then he turned back to her. "Maybe I just want to help." He slammed the door closed.

After a moment, she climbed out of the car, stiffly, and together they followed the signs to arrivals. Her chest was tight with misgiving. His motives—like everyone else's in her life—were not that clearcut. But there was nothing she could do without arousing further suspicion.

Aventurine checked the arrivals board, and then her watch. The plane had landed on time; they had just made it. Paul and Lance would be going through the new border patrol, then would collect their luggage and be out in a short time, barring hold-ups of some bureaucratic nature. The seating in the echoing hall was full, however, and she didn't feel like sitting anyway. Pacing. She felt like pacing, as though she were a wild animal. She could feel the anxiety like electricity, quivering through her veins.

Burroughs cast a glance at her. "I'll go find us coffee. *If* you promise not to do a flit while I'm doing that."

His tone was half-amused. But half not.

"I'm not going anywhere." The tension made her snappish. Burroughs shrugged and moved off.

They came through the gate together, Paul and Lance, both rolling their suitcases behind them. Paul turned his head this way and that, searching the waiting crowds, reminding Aventurine of some wary bird. Lance's dark eyes fell on her first. She raised a hand. Lance said something to Paul and jerked a shoulder, which made Paul turn toward them, tilting his head. He always tilted his head. Just like his father.

"He looks like you." Burroughs's murmur cut through her thoughts.

Aventurine's stomach clenched. Of course he didn't know about any of that, either.

"My twin sister's son," she reminded him. Let that serve as an explanation.

Dilemma: did she embrace Paul? She lifted her hands, but hesitated. He did, too, for a fraction of a second, but then compromised by slipping an arm around her shoulders for a quick side hug before stepping aside again. Lance leaned in, a hint of sympathy in his expression, and kissed her cheek.

They both glanced at Burroughs with barely hidden curiosity.

He held out a hand. "Dominic Burroughs."

"He was kind enough to give me a lift," Aventurine said quickly, skirting around the details. "Your mother took the rental car."

"Any word?" Paul asked.

Aventurine shook her head. "Nothing. She's left me on read."

"Me, too," Paul said. His skin looked pale and blotchy, dark circles under his eyes.

Lanced glanced with some concern between the pair of them. "Obviously, we need to find someplace to settle so we can work out a plan."

In her pocket, the phone sounded. All three looked up. Aventurine pulled it out and had a look at the screen, hoping for her sister. Hoping for the coincidence to end all coincidences.

Genevieve.

Aventurine shook her head, and saw Paul's face fall. "Genevieve," she said.

"Who—"

Lance cut Burroughs off. "My great-grandmother."

Aventurine pressed the phone to one ear.

"I'd like to know what the hell you're doing in London," the old woman said.

"Collecting Paul and Lance," Avi said carefully. "Their flight just got in from Milan."

"I told them to stay put as well." Genevieve sounded peeved. Obvious insubordination on all their parts.

"We're trying to figure out what to do," Aventurine said. How to explain the urge to be together to a woman who had spent her life being so determinedly independent?

Burroughs was watching her, his expression speculating. She put a finger in her other ear, as though having trouble hearing over the terminal noise, and turned away, toward the currency exchange counter.

"Since you're all together," Genevieve said, "might I suggest finding a place to establish a base, until we've got enough information to move? Which—" her voice grew steely— "we absolutely do not have, at this point."

"Yes, but have you heard anything at all from your—friends?"

"You need to develop patience," the old spy advised. "You can't just blunder about attempting to make something happen. You could just be making things worse."

"Things? What *things*? And aren't you the woman who told me to act instead of react?"

"Listen to me. I need the three of you to go to central London and *stay there*. I will forward information as it becomes available. I will message you the name of a hotel in Paddington: a small, unassuming sort of place, catering to tourists, so people coming and going are not unusual. Keep your cell phones charged, all of you. Wait for further directions."

With that, the call ended, the emptiness of cell phone disconnection in her ear. Then Aventurine felt the vibration, and clicked on her texts to find the name and address of a hotel.

She turned back to the others. "Looks like we're going to Paddington."

It wasn't until they were back in the car that she realized. *You three.* Genevieve knew she was in London, but not with whom. Something to be grateful for in that, she decided.

Twenty-seven

"Three rooms," the desk clerk said, her accent sounding vaguely middle-European. She frowned and pulled a heavy ledger from under the counter, something that Aventurine, used to computers and online reservations, found odd. Still, Genevieve had sent the name and address of this hotel off London Street, and Genevieve knew what she was doing. "I can't put all three together. I can do two near each other on the third floor—" she ran a red-nailed finger down the page, and then flipped to the next— "and one on the second floor."

Aventurine turned a shoulder toward Burroughs. "I'll pay for the two together," she said, taking out her wallet and passport. She raised a hand toward Paul and Lance, still out on the pavement, where it looked as though Paul was handing a rough sleeper a handful of change. She beckoned them inside to complete the registration.

Burroughs was watching the exchange through the window as well. "He shouldn't be doing that," he muttered. "He's probably being pegged as a mark right now."

Aventurine glared over her shoulder. "Leave him the goodness of his heart," she protested. "He's not got much else right now."

They rode the elevator silently, dropping Burroughs off on the second floor; they were to meet downstairs in half an hour, to scout out some food. Aventurine took the small room, leaving her nephew and Lance the larger. She dropped her bag on the floor in front of the mirror and slipped into the minuscule bath to get herself a drink of mildly tinny-tasting water.

"That's all you've brought?"

Aventurine had gone down to Burroughs's room; he answered the door with his toothbrush in hand, his mouth full of paste. He held the door for her and waved her inside.

On the bed lay a small rucksack, the front pocket unzipped. Aventurine could see a stick of deodorant and the cord to something that might have been an electric razor. The rest of the bag might have held some socks and underwear, perhaps another pair of pants. Not much else.

"I believe in traveling light." Burroughs finished brushing his teeth, then emerged and flicked off the light switch. The hotel room itself was small, smaller than her own one flight up, with barely enough room to get around the bed to the window. Avi pulled the curtain to the side, to look down into the road, glistening now under the streetlights.

She thought of her own small blue suitcase, and of Nicola's small red one. Then she thought of the cramped confines of the belowdecks of the *Máquina*. Oftentimes what people chose to carry with them— or jettisoned on the journey—spoke volumes about who they were. Through lowered eyelashes, she observed Burroughs as he drew out the desk chair and sat. He brushed the dark hair from his brow; she wondered if he had a comb in the rucksack's front pocket.

"You never know," he continued almost disinterestedly, "how quickly you might have to pick up and leave. You never know when."

That brought her thoughts back to Micheline, packing up in the middle of the night, and taking off with the rental car. Leaving Avi stranded in Hay. But of course knowing that Avi could always find a bus, a train, or in this case, a car. She glanced at Burroughs again: he did seem to be a master of picking up and going at a moment's notice.

133

"Did they tell you anything more about your car?" she asked. "The garage, the mechanic?"

Burroughs shrugged. "Only what you know: that the tires had been sliced. By someone who knew what they were doing. Slicing the tread would have flattened the tires sooner. Slicing the sidewall can make the flat happen long after you've driven away from the place where it was done."

"As we did."

"I don't think it was random."

Aventurine scanned the street below. Someone could be down there. Someone who was keeping an eye on them. Someone who had set the trap with the tires in Llanthony.

"It wasn't Mick," she said. "Mick doesn't know the first thing about mechanics. Less, even, than I know, and I know nothing except where the gas goes."

"And I presume that your sister feels no need to kill you." His tone was wry.

"It's not funny."

"I'm not saying it is. What I am saying is that had we met that lorry head-on, instead of that hedgerow, one or both of us might have been seriously injured or killed."

"Maybe that wasn't the intent," Aventurine protested, glancing back at him, and then quickly down into the street again. "Maybe we were just supposed to be frightened. Warned away."

"From what?"

"I don't know! Following my sister? But that might mean that she's doing something dangerous. Possibly illegal."

"Possibly both." Burroughs leaned forward with his elbows on his knees. "Look. I really have no idea what's going on with you. With you two. You three. Four, if you count that old lady."

He was watching her intently, his eyes icy. What did he know about Genevieve? About Mary Wentworth?

"Don't look so surprised. I don't think I can trust her, anymore than I can trust the rest of you. I still think there are too many coincidences here, since I first met you that night in Lincoln, to make me comfortable. And so far, you have done nothing to make me any more comfortable."

Slowly, she let the curtain fall back and came around the bed to face him. The room was growing dimmer, and he leaned back to flick on a lamp. That cast his expression further into shade.

"But you came with me anyway," she said slowly.

He turned his head away momentarily, as though caught in a weakness. "I'm curious."

"I asked you for help. You helped. You are helping."

"Am I? Or are you using me in a way that I can't see clearly yet?"

Her phone buzzed in the early morning with an incoming text, on the narrow bed on the third floor where she had tossed and turned all night. Probably Genevieve again, bright-eyed and bushy-tailed, checking to see whether they were following directions. Aventurine took her time picking up.

It was Micheline.

I'm fine. Don't come after me.

Aventurine fell heavily back onto the pillows, the bed creaking alarmingly, though she barely registered it. She was transfixed by the words on her screen. Her breathing was shallow. The screen faded, powering down, and she touched a thumb to the words, making them leap into focus again. She kept her thumb upon them, trying to absorb—something—from them. Something of her sister.

"Micheline," she whispered. She turned her head to the tall window, where she had not thought to draw the curtains against the night, beyond which now the London planes, ghostly and straggling, rose. Threadbare. That's how she felt now. "Micheline," she said again, and it seemed the name echoed up to the high ceiling, an empty, lonely sound.

Unable to be alone any more, she leapt to her feet, pulled on her robe, yanked her keycard out of the slot, and bounded down the narrow corridor to Paul and Lance's room. She pounded on the door with a closed fist.

Paul pulled the door open so quickly she nearly fell into the room. It was dim, they having drawn the heavy drapes against the lights and noise of the city, but Paul hit the light switch, and she found herself blinking blindly. Both of them were still in their pajamas.

"What is it?"

"Your mother," she gasped.

The room was so small that there was only one chair, at the vanity below the mirror. Lance stood and offered it to her.

"Mum? What about her?"

The air was suddenly taut.

Aventurine held out her phone. Paul took it, read the message, and then wordlessly passed it on to Lance.

Avi sank onto the hard chair, and dropped her head into her hands. "What do we do?"

Do nothing.

She forced Genevieve's voice away, pressing the balls of her hands into her eye sockets.

"What *can* we do?" Paul's voice shook slightly. When she looked over at him, he met her glance only for a moment, before turning to Lance. Well, at least he'd looked at her.

Lance, still holding the phone in both hands, sat on the edge of the rumpled double bed. There was the smallest of frowns between his dark brows, as though he was considering possibilities carefully. Somehow, there was something reassuring in that. As though Lance was the calm in the center of the maelstrom. She barely registered that they'd left the door ajar, barely registered when Burroughs appeared at it.

"Where's your phone, Paul?" Lance asked.

Paul jerked into life, understanding immediately what he was being asked. He looked around the room frantically, then darted around to the far bedside table, where his phone was on the charger. His fingers moved frantically over the screen, but then his face fell, and he dropped the phone on the bed, where Lance picked it up.

"Nothing," Paul said. He sank onto the bed and put his face in his hands. Beyond Lance, Avi saw Burroughs take in the action, saw the calculating glance wash over his features and disappear quickly.

She looked at Paul's hunched shoulders and wanted nothing more than to wrap her arms around them, knowing that he would, more than likely, reject her sympathy. Especially now, when his mother had contacted her and not him. Especially now, when both parents were missing, one presumed dead, one hieing off to who-knows-where, without confiding in him. Helplessly, she looked to Lance, jerked her chin in Paul's direction. Lance, who understood so much, without saying anything. He slid around the bed and to Paul's side, where he rested a hand lightly on Paul's back.

"Let's get out of here for a minute," she muttered in Burroughs's ear as she pushed past him.

He waited while she dressed in the tiny bathroom, barking her shins on the toilet, banging her elbows on the sink. Then they went out into the nippy morning air.

The wind skittered trash along the pavement, what would have been a lonely noise save for the constant honking and bustling from Praed Street. Still, Aventurine considered, hunching her shoulders against the cold, there were all sorts of loneliness. As she stepped to the edge of the pavement, sliding in behind Burroughs to avoid a couple coming toward them arm-in-arm, oblivious to anyone else, she wondered if being lonely among these waves of people wasn't the most awful kind of loneliness.

But she wasn't really lonely. There had been times over the past years, despite working so hard to get established, despite all the friends she'd made along the way, where she had just once longed for the person who would look at her the way Lance looked at her nephew, who would look at her the way Micheline looked at Shep. That one person who would lay that comforting and undemanding hand on her shoulder when things were bleak. But now? Maybe she had just grown past all that.

Even that thought made her feel cheated. She had never had someone she recognized as the love of her life, as Lance did. As Mick did. Hell, even as Genevieve did.

"You're looking quizzical again," Burroughs said, pausing to let her move up beside him once more.

"Stop looking at me," she said peevishly.

Aimlessly they wandered down onto Eastbourne Terrace, then turned to cross the bridge under which the trains rumbled on their way to the west. At the steps they descended to the canal, where several narrow boats creaked at the end of their gangplanks. Between the station and the tall glassy buildings across the water, the wind tunneled and raked at their cheeks.

"Where are we going?" Burroughs asked.

Aventurine shrugged. "No idea. I don't know where we are right now. I feel as though I'm walking in big circles."

"That's because you *are* walking in big circles." Burroughs pointed to a silver Airstream trailer, the side popped open to reveal a barista leaning on his elbows against the counter, looking glum. "Let's make or break this guy's day and get some coffee."

The barista did look happy to see them, or at least their money. Steaming large cups in hand, they chose seats at a picnic table that was partially shielded from the worst of the wind by the Airstream.

"You want to tell me about that?" Burroughs asked. The wind was ruffling his hair on his brow in a way that might have been attractive to some other woman. His eyes were on the narrow boats tied up on the far side of the canal.

"Tell you about what?" Aventurine took a drink from her cup. The coffee scalded. She squeezed her eyes shut. She knew better, but she had done it anyway, just to deflect.

Burroughs said nothing, merely waited her out. Again. She hated that about him. That he knew. He would succeed, despite her best efforts to foil him. Despite Genevieve's best efforts to train her.

"Wouldn't you be upset, too, if your mother did that?" she demanded once she had recovered. "Had a crisis and messaged your aunt, not you?"

"Maybe she thought you'd be the one she could convince. Maybe she thought telling her son not to look for her would be an absolute lost cause."

"Telling *me* not to would be an absolute lost cause," Avi countered. "I'm the one with all the research skills. I'm the one who knows people and can ask around. Paul doesn't know those kinds of people, those kinds of things."

"But you do," he said.

"I do."

"And you're her sister."

"Yes." That went without saying. She wondered where he was going with this.

"Her *twin* sister."

"You know that. Stop being obtuse."

Burroughs shrugged, tested his coffee. He apparently found it less than incendiary, for he took a big sip. "Ostensibly, she'd tell you things she might not tell him. I mean, I'm sure there are plenty of things neither of you have ever discussed with him."

Here he went again. Her hackles were rising on the back of her neck. "What are you implying? If it's something about my knowing anything about her disappearance, *I don't.* I haven't got a clue what's going on in her head, haven't got a clue where she'd head off to, or why. And I'm scared. I wish you could get that through your fat head."

Burroughs had turned on the bench to watch her; his expression was inscrutable. She stopped herself abruptly. She was *this close* to hysterics. Sitting here at this picnic table on a canal in Paddington, when yesterday she had been in Wales, waking up to a new day with her sister still in it. How did any of this happen? How was her world spinning so wildly out of control?

"I've got it," he said gently. "I know you are."

Aventurine drank some more coffee. Across the canal, a man in a brick-red puffer vest climbed onto the deck of a boat, and then disappeared below. There was a pennant on a staff on the stern, and it snapped in the wind.

"I'm sorry." He ran his hands up into his hair. This morning he looked rumpled. He gazed off down the lock for a few moments, before turning his startling blue gaze back on her. "And now I think you had better tell me the story of Shep and Micheline."

Aventurine finished her coffee. He waited.

She took out her phone, lay it on the scarred table, and opened the screen to the photos of the books. Then she began.

Twenty-eight

"I need more coffee," Burroughs said as they entered the lobby of the hotel. "See you upstairs?"

Aventurine took the elevator. She dumped her stuff in her room, then checked her phone. No new texts, not from Mick, not from Genevieve. She wandered down the hallway and tapped gently on Lance and Paul's door. When Paul opened it, she could hear the shower running. He stepped aside to allow her entry.

"Who is that man?" he asked, without preamble.

Aventurine blew out a breath. "I need to talk to you about that." She pulled out the desk chair and moved a pair of sneakers to the floor. Then she sat and looked up at him. "I'm glad we've got a few minutes to talk before he appears."

Paul's expression grew dark. "You'd better tell me."

"He's a policeman." She threw up a quick hand as he was about to speak. "It's a long story. I don't trust him, and he doesn't trust me. But I couldn't refuse his help without making him even more suspicious of me."

"Are you insane, Aventurine?"

"I've been through this before, with your mother, and with Genevieve," she said wearily. "He's going to have to go back to Lincoln soon—"

"Lincoln. Not York?"

Lance cracked the bathroom door. "Hand me some clothes, Paul," he ordered. "I can't come out wearing just a towel." Paul grabbed some things from the suitcase on the floor in the corner. In a few moments, Lance emerged shirtless, toweling his dark hair.

"What's going on?" he asked, rooting in the suitcase for a shirt, which he pulled over his head.

Paul's eyes narrowed. "My aunt here has just told me she's brought a policeman into our midst."

Lance swiveled.

"It couldn't be helped," she protested again. "He's suspicious enough. Refusing his help would have made it worse. And then he would have followed me. We were going to have him one way or another. At least this way we know what he's doing."

"What does he know?"

Aventurine shook her head. "Just about Mick being missing. About Shep, and the books. Nothing else. I swear it." She pressed her hands to her face. "I would never put you in any danger, Paul."

He tossed his head. "Well, that remains to be seen, doesn't it?"

Lance put a hand out. *Wait.* "And does he have any ideas about Micheline? Or the clues in the books?"

"He's thinking." From out in the corridor, she heard the bell as the elevator doors opened. "And if I'm not mistaken, he's coming." She stood.

There was a tap at the door.

"Did you write this?"

Burroughs held out a book. Heavy, the dark paper jacket a bit worse for wear. Aventurine thought she recognized it, and tried to place it. Among Micheline's things? No. On Sioned's bookshelf? The one upstairs, in the corridor between the bedrooms. She took it in her hands. *The Collected Poems of W. B. Yeats.*

Slowly she opened the book.

Paul Genthner.

She dropped the book to the bed and put a hand to her mouth. She shook her head, convulsively. "No. Not mine." Her voice was not much more than a whisper. The handwriting: familiar. Spiky. Incisive.

Behind her, Paul moved closer to look over her shoulder. His breath caught in her ear. "That's Dad's writing," he said immediately. His voice shook.

Lance picked up the book. Gingerly.

"You're sure?" Burroughs asked. He had the presence to move away from the three of them; he turned and pulled back the curtain to look out into the street.

"Of course I'm sure," Paul said sharply. "I'd recognize my dad's handwriting."

He threw himself into the desk chair, then stood again, unable to settle. Lance glanced at the book in his hands, and then placed it back on the unmade bed.

"Sorry," Paul said after a moment. "Sorry." He pulled his knapsack out from under the desk and rifled through it for a moment, before pulling out Shep's last letter to him, and tossing it down next to the open book. "There. Look at that."

Burroughs's gaze moved from the letter and the book, to Paul, then to Aventurine, where he held her eyes in a question. She nodded slightly, and he bent to the letter, then eased it from the envelope. Holding it in his right hand, he took the book up in his left. He examined them both for a long time before he spoke.

"I'm no expert," he said slowly, "but this was either written by the same person, or is a very clever forgery."

"If it looks like a duck…" Avi let the words trail away.

He frowned.

Lance had both hands on the back of the desk chair and rocked up on his heels. His frown matched Burroughs's. "All right, then. You should know, Paul. But it doesn't make sense."

"We need to look at this in light of the others, I think," Burroughs said. "Aventurine—the pictures on your phone? Can you text them to me?"

Avi took out her phone.

When the transfer had been completed, he turned toward the door. "Meet me at the breakfast place across London Street. I won't be long."

He was longer than expected. Both Lance and Paul had finished off their full English breakfasts by the time Burroughs came in before the wind, ordered a cup of coffee, and joined them at the table, pulling out the chair next to Avi. He carried a large manila envelope, and pushed the cutlery aside to lay it on the table. Then he took the papers out and spread them over the space.

He looked up to Aventurine. "Can you put these in order for me, the best you can remember?"

She made four sets: *Nightmare Voyage*; *Three Months Lost at Sea*; *December*; and then *The Collected Poems of W. B. Yeats*. Atop each title, she lay the copies of each respective flyleaf with the names in the corner. Three for Micheline in a handwriting she didn't recognize, one with her bastardized signature, one for Paul in his father's hand. Then she lay the photographs of the underlining with the pages for each book.

"What are we looking for?" Lance asked.

"What are we looking *at*?" Paul demanded.

Once again, Aventurine explained the appearance of the books, how Micheline had apparently found at least two of them at the Honesty Bookshop and had been so secretive about them. How *December* had been found in the wardrobe when Sioned was doing the room. And now, the Yeats, from downstairs in the hotel.

"And that's not your mother's handwriting," Avi said, pointing to the names on the first two stacks of paper.

"No, it isn't."

"So, someone left them as clues to make her do something. Make her go somewhere. Without letting any of us know."

Lance picked up the pages for *Nightmare Voyage*. "This is the first one."

144

Avi nodded. "I think so. It's the first one I saw her with at Tŷ yn y Coed."

Burroughs got out his phone, began thumbing the screen. "I remember this one. It's about a solo sailing race." He peered down at the page he'd pulled up, thumbed some more. "The participants were supposed to sail around the world."

"Dad was only going across the Atlantic," Paul protested.

Lance was sifting through the photos of the underlinings. "Chaos." He glanced up. "Well, it certainly became that." Paul's face looked pinched. "And this line, about disappearing." He tapped a finger on the page. "A book about solo sailing, and disappearing. Whoever sent this to Micheline wanted to get her attention, wanted her to know this—whatever *this* is—was about her husband."

Aventurine pressed her eyes closed. No wonder Micheline had become so pale and withdrawn. "But why didn't she tell me? Why didn't she show me?"

No one seemed to have an answer. Burroughs signaled for more coffee. "This was the second one?" He shifted the photos of the pages from *Three Months* to the center of the table. Aventurine nodded.

They all leaned forward to read the underlined section. *Disaster at sea can happen in a flash. Without warning. It can happen after a stretch of anticipation and anxiety. It does not always come in storms, but may arise when the ocean is calm and flat.*

"Disaster at sea," Burroughs said.

Paul looked sick. "The Coast Guard said there was no sign of a storm the night—*that* night." He swallowed hard. "Calm water."

"Another reference to your father," Burroughs said.

"But this?" Lance pointed to the page with the two penciled Welsh words. "*Tylwyth teg*?"

"They're fairies," Aventurine said quickly. Too quickly? "The Fair Family." She glanced surreptitiously at Paul, not quite daring to explain further.

"But what has that got to do with Dad?" Paul asked.

Avi bit her lip. When she sensed Burroughs watching her, she tried to look puzzled.

"Away with the fairies?" Lance suggested. "Another reference to his disappearance?"

More coffee came. Adjusting the cups and pages on the table took a few moments, and Avi used them to settle herself. Burroughs still had his phone in his hand, and she hoped he'd let the *tylwyth teg* go without looking them up further.

"Then there's *December*." The book was still in Aventurine's bag; she took it out and set it on the table along with the photos. "The book that sent us to Llanthony Priory."

"What did you find there?"

Aventurine sighed and pursed her lips. "That we'd just missed your mother there, by an hour or two." If only they'd got away sooner. If only she'd thought to ask Burroughs for help sooner. If only. They might have caught up to her sister and demanded answers.

"And we found out that we'd missed Nicola Hallsey by a couple of days, a week," Burroughs added.

"Nicola Hallsey?" Paul asked.

Lance and Aventurine exchanged glances. This time Avi pulled out her phone, pulled up the photo of Nicola before the Teatro alla Scala, and set it in front of her nephew. He leaned over it, then picked up the phone for a closer examination; at last, he looked over the top of it at her, then at Lance.

"This is in Milan," he said.

Lance nodded, and looked abashed.

"This woman looks like Mom. And like you, Avi."

She nodded. "Tell me about it."

"I saw her walking by us one night while we were having a drink at a little bar," Lance said. "I asked Aventurine about her. I thought at first—that it *was* her, or your mother."

"But we were in Wales."

"I thought it might be some sort of wild coincidence. Or that I was imagining things. So I didn't tell you about it."

Paul had his eyes on the photo of Nicola again, the frown chiseled between his brows. "She's younger."

Again Avi nodded. "By about ten years, we think."

"You know her?"

Aventurine felt Burroughs's calculating gaze again. She did not look at him. "I know her father. Or the person who claims to be her father." She dropped her eyes to her fingers, threaded together. "Your mother found her on one of the DNA websites. Listed as 'grandmother, cousin, or half-sister'."

"So that takes us to this book?" Lance put his hand on the prints from the Yeats. He moved the first two sheets, to find a photo of the page with "The Stolen Child." He frowned. "This Nicola—"

"Hallsey."

"This Nicola Hallsey is a stolen child. Or you two are. But either way, she's been pointed out to us. To you. In a book with your name on it, in Paul's father's handwriting."

Aventurine nodded.

"And she was following us in Milan." Paul still couldn't seem to take his eyes from Nicola's photo. His expression was fleeting: puzzlement, hurt, anger. Fear?

Aventurine took her phone from Paul and looked at the face she knew so well, the face that might have been her own but for age. "It certainly seems like it. Otherwise, that's one hell of a coincidence."

Paul met her eyes. "Genevieve says there are no coincidences."

"Genevieve?" Burroughs asked.

"My great-grandmother," Lance said.

At the hotel, Burroughs handed her the prints he'd had made.

"I had a second set printed."

Of course he had.

"But this is where I leave you," he said slowly. He put a hand on her arm, and then dropped it again, his ice blue eyes distant. "I've got to go back to Lincoln."

"Duty calls?" Avi asked ironically.

He tilted his head. "Something does."

Twenty-nine

I told you the answer might be in Southampton.

The text from Genevieve was peremptory.

The next morning, the three of them took the train to Southampton.

By Southampton, of course, she meant Hambleside, so they hired a taxi. Aventurine had called ahead, and Phil Newlan was waiting for them, crossing the yard full of overwintering boats wrapped in tarps, wiping his hands on a handkerchief. He shook hands all around, sparing a moment's curious glance at Lance, before leading them into the office.

"Good to see you," he said to Paul. "Sailing again?"

Paul shook his head.

Newlan clapped him on the shoulder. "Give it time." He led the way through the outer office, and into his cramped and overcrowded work space. "Coffee?"

They declined. It hadn't been very good in the summer, Avi recalled, and it probably wasn't much better now. There was already a chipped mug on the desk, where rings marred several papers. Newlan topped it off and turned back to them.

"More questions?" he asked.

"We were wondering—" Paul's voice failed him.

"Yes?"

Aventurine took a deep breath. "We were wondering if Shep left anything else with you. Besides that lockbox."

149

Newlan frowned. "I don't think so. Why do you ask?"

Aventurine felt as though she were scrabbling. "A book, maybe? We—keep finding his books."

"A book?" The yardman scratched his chin, where a few days' growth gave him a scruffy appearance. He frowned as he lifted his coffee cup. "What kind of book? He had his logbook with him on the *Máquina*, sure—and I think he had one or two others in the cabin. But he didn't leave any with me. Not like the box that was in that drawer." He jerked his chin in the direction of the file cabinets, some with drawers partway open, and folders sticking out. "No books in that. It was too light." But his brows rose now in a question he was apparently too delicate to ask.

"No," Paul said. "Letters. To me, and to my mother." He looked away.

Newlan cleared his throat uncomfortably. "And how is your mother? I haven't seen her in a while." He took another sip of his coffee. "Have to admit I was surprised to see her, so soon after you two—" he indicated Avi and Paul with his cup— "were by in the summer."

Everything froze. Paul glanced at Aventurine, and clutched at Lance's hand.

"You saw Mum?" he asked urgently. "When was that?"

Now Newlan looked confused. "She didn't tell you she was here?"

"Two weeks ago?" He looked up at the calendar on the wall, but it was still on September. "Maybe ten days. Something like that."

"Not today. Or yesterday." Lance spoke for the first time.

"Lord, no." Newlan laughed. "I'm forgetful, but I'm not that forgetful. It was a couple of weeks ago, something around there." He scratched his chin again. "Funny, though. She never told me about the letters. Never even mentioned them being in the box. Just letters, you say?" He leaned back in his chair and reached for the coffee pot, to pour the remaining bit into his mug. "Sure you don't want any? I can make some more."

Again, they declined.

"What did she want?" Paul asked, his voice low. "What did she ask you?"

For a moment, Newlan looked indecisive, but there was something in Paul's forlorn face that must have struck him. "I probably should let her tell you about this, but there it is. She was asking about your father. About his last day here. Before he sailed." He set his coffee cup down and threw up his hands. "I don't know why she should—I mean, she was here. To see him off. She knew what he said. She knew how excited he was. She was on and off the *Máquina* almost as much as we were, getting her ready. She was everywhere, every time I turned around. Almost like there were two of her." He stopped, looking at Aventurine, suddenly embarrassed. There were two of them, though only one of them had been there that day; Avi had been in Alaska, keeping in touch by text and FaceTime.

The memory was poignant, and Aventurine could see her sister, in her mind's eye, hovering about Shep, trying to seem as though she wasn't. Trying to be supportive without displaying any apprehension. Micheline had had to let Shep do this, because this sail was something he had wanted so much, had planned so carefully. And then disaster had struck.

Phil Newlan took out a handkerchief and blew his nose.

"My sister has been at a loss," she said evasively.

"We all have been," Paul added. Lance squeezed his hand.

"I can imagine," Newlan said. He shrugged abruptly. "So I told her everything I remembered of that day. Reminded her. Did my best. She cried a little. I felt terrible. I had to tell her that there was nothing left in the drawer where I'd put Shep's box—that I'd given you the box. I had to show her." As if to demonstrate, he hefted himself from the desk chair and moved to open the drawer, to prove it was empty.

Except, apparently, it wasn't.

"What the hell?" he exclaimed.

Aventurine licked her lips. "Is it—a book?"

"Yeah." Newlan pulled it out. They crowded around him. The book in his hands was spiral bound, with a photo of the Beatles on the yellowed and dog-eared cover: a collection of sheet music. He passed it to Paul. "She must have left it here," he said, confusion upon him again. "She must have forgotten it."

Lance leaned to turn the cover. Inside was a name. *Paul S. Genthner*.

"There, then." Newlan peered into the drawer again, and, satisfied it was empty, kicked it shut again. "It's yours—I imagine you'll be happy to have it back." He frowned. "Don't know why she'd leave it there, though. Seems strange."

There was a slip of paper tucked inside, a bookmark.

Aventurine leaned in on Paul's other side to open the book. To the sheet music to "Your Mother Should Know."

Aventurine had used her phone app to reserve seats on the train back to Waterloo: a banquette, so they could spread out. Fortunately, the train was not crowded, so they didn't have to share with a fourth, a stranger.

"It wasn't Mick," Aventurine said now with some conviction. "Ten days? Two weeks ago? She was with me. She didn't have any time to come to Hambleside."

Lance nodded. He had bought some crisps and drinks on the platform, and now handed them around. "And she wouldn't have been asking those questions about the day your father sailed, Paul. Like Phil Newlan said: she'd been there. She'd seen it."

"So, it's this Nicola Hallsey," Paul agreed. "But why? What the hell is she doing messing around with my family?"

Aventurine looked at her reflection in the window as they passed through the late afternoon landscape. Wavery, indistinct, like a face underwater. Hers, and yet not hers. Just as Nicola's face was hers, and yet not hers.

"Look her up on Amazon," Avi said bitterly.

Lance and Paul glanced at each other, and then both drew out their phones. Paul was the first to put his down.

"It's like she's trying to be you," he said.

"And now she's trying to be your mother."

Paul flipped to the inside of the sheet music book, touched his name on the flyleaf. "Is this her writing? It's not mine. It's not Dad's."

But Aventurine could only shake her head. "I don't know. I've only ever seen her signature."

Lance chewed his lower lip. He frowned when he spoke. "But we do know one thing. Micheline hasn't been to the boatyard since she disappeared. Either we've beat her there, or the clues she's been getting haven't directed her there."

"But that doesn't bring us any closer to finding her," Paul said.

Aventurine leaned back in her seat and closed her eyes. Paul was right; it didn't. All it did was further complicate a complicated situation: Micheline had received clues; Aventurine had received one; and now there was another directed toward Paul.

Your mother should know.

What should Micheline know?

Then the thought struck her so hard in the solar plexus she thought she'd be sick.

What if it didn't mean Micheline?

Thirty

"*Where were you?*"

Genevieve didn't shout. Mostly because Genevieve *didn't shout*. But her displeasure was obvious, echoing all the way down from York.

"Hambleside," Aventurine said, throwing herself back among the pillows. She felt wrung out. "Where you ordered us to go."

"And you're back now. In Paddington."

"Yes."

"Paul and Lance—are they there with you?"

"Yes."

"And did you find out anything useful?"

Report. The old woman might as well have delivered an order.

"There was another book."

"Ah. And this one was?"

She didn't sound at all surprised.

"A book of sheet music. The Beatles. With Paul's name on the flyleaf. And a bookmark on "Your Mother Should Know.""

There was a long pause.

"You think it's a message to Paul about Micheline."

"Left in a boatyard which was Shep's last port of call." Aventurine threw an arm over her eyes. "I told them. I told Paul and Lance that I thought Nicola Hallsey could be dangerous."

"Aventurine." Genevieve's voice was sharp. "Stop. You're getting

154

ahead of yourself. What do you mean, Nicola could be dangerous? Have you seen her?"

"No, but the guy who runs the boatyard has. Ten days or two weeks ago."

"He knows her?"

"He knows Micheline. He thought he was talking to Mick. But how could he make that mistake? Nicola looks younger than us."

Genevieve sighed. "Wake up to make-up, Mary Wentworth. People see what they expect to see, especially if a little make-up is involved. But that doesn't answer the question of *why* Nicola would present herself at the boatyard as Micheline."

"Two things." Aventurine held up two fingers as though Genevieve could see them. "Phil Newlan said she was asking him about Shep's last day before he sailed; Phil said he thought that was strange, because Micheline had been there on that day."

"So she's seeking information. That's interesting." The old woman's tone was calculating; Avi could imagine Genevieve sitting back in her brocade high-backed chair, stroking her foul-tempered cat, considering. "What's your second thing?"

"We think she left the book in the file cabinet. Phil was adamant that it wasn't there before."

"When had he last looked?"

"She asked to see the drawer where the lock box had been kept. She wanted to make sure there wasn't anything else left in there. So there wasn't—until this book was left in there."

"Yes. I can see the logic of your conclusion."

But there was something uncomfortable niggling at the back of Avi's thoughts. "Did you know there'd be a book there?"

"I didn't know anything would be there. But I did suspect."

"You said the answer might be at the boatyard."

"And you found some answers. We just haven't figured out what the questions are yet. This is going to take some thinking."

A dismissal.

"No, wait," Aventurine tried to forestall her. "If it was in fact Nicola who left the book, and left it for Paul, she's playing a long game."

"Shep has been missing for a long time. Well over a year. That would definitely indicate a long game."

Missing. Even Genevieve was now using that word. Instead of *dead.*

"Missing," Aventurine echoed slowly.

Genevieve clicked her tongue, the sound sharp in Avi's ear. "Listen to me, Aventurine. Listen carefully. From what has been happening over the last couple of weeks, what with the hidden books, with your sister's behavior, and now with Nicola, I think it might be a good time to entertain the possibility that Shep might not have gone down with his ship."

"And that Nicola knows more than she should."

But what did Nicola know?

Thirty-one

They were seated on a bench in Norfolk Square Gardens, beyond the Paddington Bear statue and the now-empty chess board. A fitful breeze rattled dying leaves and skittered trash along the walkway at their feet. Beside her, Lance and Paul held hands, Paul's grip tight as though to let go meant to be blown away by the mean November wind. Aventurine leaned back against the cold seat and pressed her hands to her face. She had thought, perhaps, to find solace in the tiny green space in the middle of the noise of Paddington—even now a siren sounded, making her jump—but her thoughts ran faster than the trains from the station, and were more tangled than the network of tracks.

Aventurine found herself wishing that Burroughs had not returned to Lincoln.

Then she found that she was kicking herself for being so stupid. But it was difficult to remember that she had to stay away from the police detective, especially when the person who had instructed her to do that was the person she was so irrationally angry with at the moment.

It would help, though, to have someone to work through this mess with. And both Burroughs and Genevieve were out of the question.

"Talk to me," Lance said. A gust of wind whipped his words away.

When she opened her eyes, Aventurine was surprised—and somehow touched—to find that he was looking at her, rather than at

Paul. His dark eyes were intense, his brow under that shock of dark hair furrowed.

Paul did not look up. He seemed somehow smaller this afternoon, and desperate, his head down, his eyes studying the walkway at their feet.

"I always believed the authorities," Aventurine said slowly. She bit her lip for a moment. "When they said there was no sign of Shep? I believed them when they said that he was, more than likely, dead."

On the bench beside her, she felt Paul wince at the word.

"I never believed it," he said roughly. He did not look up.

"I know."

"And Mom never did, either," he added fiercely.

Micheline had, though, Aventurine thought. At least her sister had come to that belief when, day after day, week after week, there was no sign of Shep, no word from Shep. They had been together for so long that Micheline *knew* in every part of her that Shep would have contacted her, had he been able. But there was no point, right now, in arguing with Paul about this. He was in no mood—in no shape—to listen to her.

"And Genevieve hasn't been able to find out even a quiver of anything to the contrary," Lance said. "None of her contacts gave her any information that indicated that—your father—wasn't lost at sea."

"Genevieve doesn't know everything," Paul retorted swiftly.

Aventurine refused to argue about that at this point, either. She leaned forward now, elbows on her knees. Two boys zipped past on skateboards, though she was fairly certain that the park rules prohibited that. She thought about glaring after them, then decided she didn't care enough; they wouldn't have seen it anyway. She had enough problems of her own. She cupped her chin in her hands.

"But now she's the one who wants us to consider the likelihood of your father being alive after all." Lance seemed puzzled, uncertain.

"He can't be," Aventurine protested unhappily. "He wouldn't have done that to Micheline. Or to you, Paul. He wouldn't have put either of you through this." But did she know that for certain? Did she know anything for certain anymore? She never would have thought Micheline would keep secrets—any secrets—from her, but here they were, huddled in the darkness of an early November evening, trying to figure out where she would have gone, and why. And coming up with no answers. Because this, apparently, was a long game.

Genevieve doesn't know everything.

Well, Aventurine was inclined to believe—somewhat resentfully right now—that Genevieve knew a hell of a lot more than most of them. And far more than she was letting on.

None of them had been all that hungry, but they'd eaten a subdued fish and chips at the Sussex Fish Bar, and then had retreated next door to the purple splendor of the Sussex Arms.

"I just feel like I should be *doing* something," Paul said helplessly, taking his pint. The bartender handed him a coaster. Pointedly.

Aventurine slapped her card on the machine, then followed the pair of them under the Business Class Lounge sign into a cozy back room, uninhabited, in which a fireplace stood empty and cold, and a snooker tournament was underway on the giant television. The TV sound was off, and instead, the ambient music was—she listened—the Electric Light Orchestra.

"Evil Woman." She wondered which one of them was. Nicola, probably.

"We all feel as though we should be doing something," Aventurine agreed. "Genevieve said to stay put, then she said to go to Southampton, and now she's pissed off because we did and didn't follow her directions. She warned me against trying to force something to happen, and making the situation worse."

"My dad is missing, and my mom is missing now, too. I'm not sure how it can be much worse," Paul protested.

Aventurine dropped her coaster onto the low table before the leather sofa, but took a drink from her pint before setting the glass down on it. Sadler's Peaky Blinder black ale. She frowned, considering, never having had a black ale before. She liked the lingering bitterness on her tongue; it suited her mood.

"Besides," Lance said, setting his own pint of Boddingtons down on his coaster. "We don't know what the hell we're doing. We don't know what the hell we're looking for. We don't know where the hell we're going. We're just flailing. Flailing in the dark."

Aventurine nodded unhappily. "That's just it. I keep looking around for direction, but since we have nothing to build on, I don't know where to go or what to do. Maybe Genevieve was absolutely right the first time. Maybe we have to sit tight and wait for the clue that tells us what our next move is supposed to be."

Paul looked obdurate. He opened his mouth as though to protest, but Lance laid a long-fingered hand on his knee. After a moment, Paul set his pint aside and covered Lance's hand with his own.

"We do have clues, though," Lance reminded her slowly. In the dimness, his expression was hard to read. "The underlines in the books. The books themselves. The sheet music from the boatyard."

"That was in a book," Paul said. "What should my mother know?" He looked at Avi so intently she had to look away.

A waitress peered around the corner, no doubt to check on their drinking progress, which was not much. Seeing Paul's pint, she slipped over wordlessly, picked up the glass, and then slid a coaster beneath it before disappearing back into the main room. Oops?

"And the ones that started it all," Aventurine said. She frowned.

"What?"

"The notes that started it all," Avi repeated. "The original notes in the lockbox. The ones from your father."

There was a long pregnant pause. Aventurine drank from her pint—it was suddenly nearly empty, and she wasn't sure how it had come to be that way. She should have flagged down the waitress. Of course, as a lightweight, she knew perfectly well that she shouldn't have another; but as a person who was, perhaps, about to reveal the most shameful thing she'd ever done, she probably could use the jolt of false courage. Her hand holding the glass shook. She stood.

"Anyone need another?" she asked. Both Paul and Lance shook their heads.

Aventurine took her time, aided by a couple of customers ahead of her at the bar; the place had filled up, at nearly nine o'clock. She didn't mean to fumble her credit card out of her wallet and drop it to the floor, but that bought her a further respite, as she scrambled to find it. Then, pint in hand, there was no help for it.

Returning to the lounge, she found herself wishing she had not chosen the seat against the far wall; when she dropped back down into it, both pairs of eyes turned on her expectantly, as though she were a witness on the stand.

"Go on," Paul said, much as though the break in the conversation had never happened.

"The first letters," Lance prodded, when she hesitated. "The ones, as you claim, started it all."

There was nothing for it. This was not the way she would have chosen to tell them about the note; she would have chosen not to tell them at all. Going through your sister's things wasn't an admirable activity; and it was an activity she had never participated in until now. She could only hope that Lance and, especially, Paul would understand that this was not business as usual.

And Micheline had begun keeping secrets first.

Aventurine pressed her eyes closed, doubly ashamed of herself. *Micheline started it.* That thought made her entire action seem petty, like some childish tit-for-tat, rather than because of her desperate concern for her twin.

"I found Mick's," she said. "I read it."

The air around them stilled.

Aventurine slowly dug out her phone and flipped through the photo app until she came to the picture she had taken of Shep's letter. She enlarged it as best she could, and held the phone out.

After a moment of holding his burning gaze on her face, Paul took it from her.

She watched, chewing on her lower lip, as the two bent their heads over the screen and read.

They were both complicit now. This did not make her feel much better.

My darling Micheline—

Aventurine felt as though she knew every single line, every single word. She felt as though she could recite the letter by heart. Her hands shaking, she lifted her pint of Peaky Blinder and took a long drink, welcoming the bitterness on her tongue. It might have been the beer; it might have been the stress, but her head immediately felt lighter, and the snooker table on the giant TV began to swim.

After an interminable few moments, Paul set the phone down on the glass-topped table with a click. Lance leaned over it then, and scrolled with his finger. An incongruous roar of laughter erupted from the bar in the front room.

"Where did you get this?" Paul demanded hoarsely. He did not look at her.

"Your mother—carries it with her." Aventurine licked her lips and took another drink. Her stomach, as well as her head, was beginning to protest.

"And she let you read it?" he pressed. "She let you take a picture of it?" His voice was hard. He knew the answer.

"Not... exactly." She dropped her eyes.

Another long and painful silence. Lance had pushed the phone away, and now slumped against the back of the leather couch.

Paul's silence was an accusation. Aventurine felt it like a knife between her ribs.

"He knew," Lance said after a moment. Somewhere in the background, the Traveling Wilburys launched into "Handle Me with Care."

There it lay, between them. Out there in the open. The idea that had been simmering just under the surface for a while now. The fear that she carried in her belly.

"It sure reads like it," Aventurine said. Her voice sounded odd to her own ears. Disembodied.

"He knew that the *La Máquina de los Vientos* wasn't coming back," Lance said. He sat up again, tried to put an arm around Paul's shoulders—but Paul jerked away. Lance dropped his hands into his lap and twined his fingers together.

Aventurine slugged down the last of her pint. A mistake. The room whirled. Across from them, through the fire door, the spiral staircase and its fairy lights seemed to spin like a drill bit.

Hurriedly she set the glass on the table, aiming for the coaster and missing, and struggled to her feet. The ladies' toilet was downstairs and around a corner. She barely made it.

"We've got to figure this out," Paul insisted angrily. "The books. The clues. Where Mom is. And Dad."

"We can't do it tonight," Lance countered as he pulled open the door to the hotel. "Your aunt isn't well."

"My *aunt*," Paul snarled, "is drunk."

The night clerk looked up and nodded as they navigated the lobby to the elevator, all lights and mirrors. Aventurine closed her eyes against the brightness, which was a mistake, as the movement upward exacerbated her nausea.

She *was* drunk. Aventurine cursed herself, for knowing better, but drinking that second pint anyway. When the door opened on the narrow hallway, she pushed herself out and down to the corner, where she found herself fumbling in her bag for her key card.

"Do you need help?" Lance asked. Paul had already opened their door and now stood just inside, holding the door with unconcealed impatience.

"No," Aventurine managed, shoving the card into the slot. The green light flashed and she shoved her way inside. "Thanks," she called over her shoulder, and let the door close. Once inside, she dropped the key card and it fluttered away into the darkness. She needed it to turn on the lights; but for now she could not think ahead to finding it. She stumbled to the bed and fell down across it.

Tomorrow, she knew, she would have to gather up all the photos from the books and try again to fit all the puzzle pieces together. Tonight, the idea of reading made her head—and the bed on which she lay—spin.

She had dozed off when her phone rang. Opening her eyes was like prying open a rusty gate. The number was Genevieve's. She ignored it.

Thirty-two

Somewhere in the small hours, Aventurine woke abruptly in a sweat, from a dream of her parents, which had quickly degenerated into a nightmare. She groped for her phone, which read 3:02. Outside, even at this early hour, the street hummed, with the punctuation of a faraway siren. She'd left the window cracked a few inches, and the heavy curtain moved in the dimness. Overhead, the tiny red eye of the fire alarm blinked.

She stared up into the darkness. They had been dead for a long time now, her parents; the accident took their lives when she and Micheline were still in college. Half her life plus some. A car accident traversing the Rodovia Regis Bittencourt, outside Curitiba, a place which, had circumstances been different, Avi might have liked to have visited, wandered around in, until she stumbled across a story. But she knew now that she'd never be able to: never be able to look at the Andes, never be able to drive over that pass without thinking of that one fateful moment when her father had lost control of the car on one of the switchbacks, and the car had plummeted from the road in the deserted darkness.

Slowly now, Aventurine drew herself up until she was seated on the rumpled bed, her back to the headboard. Traffic outside hushed along the London Road. No one was crashing a car. No one was plunging to his or her death. It was another quiet night in England.

Somewhere out there, Micheline was probably lying awake,

staring at the ceiling of whatever mean little room she was inhabiting. Planning her next move on her quest, whatever form that was taking. Avi felt the deep knot, somewhere in her rib cage. It was fear, she recognized, and frustration. That she could not help her sister—was not allowed to help her sister. She missed her twin. Desperately. More than any other time they had been separated, because then, unlike now, they had not been separate.

The phone, charging on the bedside table, buzzed with an incoming text. Aventurine drove the balls of her hands into her eyes. She didn't want to talk to Genevieve right now. She didn't even want to think of Genevieve right now. But when she closed her eyes against the dark hour in the city, all she could see were the wispy remnants of her dream, of her mother and father as she last remembered them, though now both their mouths were open in silent screams as they plunged off the road.

Sucking in a dry gulp of air, she picked up her phone, still tethered to the outlet. Her breath caught as she saw: it was Mick.

I dreamed of the accident.

Where are you?

What's going on?

No matter what she texted, Micheline didn't answer, having fallen determinedly silent.

Are you okay?

I want to help you.

Nothing. Dead air. None of Aventurine's texts were even opened.

I miss you, she threw out there at last. Desperately. Into the void where her sister could not be reached.

In frustration, she opened the Find My app again, but Micheline was still disconnected. There was no way to know where that phone was. Where Micheline was.

Hell, she could be well out of the country by now. She could be, for all Aventurine knew, in South America. Or somewhere in the middle of the Atlantic Ocean. Or in the room next door.

This, then, Aventurine realized, was despair. The despair she had watched Paul wallowing in for months, but which, despite her best efforts, she had never understood: it had taken Lance to convince Paul to open up. She touched her phone screen again as it threatened to go dark, then put her finger on Micheline's text message. Trying, desperately, to reach her through the words, and failing miserably.

She rolled down onto her back, and pressed the phone to the place where she knew her heart was supposed to be, but which held only a great throbbing pain.

Thirty-three

Meet us in the breakfast room, Lance texted.

Breakfast, Aventurine had discovered the previous day, was in a cramped room in the basement. After a quick shower and a handful of Panadol, she dragged herself down to find Lance and Paul at a table across from the door, sipping coffee, with a family-sized rack of toast between them, which neither had touched. She slid into the empty chair across from Paul. He looked worn and tired, exactly how she felt, but she was willing to bet that he wasn't as hungover as she was. A woman in a blue smock hovered and asked whether she'd like tea. She nodded.

"I heard from your mother last night, Paul," she said without preamble. "Or rather, this morning. Around three."

He sloshed his coffee. "Where is she?" he demanded. "What did she say?"

Aventurine opened her phone with a touch, and slid it across the crowded tabletop toward him. He read the exchange quickly, then sat back. Lance looked at him, then at her, and raised an eyebrow. She waved him to the phone.

"What is she doing?" Paul's voice was anguished. "What is going on? Why won't she contact me?"

Aventurine wished she knew.

"But she's safe, Paul," Lance said reassuringly. "Even if we don't know anything else, we know she's safe." He set the phone back down again, and Aventurine watched the screen fade.

"Safe," he spat bitterly. His face twisted, and his laugh was short and angry. "Safe, but selfish." He dabbed fruitlessly at the spilled coffee with his napkin, only managing to smear it around on the tabletop.

Aventurine closed her eyes, feeling his despair, feeling his useless fury. "I know, Paul," she said quietly. "I know." She took a deep breath, which only exacerbated the headache that had settled behind her eyes. "But I also know how much she loves you."

He made a scoffing noise, turning his face away.

"She does," Aventurine insisted. "It would have to be something huge to make her put it before you."

Suddenly, she caught a glimmer of something. An idea. Something. But when she turned her whole attention to it, it slipped away.

"The only thing she'd *ever* put before you," she breathed, "is your father."

"We're going to wait," Lance said at the elevator.

"For what?" For a moment, Aventurine had a sensation of being caught in limbo. In waiting, possibly forever, for news. Any news. Waiting for the remainder of her life. "For what?" she demanded again, when all the other two did was glance at each other.

The elevator came with its cheerful ping, and Aventurine felt an impotent rage at the sound. *Get a grip*, she ordered herself. They climbed aboard, and in a matter of moments, were before Lance and Paul's door.

Paul shrugged. "Genevieve."

Her anger transferred to the old woman, which was easier, and made more sense.

"I've got to walk," she said. Then she realized what she had said. *Damn you, Genevieve.* "I've got to think." She took a step toward her own room, for her coat, for an umbrella against the unsettled day. "Will you be here?"

"We'll text you if we go somewhere."

"Or if you hear anything?"

Lance nodded. Their door closed behind them.

Thirty-four

Her phone vibrated as she was sitting beside the boating lake in Regent's Park, now cold and empty of boats. The bandstand, over her shoulder, was deserted and silent. Some geese paddled lazily by and took no notice of her. She fumbled in her bag for the cell, hoping for Paul, or Lance, or Genevieve, or, please God, Micheline.

Nicola.

Nicola?

She opened the message, and found a map, a red location indicator back in Paddington.

Lunch. 12:30.

Furious, Aventurine hit the call button. Two rings.

"What do you want?" she demanded.

"It's something my father told me." There was a note of something—triumph?—in Nicola's voice, and then that empty ringing silence. She'd ended the call with that enigmatic statement. Aventurine stared at her phone screen, the number pad, the phone icon. *Call ended.*

It was something Nicola's father had told her.

But who the hell was her father?

Henry? Was there something Nicola wished to convey from Henry?

Staring at the boating lake, Aventurine had, for the slightest of moments, a flash of Nicola as a child, seated on Henry's lap, as he regaled her with stories of sailing ships and pirates. It was a winsome imagining, and, Avi realized, the child on Henry's lap could have been any of the three of them.

Then Henry Hallsey morphed slowly into someone else, whose features were all too familiar. Daniel Morrow?

It all came back to that damned DNA test. She needed to know more about it, and Nicola was dangling the hook. *Knew how* to dangle the hook. They were half-sisters: Nicola on one side, the twins Aventurine and Micheline on the other. One of their fathers was not who he seemed, and, without getting Henry's DNA involved, there was no real way to figure it out at this point.

No longer wanting to walk, Aventurine jumped on the Tube at Baker Street and swayed through the two intervening stations to climb off at Paddington. She held her phone in her hand as she came out of the long entrance to the station and turned to her right. In two minutes she was at the place, and through the window, she could see Nicola, seated at a small table, sipping from a glass of white wine. Avi slipped inside.

The maitre d' held the chair for her; Nicola Hallsey smiled at him without once glancing at Aventurine. "Another glass of this for my sister," she said.

"I'm not staying," Avi said. Her face felt stiff. "What have you got to tell me?"

"Such a rush." When Nicola looked at her now, the smile did not reach her green eyes, which were narrowed and speculative. She took up the menu and made a show of examining it with her full attention. "Where have you got to go?"

Aventurine paused. The question unnerved her: what did Nicola know of her situation? How did Nicola know where to find her, for that matter?

A waiter appeared with a glass of wine on a tray.

"Caprese salad, I think," Nicola said, closing the menu and handing it to the waiter with her still-bright smile. She shook her blonde hair back. "Thank you."

Across the table, Aventurine felt the rebellion born of resentment, and let her eyes run down the list of pastas in heavy sauces. All of them looked wildly attractive; and all of them, no doubt, contained ten or twenty thousand calories. None of them healthy; all of them conducive to clogged arteries and heart attacks. *That'll show you, Nicola.* At the same time, Aventurine was appalled by the depth of her own pettiness, and she attempted to extricate herself from it, much as a wild thing caught in a snare might do. "I'll have your chicken Caesar, please," she said, her own voice more strident than she meant it to be. When the waiter had sashayed away with the menus, skirting the tightly packed tables, she picked up her wine glass and smiled virtuously.

For a long moment neither said anything. Outside in the street, Paddington bustled, cars and red buses passing, with the occasional blare of a horn.

"Why are you here?" Aventurine asked at last.

Nicola picked up her own drink again, her familiar green eyes level and hard, her expression watchful, traveling quickly around the restaurant. Then she leaned in. "I needed to talk to you."

"A text would have sufficed." Avi didn't like white wine. It wasn't sitting well on her stomach, or with her lingering headache, either; she wondered why Nicola had ordered it for her, wondered why she hadn't objected. She pushed it daintily away on the white tablecloth, suspecting she'd need a clear head for this conversation. Instead, she lifted her water goblet. "I mean, there was no need to rush back from Italy."

If she had scored a point, Nicola did not let on. Neither did she deny it. With a movement of her wrist, she swirled her wine and looked at the bubbles. Then she took another delicate sip. Aventurine noted that she hadn't even left a lipstick mark on the rim of the glass.

"You don't trust me."

Aventurine shrugged. "Only as much as you trust me."

A tiny smile lifted the corner of Nicola's mouth. "You've learned well from your friend Genevieve."

"I have."

"The spy."

Aventurine locked eyes with Nicola. It was going to be like that. The weird dance. The oneupmanship. She could play as well. She didn't even crack a smile.

The waiter came, accompanied by a second, and, using a white cloth over his hand, placed the heavy white dishware on the table before them. They busied themselves for a moment with cheese and pepper grinding, and then both servers sailed off again.

"Your father has been in contact with me. By text. He was wondering if you were spending time with Micheline and me."

Nicola paused with her silverware in hand, and now appeared to be examining her salad for imperfections.

"He's not my father," she said. "Henry."

The statement was bald. Explosive. Yet now Nicola cut a piece of cheese and speared it with a sliver of tomato, as though she was simply remarking upon the weather. Avi felt her jaw slacken with the shock of it. The incongruity. The casual bomb.

She was surprised at the pang she felt. *Poor Henry*. She thought of his distress that afternoon in the tea shop in Lincoln, when he had talked about Nicola missing their lunch date; she remembered the fear underlying that distress. How much he loved Nicola, the daughter of his beloved wife.

"Does he know?"

"We share a father, Aventurine. You, me, Micheline."

"That tells me nothing. Henry could be my father."

"Do you really think so?" Nicola's tone was derisive. "Look. I love him. I would never do anything to hurt him. But—I found my mother's diaries, in some boxes in the attic. Hidden, probably by her, so my—Henry wouldn't find them; all of her others, from the past twenty years or so, were in her closet." For a moment, there was the faintest echo of a far-off tragedy in Nicola's expression, but it quickly faded away. "We share a father, Aventurine. And it's Daniel Morrow."

"That's why you took the DNA test." Every sound in the restaurant had faded to a background hum; every other table had blurred to a late Monet painting. Only Nicola's face was clear; only Nicola's voice was discernible.

"Of course, it was. I was hoping to find you."

That didn't ring true.

"The books," Aventurine said. "You knew I was out there. You knew we looked alike. These hidden diaries of your mother's—they didn't give you any new information. They confirmed what you already believed."

Nicola waved a hand like it didn't matter.

Aventurine moved an anchovy to the side of her plate. She'd never felt less like eating lettuce and cheese. Chicken: she forked a bite up, but it was like chewing cardboard.

"So, you wanted to talk to me about my father." Aventurine chose her possessive carefully. Nicola registered no expression. "Why? He's been dead for half my life. More than half yours."

"And he died how?"

The dream rose up before her eyes. Aventurine shivered, and then realized that Nicola was watching her intently. She fought to regain control.

"A car accident, if you must know."

"I must, as you put it."

"Surely your mother wrote about that in her diaries," Aventurine said. Meanly. But she felt mean.

This time Nicola flinched, and was the one to fight for control.

But Avi was finished. She pushed her plate away, crumpled her napkin and threw it on the tablecloth. "I have questions, since you're here. Things maybe you'd tell me, and perhaps we could trade information."

Nicola finished her wine.

"Have mine," Avi said, flicking a nail against the glass. "I don't want it."

Nicola lifted a hand to the waiter instead. "What do you want to know? I'll decide whether the answers are worth trading for."

"Why were you following my nephew—"

"*My* nephew."

"—in Milan? How did you know he was there?" Aventurine narrowed her eyes and ticked off her questions on her fingers. "Why did you go to Hambleside two weeks ago? Why were you at Llanthony ten days ago? Why haven't you checked in with your father? Why does Gio think you're with Micheline and me?"

Her smile was arch as the waiter brought her another wine glass and whisked the empty one away.

"I *am* with you," she said.

"But not with Micheline. Do you know where she is?"

Nicola looked around the restaurant. She raised her fair eyebrows. "Not today."

"So, you won't give me a straight answer."

Again that flick of blonde hair over her shoulders. "Suffice it to say that I need to find out all I can about you. You are my family, aren't you?"

"DNA does not make family."

She took a leisurely sip of wine. "No, but it helps, doesn't it? Especially with twins?" She laughed at the look on Aventurine's face. "Oh, don't worry. Your secret is safe with me. For now." Her expression grew more calculating. "It's just nice to know that I'm not the only stolen child."

Aventurine's eyes locked on Nicola's face. There was a hardness there. A cruelty. She touched her own chin, her cheekbones. Did she share that expression?

Nicola gathered her bag and stood. "The ladies?" she asked a passing waiter, who pointed to the back of the dining room. "I'll be back," she said to Avi, and took only a few steps away before returning. "Did you ever think," she murmured, leaning in close, "that your sister's beloved Shep scuttled his boat intentionally?"

Thirty-five

Nicola never returned.

After waiting uncomfortably, Aventurine called for the check, then hurried back to the hotel. No one answered her knock on Lance and Paul's door.

Where are you? she texted. There was no reply.

Walk, she told herself sternly. Back in the street, she headed down toward Lancaster Gate and entered Hyde Park near the Italian gardens. The sky, like her mood, remained unrelievedly grey, though it did not rain.

Aventurine barely registered anything until she'd left the Serpentine behind and the Albert Memorial loomed to her right. She paused, staring upwards. She liked the over-the-topness of the Albert Memorial, that overwrought monument to great love and even greater grief; she wondered what kind of memorial her sister would build to Shep. Who wouldn't want to commemorate the greatest thing in one's life by building a statue to one's love, and then placing it so high above the ground that no one could really make out its features without binoculars? Except that the gold of the prince gleamed, even on this dreary November day. Avi particularly liked the elephant to the side, though the imperialism of the remainder of the decoration really made her uncomfortable; and the camels looked as though they'd like to spit.

Wearily, she sank down onto the cold marble steps, mindful of wet spots. Albert peered over her shoulder, and they both looked across at the Royal Albert Hall, where the front was partially hidden by scaffolding. The last time she had been here, at night, the dome and the pillars on which it floated were illuminated in red. Now, like everything else on this day, it looked cold and mean and grey. She sighed and took out her phone, checking the battery. Still at 87%, and she had had the foresight to pack a couple of portable chargers in her bag. No messages there, though. Nothing from Mick. Nothing from Genevieve, or Burroughs, or Paul and Lance. Nothing more from Nicola, though after the fraught luncheon, she barely expected it, and wanted it even less. She couldn't help but feel her aloneness in this largest city in Europe, and hunched her shoulders against that thought.

Quickly she typed a truncated report of her lunch and texted it to Genevieve. Information flowed both ways.

I'll text you, Lance had promised. Kindly. He really was a nice young man, and she desperately hoped that Paul was able to see that through his darkness, and recognize Lance for what he was. How dependable. Especially now, when it seemed, at least to Paul, that there was no one to depend on in his life. Nothing solid.

Of course, Micheline had left them all to go after Shep. Almost viscerally, Aventurine could feel her sister's shaking body in her arms, that night in Lincoln, where she had sobbed out how much she missed her dead husband. But was he really dead? He had to be, Aventurine thought wildly, again, feeling the fury building inside her. Overhead, the scudding clouds broke apart just enough to let a patch of blue peer through, but soon enough, that disappeared again. Shep had to be dead, she reasoned desperately, because if he wasn't, he had been immeasurably cruel to Micheline, and to Paul, for the past year and more. Immeasurably cruel. Through the sunglasses she didn't really need, Aventurine glared upwards into the changeable sky, and when the first of the raindrops spattered on her lenses, she couldn't tell whether she'd willed them into being with her fury. All she knew was that, if Shep was not dead, then Micheline had better find him first, because otherwise, she, Aventurine, would kill him for hurting the two people she loved best in the world.

The rain was picking up. Umbrellas were appearing in Kensington Gore: red, blue, but mostly serviceable black.

Aventurine hadn't brought an umbrella; she'd forgotten it somewhere between the Italian restaurant—damn Nicola; but she couldn't think of her right now—and here. Now she pulled the hood of her rain jacket over her head, got to her feet with the ease of a ninety-year-old woman who was not Genevieve, and hurried across the road when the traffic broke.

She had to stuff her phone into her pocket to keep from checking it compulsively. She'd texted everyone; no one had messaged back.

In the Victoria and Albert Museum, she studied the signage at the entrance, with the lists of what exhibits were on which floors, and in a fit of desperation, finally slipped into the elevator behind a woman in a black leather jacket. She pressed 4, and Aventurine, considering this a kind of divination, nodded. They rode in silence until the door opened.

Furniture. Cabinetry. Things about which Aventurine knew nothing. For a moment she considered turning back to the elevator, but then she realized that it hardly mattered. She was in limbo. Until she heard from someone. Anyone. Her footsteps echoed as she entered the gallery. The woman in leather was suddenly nowhere to be seen; she obviously knew where she was going and what she was looking for. Avi found that she envied that in a person.

Joinery tools. Aventurine leaned in and examined them, trying to understand the work they did in the proper hands. There was a film, but she found that she couldn't watch it; her head ached too much, and her attention span was at an absolute low. Guiltily, she thought she perhaps should take notes, in case something came up she could use in her work later, but she did not reach toward the notebook in her bag. She moved on, pulling her phone out again and checking it, though it had not vibrated nor rung. She might have missed something, she told herself. But no. No new messages.

Partway along the gallery was a flat bench. She sat, with a sideways view of one of the most ornate and ugly carved Victorian sofas imaginable. Aventurine wished for her sister, who would die laughing looking at this monstrosity, who would pose at her most faux-seductive before it. No, that wasn't true. The old version of Micheline, before the loss of the *La Máquina de los Vientos*—she would have done those things, would have insisted Avi take a picture of her, would have laughed in a way that would have echoed down the long gallery, causing anyone else viewing the exhibits to look up at the joyousness of the sound. This new Micheline: no. Something in her had died, with Shep.

So it was no wonder that Micheline was doing what she was doing.

Not for the first time did Aventurine wonder what it would be like to feel that great love. To bask in that great love.

But if Shep were still alive—his *great love* apparently wasn't so great at all.

Aventurine heard footsteps, and in her almost fugue state, expected to see her sister materialize before her. She shook herself.

The footsteps stopped. She saw no one. Someone examining a piece of furniture in one of the glass cases? Perhaps the woman in black leather.

She fell again into a fitful examination of the sofa, the purplish-red upholstery with its floral design, echoed in the rosewood carving at the back. She would never be comfortable sitting on that sofa, imagining it hulking over her, a kind of *Little Shop of Horrors* vegetation coming to life and devouring her. Perhaps, she mused, that was just it: you invited unwanted visitors to sit there, knowing they'd leave quickly. Or be eaten.

The footsteps drew nearer, stopped again. Still she could see no one. It made her rather nervous, but she chastised herself. Lots of people came to this gallery, in which there were pieces they understood and came purposely to study. Lots of people stopped to more closely examine this table, or that chair. She was just being stupid, because of her heightened level of anxiety.

Aventurine drew out her phone again. Still nothing.

There was something strange about the footsteps echoing down the gallery. Quiet. Exaggeratedly slow, as though the maker were placing one foot on the hardwood and waiting a moment before taking the next step. Waiting to see if there was a reaction. Waiting to see if the maker was noticed. Aventurine's neck prickled. She felt as though she were being watched. But that was impossible, surely: if someone were watching her, then wouldn't that person, in this long well-lit room, be visible? At least reflected in the long glass display cases? She glanced around, biting her lip. She couldn't even make out a shadow, a liminal edge.

Okay. She was being stupid. She knew it, but she couldn't shake the anxiety. Any interest at all in the furniture had flown. Shoving her phone into her pocket once more, she got slowly to her feet, listening. Listening.

The footsteps receded briskly.

"Nicola?" she called. She didn't know why. There was no answer.

Aventurine moved hurriedly toward the entrance and the elevator, but the gallery was empty. There was no sign of anyone else. She heard a ring as the elevator doors, just out of her sight, opened; but when she turned the corner, the elevator had gone again, the arrow only pointing down.

There was a book on the chair near the doors.

Thirty-six

Aventurine shook. Still. She had known, as soon as she saw the book, that it had been left for her. That it was meant for her. That her anxiety had not been unfounded. That there had, in fact, been someone in the gallery with her, watching her, waiting for the precise moment to leave this—message—where she would not miss it.

Dracula. By Bram Stoker.

With shaking hands, she had flipped back the black cover to look at the first page, where her name was boldly written in that familiar—unfamiliar—handwriting. *Aventurine D. Morrow.* She couldn't help but think someone was mocking her, using the middle initial where she never did. A bizarre kind of finger in the eye.

Avi had thrust the book into her bag as quickly as possible, not wanting to touch it in case it burned, like the host had burned Mina Starker. The elevator had taken forever to reappear: no doubt the silent messenger had ridden it all the way down to the ground floor. Aventurine climbed aboard and then immediately hit the button to close the door, to obviate anyone else getting in with her, even though her rational mind told her that anyone else would just be a stranger, no one to fear. Still, she held her finger on the button for the ground floor, hoping that what people said about causing a non-stop trip was true. Her skin didn't stop prickling until she was out in the street, where the rain had let up, and the cars hissed along the wet tar.

She stood on the pavement, trying to catch her breath, trying to still her rapidly pounding heart. A couple wandered by arm-in-arm, and a woman marched past with an enormous poodle on a long sequined leash. Aventurine turned, looked the other way along the street, eyes straining for someone, anyone, she might recognize. There was no one.

She was certain, as she made her way along the Brompton Road, that she must be reeling, much as a drunken person would do. Her head was pounding. There was a tea room just down to the left, and she turned in gratefully, but not before scanning the pavement in either direction, to ascertain that she wasn't being followed.

Inside, she ordered a scone with jam and cream, and a pot of tea, fumbling to pay, watching the street through the window. Then she threaded her way toward the garishly decorated room at the back, where she hoped she could find a seat from which she could keep her eye on the door. But when she passed through, she heard her name, and nearly dropped her tray.

"What a coincidence, Aventurine," Sioned Davies said, rising from her chair. "Do come join me."

Aventurine sat slowly, warily. *Of all the gin joints in all the world...*

Sioned smiled, indicated her muffin with a single bite taken from it. Her teacup was full. "I thought I was feeling peckish, but then I realized I just didn't have the stomach for it." Her smile turned to a grimace. She pushed the plate with the muffin to the side, and lifted her cup.

Avi stared dumbly at Sioned's plate. After all that, it was Sioned. Wasn't it? She lifted the strap of her bag off her shoulder, but kept the bag in her lap. Inside it, the book. Had Sioned been the person in the furniture gallery, there had been time for her to duck into the tea shop and take that one bite, to establish her presence. But—and the reasoning made Aventurine's head hurt more—Sioned would have had to know that she, Aventurine, would decide on tea, would choose this particular shop. There were very specific difficulties in following someone while walking ahead of them.

Aventurine had not seen Sioned in the street. Had she? Would she have recognized the head of grey hair, had it been on a person walking away from her? Sioned could have had her hood up; Sioned could have had an umbrella. The possibilities were enormous.

"I'm sorry, Aventurine, but are you all right? You look as though you've seen a ghost."

"No, no—it's just been a trying morning." And lunch, and afternoon. She put a hand to her phone, but did not draw it out. "It's good to see you." But was it? "I didn't know you were in London. It is an amazing coincidence meeting you here." Aventurine poured out some tea, and her little pot clattered against the cup. She hurriedly set it down again.

What would Genevieve do?

And then, *what would Mary Wentworth do?*

The answer was obvious: both would play it incredibly cool, as if they weren't profoundly rattled by everything that had happened today—everything that had happened in the past few days—and by a hangover. Hell, neither of them would *have* a hangover. Genevieve would be so disappointed.

She drank some tea.

Sioned's forehead creased in a frown. "I didn't know I'd be up to town, either. It's to do with my brother-in-law Dafydd's estate. His solicitor is here."

Aventurine nodded. It was a very good cover story, she had to admit. If it was a cover story.

Now Sioned sighed and leaned back in her seat. She picked idly at her muffin without seeming to realize it. A shaft of light from a high window skimmed her hair, turning it from grey to silver. "I thought it would be a matter of signing some papers and letting the solicitor do what solicitors do. But it's become a bit more complicated than that."

Sioned seemed to want to talk, and Aventurine caught herself falling for it. Unless it wasn't a set-up and the other woman was totally sincere? She had to watch herself. She lifted her tea cup to her lips.

"His wife—"

"He had a wife? I thought you said—he was divorced."

Sioned shrugged. The muffin lay in crumbs on her plate. "He married ages ago, but I *thought* they were divorced. Now it turns out that they were only separated. And there are provisions in the will related to her. Alyona, her name was. Something-ova Davies."

Alyona Something-ova. The jangling of bells erupted in her mind.

"She's Russian?" Avi tried to keep her voice neutral, just a passing curiosity.

Sioned shrugged again. "I know. Strange, isn't it? She was someone Dafydd met through business, I think in Lincoln. She'd only come out to the farm a couple of times—didn't like it, Dafydd said, and he seemed really disappointed by that." She half-smiled, a fond remembrance. "I think he had this picture in his mind: he'd retire to the farm, and Alyona would come with him, and they'd probably live some idyllic bucolic lifestyle."

Lincoln.

It always came back to that.

"But she wasn't bucolic."

Sioned shook her head. "Some people just don't take to it, I guess. Dafydd wanted to stay on the farm; Alyona didn't. So they went their separate ways. My brother-in-law was always talking about finalizing the divorce, and I never realized that he hadn't carried through. So now the solicitors have to try to find Alyona—"

"In Lincoln—"

"In Lincoln, and I don't know how they'll do that." She wiped a weary hand across her brow, and then took up her tea cup.

"Did they communicate, do you suppose?" Aventurine asked. She needed to talk to Dominic Burroughs. "Phone calls, emails, letters?"

"I don't know, really," Sioned sighed. "It always seemed like a place you didn't go with Dafydd. He didn't like to talk about his marriage, his ex-wife—plain old wife, I suppose." She drained her tea. The passing ray of light had disappeared, and now she looked like what she was: a tired, grey-haired woman, grieving the recent loss of her dead husband's brother. "I'll have to go back and go through his things, see if I can't find any answers that would make finding her easier for the solicitors."

"I'm sorry." Aventurine, too, leaned back in her chair. She studied the other woman through lowered lashes, wondering. Her anxiety had eased, and now, looking across the table, she couldn't see Sioned as the presence in the gallery. It didn't make logistical sense. And no one who would take such care not to be seen there would place herself in Aventurine's path like this.

Avi put a hand on her bag, still in her lap, still with that book inside. Another thing she had to look at more carefully, but she knew she had to do it in the relative safety of the hotel room. Surreptitiously, she glanced at her watch. How long had she been here with Sioned? But she had to stay, had to glean the rest of Sioned's story of Dafydd; it could be important. The story of Alyona, a missing Russian bride.

"What did Alyona do for work?" she asked.

Sioned now made a face. "I think Dafydd said something about her being a free-lance journalist. I don't recall the details."

Oh, for God's sake. Another writer? Then Aventurine felt the jolt, the spike in her blood pressure. *Surely not.* Surely, absolutely not. But after Nicola Hallsey, anything was possible.

"What does she look like?" Did Aventurine's voice wobble?

If Sioned thought that an odd question, she didn't let on. "Oh, I can hardly remember. Dark hair, dark eyes. I used to think of her as the Dark Lady." She shook her head. "It's been so long since I've seen her. But now, I suppose, I'll have to help find her, wherever she is."

Slowly Aventurine's blood pressure was receding. She steadied her breathing. "I'm sorry. I know how hard that can be. Especially if she doesn't want to be found."

Sioned paused with her cup in midair, before slowly setting it down again. "Oh, Aventurine," she breathed. "Your sister? You haven't met up with her?"

Aventurine shook her head, pressing her lips together for a moment. "No. Because she doesn't want to be found."

"You've heard from her, though. She's all right?"

It was Aventurine's turn to shrug. "She says she's fine. But no one is fine who cuts themselves off from family—including her son—who are desperately worried about her, and who want to help."

Sioned reached across the table to touch the back of Avi's hand lightly. Then she drew back, looking away. "I'm sorry. I'm so sorry. If there's anything I can do to help—"

"No." Aventurine pulled on her jacket and made a sorry attempt at a smile. "I don't think anyone can help. We just have to wait this out."

Thirty-seven

"I might be able to help," Burroughs said. Avi had called him and slipped into the park on the way back to the hotel from Paddington. She had not wanted to walk all the way back from the Victoria and Albert and the Brompton Road; she was too worn out entirely. "It's public knowledge now, as we've put out an all-call for help." There was the sound of a chair scraping back on the floor, and a few footsteps. "Her name was Alyona Morozova." He coughed. "She seemed to be a free-lance writer; we've come across a few pieces she'd published, most in Russian, a few in English, one in French. Nothing in the past several years, though." Another cough, obviously fake, more pronounced. "Now you'd better tell me why you're asking this, Aventurine. Because you owe me."

Aventurine bristled. Owed him? The air, damp and cold, hung about Norfolk Square like a gossamer veil. It would start raining again soon.

"You owe me, Aventurine," Burroughs repeated when she did not answer. "Why do you need to know this?" His voice was strangely neutral, as though their first meeting had not been over the Russian woman's body. As though he hadn't, just the other day in Sioned's front room, made that cryptic remark about the frequency of people plummeting to their deaths in her wake.

She shifted uncomfortably on the damp park bench, looking up into the skeletal tree branches. A lone pigeon landed nearby, cooed, and took off again with a whirring of wings. "I think I might have some information for you about her. Unless you already know."

"We won't know until you spit it out," Burroughs prodded. Was that impatience creeping into his voice?

"My bed and breakfast landlady, back in Hay? Whose brother-in-law died while I was there?" She flushed now, her skin growing hot as she realized what she was saying; but it couldn't be helped—Dafydd Davies had died while she was there, but surely that wasn't her fault, surely she couldn't be blamed for that.

Burroughs made a rude noise down the line from Lincoln.

"I ran into her in a tea shop near the V & A," Aventurine pressed on, squeezing her eyes shut. "She had an appointment with her brother-in-law's solicitors, and—you won't believe this—"

"Try me."

"She told me his wife—or ex-wife—was a Russian named Alyona *something*. She couldn't remember the patronymic. Sioned said she hadn't seen nor heard from her in years, and that this Alyona and Dafydd were estranged. Sioned thought they were divorced, but the solicitors said no."

"Alyona *something*."

"I thought it too much of a coincidence when Sioned said Dafydd's wife had left him and returned to Lincoln. Lincoln, of all places. Your patch."

"Lincoln," he said. "My patch." Again the scraping of a chair on the floor, a rustling of papers, and then a tapping of keys. "Do you know where I can get hold of this Sioned? Davies, is it? Where she's staying? Maybe the name of the solicitors?"

"No, none of that—but I've got her phone number, from making the reservation and from staying with her. Hold on."

Quickly, Aventurine scrolled through her contacts until she found the number, then read it off. Burroughs repeated it back to her.

"I'll give her a ring," he said.

"Did you know any of this already?"

"I'll give her a ring. Thanks, Aventurine."

189

He cut the call.

Aventurine felt the first drops of rain.

She pounded on the door of Lance and Paul's room on the way past, hoping they might be in. No answer. She let herself into her own room, then texted them both.

Where are you?

Then, **I've got another book.**

They were back within the hour. Aventurine had dozed on the bed, and woke to the frantic knocking on her door. When she opened it, Paul tumbled inside, gripping a book to his chest, with Lance at his shoulder.

"It was in our room," he said without preamble. "On our bed. Did you leave it there?"

There was barely room for the three of them. She put the 'Do Not Disturb' sign on the knob, then double-locked the door.

"I don't have a key to your room," she said. She sat back down on the bed, drew her knees up. "Did you look inside?" Her throat felt weird, her tongue thick. She put a hand to her neck. "What book is it? Another on sailing?"

"I haven't looked inside yet." Paul sank into the desk chair and set the book on the coverlet, so she could read the title. *The Blues Line: Blues Lyrics from Leadbelly to Muddy Waters*. On the cover, a line drawing of a man playing a guitar. Lance found a place to lean against the windowsill.

The inside bore Lance's name. Avi picked up the book, gingerly, as though picking up a live coal, or a venomous snake. "On your bed. In your room. Was the door locked?" As soon as she spoke the words, she knew how ludicrous they were. The doors locked automatically behind them; someone would have needed a key card—either the room key, or a master—to get in to leave this on the bed. She looked

190

at her watch: too late to check with housekeeping to see if they'd let anyone in, or if they'd been asked to leave off the book for someone.

The book Burroughs had found in the coffee room meant that someone knew what hotel they were staying in, and that idea had been unnerving. This book on the bed in Paul and Lance's room meant that someone knew exactly which rooms they were in. And perhaps had access to them. That idea was frightening.

"That's my name," Lance said hoarsely. "Mine, this time. On a book in our room." He shifted uncomfortably. His expression was that of a confused puppy, an endearing look. "Why, though? Why me?"

Paul put a hand on his forearm. "Why not you?"

"But—I'm not in your family." Lance's voice trailed off awkwardly.

"Don't be silly," Avi said. "We're all in this together, since you threw your lot in with ours." Genevieve had said that the two would be inextricably bound together, after York.

Lance bowed his head, ran his hand up into his tight curly hair.

Aventurine closed her eyes and took a deep breath. "Nicola Hallsey knows we're in Paddington."

"Nicola Hallsey? What's she doing now?"

Avi glanced from one to the other. "She is in our family, if Micheline's genealogy work and DNA testing are to be believed. Our half-sister?"

"Who *is* she?" Paul asked.

Lance grimaced and pulled out his phone to dial up the photo of Nicola in Milan again.

"I know *that*." Paul looked up from it into Aventurine's face, his expression beyond confusion. *"Who is she?"* he repeated.

"I met her in Lincoln," Aventurine said slowly. "Then your mother and I went to Wales, and she—Nicola—apparently went to Milan, after you two."

"Following us." Lance frowned. "But why? We'd never met her. We didn't know she existed. How would she know we did, or where we were?"

Aventurine could only shake her head. *Wheels within wheels*, Genevieve would say. "I don't know. But Nicola's here, in Paddington. Or at least she was, at lunch time."

"So she's followed us back," Lance said.

"And before she went to Milan, she was in Wales," she reminded them. "In Llanthony. Burroughs and I followed your mother's trail there. But Micheline missed Nicola by a week, and we missed Mick by a couple of hours." *A couple of hours.* That was all. That still stung. "And before that, she was at the shipyard." She tried to map out Nicola's movements in her mind's eye.

"She could have left us this book," Paul mused. He was still transfixed by the photo on Lance's phone.

Lance and Avi locked eyes. "But she couldn't have left the ones for Micheline," Lance said at last. "Could she have?"

Avi nodded in agreement. "No. Whoever left them knew that Mick and I were going to go to the Honesty Bookshop *that afternoon.* So they had to leave the books for Mick when we were going, or there was a chance she wouldn't find them." Who had been there? She remembered the man with his dog, but no one else. "And if Nicola was trailing you two around Milan, she couldn't have been trailing Mick and me around Hay."

Avi picked up the book. She opened it again to the flyleaf, examined Lance's name. The handwriting looked enough like the handwriting in the other books to indicate the names were written by the same person. *Music again?* she wondered. *What now?* The sailing books made perfect sense, if this taunting, tantalizing leaving of book clues made any sense at all. But blues? Did Shep have any interest in blues music at all? Aventurine shifted through scenes of Shep in her memory, in all the years she'd known him. Shep in his bespoke suits. Shep at a party at the apartment of friends. Shep in his collared sailing shirts, and shorts. In no memory could she place her brother-in-law with any particular music. It was incidental to his life, rather than close to central, as it was to hers. She began to flip through the pages, until she found what she was looking for: the underlining.

The lyrics were to a Lead Belly song. She felt paralyzed.

Paul must have seen her reaction, for he took the book from her hands. When his eyes fell on the lines, his complexion went as pale as the pages. His mouth worked, but no words came out.

Now Lance leaned forward, frowning, to read the lyric.

Sometimes I get a notion
To jump in the river and drown

Aventurine grabbed the book from her nephew's hand. The two lines from the Lead Belly song were underlined in pencil, but the person who had done it had pressed down so fiercely that the lines were nearly incised into the paper.

"What the hell does this mean?" Avi demanded. Of no one, of everyone. She felt her chest constricting: it was hard to breathe.

Did you ever think, Nicola's mocking voice answered in her head, *that your sister's beloved Shep scuttled his boat intentionally?*

And the man from the first book, the one who falsified his log of the race around the world, and finally drowned himself when he was found out.

For a long time they only stared at the book.

"Have you ever—" Aventurine swallowed and tried again. "Have you ever considered—the possibility?"

The look Paul turned on Avi was pure fury, almost as dreadful as the one he had turned on her that horrible day in Southampton. He stood abruptly and whirled away toward the window.

"He wouldn't," Paul said.

Aventurine stared at her nephew's back: one quick shake, like a single sob he would not allow them to see. She bit back the urge to sob herself, not for the lost Shep, but for Paul, who was not her son. She could read that single movement as clearly as she could read the underlined song lyrics on the page in front of her. Yes, Paul *had* considered the possibility.

"He wouldn't," Paul repeated. He did not turn around. Neither did he push aside the curtain to look out into the street.

"Have you—or has Micheline—got hold of his medical records?" Aventurine pressed. Her voice was low.

A fire engine passed somewhere near, siren blaring.

"She's never said anything to me," Avi continued when Paul did not speak. "Do you know anything about it?"

Paul shook his head sharply.

Lance glanced between them, the expression in his dark eyes stricken. "You mean—to see if there was something—an illness—cancer—"

Aventurine nodded miserably. "Something like that could make a person—take his own life. Something incurable."

"No," Paul said, pounding his fist against the window frame. "Dad wouldn't have done that. He would have let us help. He would have fought. He would never have—ever—" But his voice was wavering, the doubt creeping in despite his words of conviction.

"I'll text Mick," Aventurine said hurriedly. Helplessly. What if Micheline simply ignored her text, as she had all the others? Nevertheless, she retrieved her phone and tapped in the message. *Was Shep ill?*

Then, without telling them, she sent the text to both Genevieve and Burroughs, hoping they would be able to understand what the cryptic message was asking.

The silence that descended now, like all the silences that frequently descended between them, was awkward and uncomfortable. Paul still stood in the window, unseeing; when Lance moved to his side, he did not respond. Aventurine, for her part, found the lyric playing on a loop in her head, alternating in the voices of Lead Belly and Jon Boden. She squeezed her eyes shut.

What if Shep had discovered he was suffering from some terminal disease? Would he have sailed off and purposely scuttled *La Máquina de los Vientos* to avoid a lingering and painful death? To avoid forcing his wife and son to share his agony?

Yet if this was the case, he'd delivered them into the hands of a further, different agony, that of *not knowing*. To use the trite parlance, that of having no closure.

She opened her eyes only enough to watch her nephew through lowered lids. Where Paul's initial reaction had been explosive—a kind of spontaneous combustion—now he seemed to have collapsed in on himself. His expression had fallen, his shoulders slumped, and his knees buckled as though they could no longer bear his weight. He leaned against the wall for support.

"Lance," he said despairingly. "I can't do this."

Immediately, Lance was at his side, holding out his arms. Paul slipped into his embrace and buried his face in Lance's shoulder. Defeated. Exhausted.

Aventurine felt her heart constrict in her chest. The pang of jealousy made itself felt, and she attempted, furiously, to force it back. In this moment, Paul had turned to Lance, not to her.

That was the way it should be, she reasoned, biting her lip. His father missing, presumed dead; his mother missing, on a quest none of them quite understood. And she, Aventurine, his mother, not his mother. Lance must seem a relief: a man who had not lived his life withholding secrets from Paul.

"You can," Lance murmured into Paul's hair. "You *can*. Just take a breath."

"It's hard," Avi said. "And I'm sorry."

"You don't know." Paul's voice was muffled, but his words still pointed.

Aventurine unfolded her cramped legs and stood from the bed. Everything hurt suddenly, her muscles, joints, head. "She's my sister. Twin sister. I've shared everything with her since before we were born. I'm terrified."

"They're my parents."

It was a game of who loved more than whom. Avi sighed. There was no winning this sort of game. None at all.

"I've also lost my parents, as has your mother. Don't forget that." Aventurine met Lance's eyes over Paul's shoulder. "In a car accident.

At the same time. In South America. We were just a bit younger than Paul." The admission was made of echoes, the story coming in bits and pieces down all the years. Aventurine winced. It didn't make her parents' deaths less real, or less painful. "But that's done. We're going to find Micheline, and we're going to find out what happened to Shep." She gripped the carved headboard until her fingers ached. "You just have to prepare yourself to find out things that you might not like. And to accept those things. The truth isn't any less the truth because you refuse to accept it."

When Paul straightened to look at her over Lance's shoulder, his face was hard. Furious. Determined. For once, Aventurine took a deep breath and met the furious gaze, an expression so unlike she'd ever seen on Mick's face. This was an expression Paul had inherited from his father, and it made her shiver.

"I need to know," he ground out.

"Like your mother needs to know?"

"I need to know," he repeated.

Aventurine's phone buzzed. A text. Everything between them was suspended as she looked at the screen. Mick.

What do you mean?

Hurriedly, Aventurine typed.

Did Shep have an illness? Cancer? Like that?

She found herself wishing that she could reach through the phone and grab her sister by the shoulders, to hold her as Lance was holding Paul. Micheline had answered almost immediately this time, but there were all those other times when Avi had been left on read. By her twin, by the person she had thought she was closest to in all the world. *Answer me, Mick*, she willed. *Don't let go.*

Another buzz from her phone. Burroughs. Aventurine set the phone facedown on the bedside table. It vibrated again almost immediately, and she snatched it up.

No. No cancer, Parkinson's, nothing. Investigators looked at medical records.

Aventurine read the message aloud to them.

Mick again.

Don't you dare suggest Shep killed himself.

Then, **DON'T YOU DARE.**

Aventurine dropped the cell phone onto the coverlet, shocked at her sister's vehemence. Silently, Paul leaned across the bed to pick it up, then, casting her a look of angry triumph, he let it fall again.

"Don't you dare," he whispered, his eyes burning in his pale face. "Like Mom said."

Thirty-eight

They decided on pizza and a pint, and when the others went to gather their things, Aventurine hurriedly took photos of the cover and pages from this new book. She texted them to Burroughs and to Genevieve. Genevieve, she realized, who had been surprisingly silent.

Information flows both ways.

Or maybe it didn't.

Then she remembered the text from Burroughs and read it.

Call me.

"I've put in a request to my U.S. contacts from BARD and the law body responsible for the investigation into Shepherdson Genthner's boat's disappearance," he said as soon as he'd picked up. "She said she'd get back to me as soon as she found the reports."

"How long will that take?"

"I don't know." Aventurine could imagine his shrug. "As long as it takes, I guess. She'll send them to me, she said, but she'll call with the gist of what she finds."

"Mick says no cancer, no Parkinson's, nothing like that in the medical records."

"You talked to her? Where is she?"

Avi sighed. "I didn't, no. She texted. I asked because Nicola suggested the loss of the *Máquina* wasn't accidental."

"You talked to *her*?"

Quickly she gave him the story of lunch with Nicola.

"What is she playing at?" he demanded.

Aventurine thought of Nicola excusing herself from the table and never returning. She hadn't taken her coat; she must have checked it at the door or something. "I don't know. A long game, I've been told."

"By whom?"

Shit. "By Lance's great-grandmother."

They were all so careful during the pregnancy. Once it became obvious Aventurine was carrying, she moved into Micheline and Shep's house, and wore only Mick's green, in case they were seen— by the mailman, the hired yard crew, anyone. They agreed that there would be no photographs, no record of their deception. As the due date neared, they went on vacation at an AirBnB in the Green Mountains, and Paul was delivered in Vermont, where no one knew them, and no one would be able to point to either of them as his mother. A plan that worked so well for more than twenty years, until Neil appeared with that old photograph from the party. Their one mistake: one they had no idea existed until Neil dropped it like a bomb.

You never smoked, Aventurine, he'd said, sneering.

Even a DNA test would not have given them away. No, it was Aventurine's former lover—another mistake—who had found such sick delight in revealing the secret to the one person who could be hurt the most.

"You're identical twins," Paul said now, his voice bitter. They were back in the pub. "*Identical.* I should have known you would *both* betray me."

He knew how to hurt, at least. How to go for the jugular.

"Paul, what's got into you? What's going on?" Aventurine looked for Lance, forgetting he'd gone for another round.

"Do you *want* my dad to be dead? Is that how it is?" Paul continued.

"It would work out really well for you if he had committed suicide, wouldn't it?"

"*What are you saying?*" Avi quickly set her tonic water down on the mat. She couldn't control her shaking, and probably wouldn't be able to control her stomach, either. "Where is all this coming from?"

"Then you wouldn't feel so guilty about having my father's baby. About me, being my mother's *stolen child*."

Nicola.

She stared at Paul in horror.

Nicola had said just those words as a parting shot in the restaurant. Before disappearing.

"I thought—I thought—you were coming to grips with this," she whispered.

"That I am not who I thought I was? That you, and your twin sister, knew, and never bothered to tell me?"

"Nicola—"

For a fraction of a second a wary look crossed his face, but then was gone. "This has nothing to do with Nicola. Whoever she claims she is." But he was backtracking, and she could read it in his demeanor. Nicola Hallsey had got to him. When? How?

"I wish I could make you understand," she protested, trying to form coherent thoughts. She spread her hands out before her, which would probably not have any effect. "My decision to carry a child for my sister and her husband had nothing to do with you. And everything to do with your mother."

He looked away. The snooker was on the TV again, but none of them paid it any attention.

"Listen," Aventurine said, still with her hands before her, still desperate to be understood. "Micheline wanted it that way. And I agreed." She took a deep breath. "I love you. To the ends of the earth, and to the ends of time. *But I love Micheline more.*"

Lance came to the table, carrying two full pints and another tonic water with an incongruously cheerful lemon slice bobbing in it. He slowed and his expression darkened as he sensed the atmosphere between them. Paul took up his glass and drank long.

"Easy, there," Lance murmured, placing a hand on Paul's shoulder and sliding onto the sofa beside him. "What did I miss?" He looked wary of the answer.

Paul's mouth was tight, his eyes angry. "Aventurine was just telling me how she loves my mother more than she loves me."

Lance's laugh was not the reaction Paul was looking for. "Of course she does," he said. He too took a drink, and wiped his upper lip. "That's her twin sister we're talking about. Don't be so selfish."

Paul's expression turned mulish, but then seemed to collapse. He said nothing. The sip he took now was considerably more moderate.

"And," Avi said quietly, repeating what she'd said earlier, "there's only one person your mother loves more than you. That's your father."

Paul appeared determined not to acknowledge her words. She could see his throat working. Lance, for his part, slewed a glance between the pair of them.

"I'm sorry you feel that she's betraying you. But you're looking at this from the wrong end. She would move heaven and earth to bring your father back—and she probably thinks she's doing that now. And that would mean bringing him back to you, as well. So I think, Paul, that it's time for you to stop feeling like everything is a personal attack, and start thinking about how you can help your mother find out what's happened to your father." Aventurine surprised herself with the force of her words. "Think of *her* for once, instead of yourself."

Paul was still, so still that she wondered whether he was still breathing. Beside him Lance looked uncertain, and anxious, waiting for a reaction. Aventurine couldn't blame him. But at the same time, she knew it was high time for Paul to widen his tunnel vision.

Her tonic water tasted sour, and she set it aside next to her empty pint glass, her eyes still on her nephew's face. The face in which she could plainly see his father, as well as his mother. His two mothers. And his half-aunt as well, but she thrust all thoughts of Nicola aside. She saw the single tear leak from the corner of his eye and begin its track down the side of his face.

The moment was balanced. She didn't breathe. She didn't move.

Then, savagely, Paul wiped his face and rose to his feet so suddenly his pint tipped, spilling over the table and the floor. He turned and left the room.

"I'm sorry," Lance murmured, and set his glass aside to follow.

Thirty-nine

A venturine didn't sleep well, and in the morning, headed to Bar Torelli for a large latté. She decided to forgo the *pastel de nata*; her stomach, though empty, did not feel sturdy enough for breakfast. Coffee in hand, she cut through the station and out the Praed Street entrance, then crossed to London Street and Norfolk Gardens.

From the bench she chose, she could see her window on the third floor; and a couple of windows over, Paul and Lance's. Hers was open just a crack; theirs was closed and the curtains pulled tight. As she watched, the front door opened and Lance emerged. He looked around as though searching for someone, and when she put up a hand and called his name, he bounded down the steps and crossed to the gate. He sat down heavily next to her.

"You look beat," she said.

He half-laughed. "That's because I am." He cast a sideways glance at her. "You do, too."

"That's because I am."

She held out the coffee cup, and after a moment, he took it for a sip, then handed it back.

"Thanks."

The rain had stopped, and this morning was bright, but cold. The seasons were really changing. It smelled like winter.

"Paul told me," Lance said now, his voice low, "that he's kept that photograph—the one of Micheline and Shep and him, at his graduation. Always. In his wallet." He looked down at the pavement, and then up at the scraggly trees. Anywhere, it seemed but at Aventurine's face. "He showed me, you know. On our very first date."

"You had no idea what you were getting into with all of us," Avi said. She laid a hand on his arm. "I'm sorry, Lance."

He only shrugged. "It's all part of everything, isn't it? If I want to be with Paul, I have to put up with the good, and the bad, and the *weird*." His dark glance darted in her direction, and he let out the smallest of chuckles. "And I *do* want to be with Paul. Because I love him."

It was a quiet declaration; everything about Lance was quiet. And dependable. Aventurine leaned in to kiss his cheek. "I'm glad. I'm glad Paul has you."

Lance shifted on the bench uncomfortably.

"Where is he?" Aventurine glanced around, back up to the doorway to the hotel, to the room with the tightly closed curtains. One of the maids struggled with a heavy bag and set it on the steps beside the other door. "Where's Paul?" He could be still sleeping, she supposed; he slept quite a bit, but at least, since he'd been spending time with Lance, his drinking—at least his hangovers—had lessened, and she was grateful for that.

Now Lance shoved his hair away from his brow in that way he had when he was agitated, and seemed to force himself to look at her. "Aventurine—"

Everything grew still.

"Tell me. Tell me what's going on." Her touch on his arm became a grip which tightened.

"He's at the station," Lance said unhappily.

"*At the station?*"

Lance licked his lips. "He didn't want to say anything. To you. He wanted to just go. We got down there and I told him I thought I'd left my phone behind, and I just needed to run back."

Norfolk Square was spinning.

"What are you saying?"

"I wanted to tell you. And to tell you not to worry, that I'll look after him, and I'll keep in touch. Wherever we end up." Lance shook his head, his eyes peering beyond her shoulder towards London Street. The wind was picking up, cold against her face. The traffic at the intersection was growing more noisy.

"*What are you saying?*" Aventurine's voice was shrill. She couldn't control it. Her vision was tunneling, and all she could see was Lance's expression, and amalgam of worry, anxiety, and pity.

"He's angry."

"With me."

Lance shrugged. "With everyone. But yes—mostly with you, because you're *here* and the others are not." He blinked against the cold wind. "He's angry that you won't consider the possibility that Shep is still alive."

"I—"

"He's angry that you would think his father killed himself. He certainly can't bring himself to consider that possibility." Lance took a deep breath and straightened his shoulders. "So, he feels like he needs to get away from you—"

Aventurine let out a little cry. "He's running away. Again. No. Don't let him go, Lance. Don't let him go."

With his free hand, Lance slowly detached her fingers from his arm and stood. He took a step away from the bench, away from her. "I have to, Aventurine. And you have to, too." Looking down into her face, his expression was momentarily heartsick, but then he drew his shoulders back again, in resolve. "I'll keep him safe. I promise you that."

"Lance—"

"No, Aventurine. You have to let him go."

A quick crush of a hug, and then Lance was gone, running along Norfolk Square to the gate. He dodged a couple with some suitcases, turned the corner, and disappeared.

Part III:

Whitby Bull

Forty

The countryside grew wider, all fields and hedges, sheep and the occasional horse, the further north the train drew her on from King's Cross. After the initial glance, Aventurine did not look at it again, though, nor at her reflection that stared back at her from the window, pale and peaked, with wide, frightened eyes.

In her lap, *Dracula*.

The book had borne her name. The one book had been directed to her. With a clue, perhaps, that only she could figure out.

I've got to go to Whitby, she had texted to Genevieve.

Don't, came the reply.

She had thumbed through the pages repeatedly, but nothing was underlined in this book. Of course, some of the story took place in London—but she was already there, and this slim paperback, it seemed obvious, was meant to direct her away from the city. She was fairly certain—though she could be wrong, and she hoped she wasn't—that she wasn't meant to travel all the way to someplace in Transylvania. No, Whitby seemed the choice.

It was like clutching at proverbial straws. Or like feeling one's way through an unfamiliar house with no light, only touch to guide one. Aventurine despaired, turning the book over and over in her hands. They would be pulling into York soon, and she had eight minutes to change to the train to Middlesborough, and then on to Whitby. She thought about calling Genevieve, but the single word—don't—was like a cold slap to the face. Whatever was—or wasn't—in Whitby, she'd have to see it through herself.

When the train came to a stop at platform 9, she found to her dismay that she had to hump the suitcase over the bridge to platform 10. As she made her way down again, the train eased into the station, and a voice over the tannoy announced something she couldn't quite hear; but she asked a guard, who ushered her on. She left the suitcase on the shelves near the door, and looked for a free seat facing forward, near a phone charger.

Just as the guard raised his circular sign and blew the whistle, her eyes fell on a familiar figure rushing onto the platform.

Dominic Burroughs.

The train pulled out.

She changed at Middlesborough for the Whitby train, and then struggled down with her small blue suitcase at Whitby Station. Her phone directed her along the road, then up Brunswick Street, past a large church and up a curving hill. She'd managed to book a room overlooking the beach on East Terrace; she'd have to find her way about half a mile, and glancing up into the cloudy sky, hoped any incipient rain would hold off.

Despite having found a USB outlet on the train, she discovered now that her phone hadn't charged at all, and the battery was at 27%. She hoped that would be enough to allow her to follow the map to the hotel. When she got the notification for the text, she ignored it.

The hotel itself was on a corner and had, no doubt, been one of the grand ladies of holiday establishments from the Victorian age. Aventurine recognized the faux Gothic ornamentation as she entered the glass doorways, an obvious addition at some point by management that didn't understand coherence in style. She had made sure to book a room with a sea view—she had no idea what she was looking for in Whitby, and no idea how long it would take—so she had decided to splurge and pay the extra twenty pounds per night just to make herself feel better.

She didn't begrudge them installing a lift, though, once she discovered her room was on the second floor. When she finally reached it and inserted the key card, she could do no more than flop onto the double bed. Another splurge: she didn't envision herself being able to sleep well, but at least she'd lie around restlessly in relative comfort.

Even *now*, though, she was restless. She plugged her phone in, and checked this time to make sure it was charging as it should be. Then she opened the text.

Where are you?

She closed her eyes. How many times had she asked that question over the last several days? How many times had someone demanded that of her? But this time, it was from Dominic Burroughs. Who had stood on platform 10 back in York, a hand raised toward the departing train as though he would stop it. Would stop her.

In York. Aventurine had no idea what he could want. Had no idea what he was doing in York.

Genevieve was in York.

Unless, of course, she wasn't.

The coincidence made her anxious.

But there was no one else. She looked around the otherwise empty room and felt an incredible loneliness descend upon her.

Whitby.

There was an electric kettle on the dresser. She filled it and set it to boil. The cups were sturdy and large, and she tore open a Yorkshire tea packet and plunked the bag into one. Once the water boiled, she poured it and took her cup to the windows.

It was a corner room, and there were two windows, one overlooking the North Terrace, and beyond that, the sea; the beach, she knew, was tucked down out of sight under the cliffs. Off to the left, the sun was setting, casting shadows of cars, streetlamps, park benches. If she turned her head, she could make out the statue of Captain James Cook, proudly claiming all he could see. A couple pushing a pram passed, their figures strangely foreshortened from this height.

She moved to the other window, the one overlooking the Whalebone Arch, and the pavement leading to the stairs down to the harbor. She sipped her tea and tried to convince herself it would make her feel better. Across the river, she could see East Cliff, topped by St. Mary's Church and the ruins of the Abbey beyond. This was where, she knew, Mina had seen her friend Lucy prostrate on a bench in the graveyard, and she was appalled to realize how much liberty Bram Stoker had taken: there was no way in hell Mina would have been able to see a cloaked figure with a red mouth from here. Glaring, she wondered again what she was even doing here.

Then Aventurine saw her. Coming along the pavement on the other side of North Terrace. A woman in a green raincoat, hands in pockets, a purse slung over her shoulder. She strode purposefully toward the Arch, but as she reached it, she cast a look behind her, her chin-length blonde hair swinging about her jaw, and then dashed through it toward the stairs.

Micheline, her heart cried out, and maybe her voice did, too. Aventurine set the tea down, grabbed up her purse and rain jacket and key, and ran for the door. She hit the button for the lift, but it was all the way down on the ground floor; she dashed through the fire door to the stairs and hurtled down them. She met no one and was grateful. Bursting into the lobby, she pushed out the door into East Terrace.

Avi heard the squeal of tires and the blare of a horn, but she kept on across the road and to the Arch. She could see no one in the little park. The woman—*Micheline, please God make it be Micheline*— must have gone down the stairs. They curved, and Avi cursed; the turn blocked her sight line. She pounded down.

212

"Micheline!" she called down, and her voice echoed weirdly. "Mick!" But there was no answer. Her side was starting to ache, and she couldn't breathe; she couldn't stop, though she was terrified of tumbling down and breaking her neck. "Mick, wait!"

She came out on Khyber Pass—what the hell kind of name was that, anyway?—and there was no one to be seen, either to the left or the right. But the left turn led past a coffee shop to a path leading to a street even lower down. Aventurine hitched her bag over her shoulder and ran.

No one there, either.

She slowed her pace, clutching her side. There were some people down on the Battery Parade and Pier Road, all looking vaguely dissatisfied with a seaside resort in November, and none of them looking like her sister.

Where had Micheline gone?

She had lost her sister, again.

Despondently, Aventurine crossed the road toward the bandstand, deserted and lonely. The wind off the water scuttled dirt and some litter along the pavement. Avi found a park bench, and leaned against the wall behind it, looking out to North Pier. There was no movement along it; she squinted to be sure. Even if Mick had decided to go out on it, she wouldn't be that far away anyway. The lighthouse mocked her, lifted into the air like a middle finger. She collapsed onto the bench.

Where had she gone?

Hungrily, she thought over every second of her sighting, every moment, every movement. The purposeful striding—she would know that stride anywhere. And the swirl of hair as she turned: Aventurine's would swing in exactly that way, should she turn quickly. And then the woman had looked over her shoulder and quickened her pace, as though fearful of being followed. Avi's chest constricted. She moved like she was in some danger. Aventurine needed to help—but how could she help, if she couldn't catch up?

"Oh, Mick." Avi dropped her head into her hands.

And then the thought struck her.

Nicola.

Maybe it hadn't been Micheline at all.

Aventurine felt dizzy and knew she needed to eat. When was her last meal? It might have been the scone in the tea room on the Brompton Road, or the pizza, of which she had eaten very little. She couldn't remember eating anything since then—only drinking coffee. And more coffee. And tea.

Discouraged, she got to her feet and wandered along Pier Road, leaning into the walls as she went. There was a small line at a restaurant just beyond the arcades; as she approached, the last couple went up the stairs and entered. She pulled herself up behind them.

"Just one," she told the hostess inside the door.

The woman frowned, peering at her closely, then adopted a professional smile. "Right this way."

She seated Aventurine at a two top in the dining room to the left and handed her a menu. "Can I get you a drink?"

"Just water."

The hostess zoomed off, to be replaced almost immediately by a girl half her age, who placed a water glass before Aventurine.

"I'll have the regular cod and chips, please," she ordered.

The server smiled. "Liked it, then, did you?"

Aventurine's smile froze in place. "I'm sorry, what?"

"Yesterday," the server said cheerfully. "When you were here for dinner? You ordered the same thing. Same size. But with a pint of Farmer's Brown Cow."

Aventurine licked her lips and managed a small laugh; she hoped the girl couldn't twig how fake it was. "How'd you remember that, with all your customers?"

She shrugged. Her face was freckled and her smile wide. "Not too busy out of season," she said. "And besides. The tip was *huge*." She flitted away.

Hurriedly, Aventurine scanned the rest of the tables. Micheline had been here for dinner last night. It *had* to be Micheline. And of course, she'd ordered a brown ale; they both drank browns.

Unless it *was* Nicola...

She had no idea what kind of beer Nicola drank.

But—British people usually didn't tip, not like Americans did. It *had* to be Micheline.

Unless Nicola wanted her to think it was Micheline.

When the fish and chips came, she forced herself to eat it, though her appetite had gone again.

Forty-one

Aventurine sifted the sand through her cold fingers, staring out into the shimmery air at the encroaching morning tide. When they were children, she and Micheline had played at being goddesses, Mick of the clouds, Avi of the water. Even now, holding her hand out toward the waves, she could flex her fingers and almost believe that she was drawing the ocean toward her, then pushing it away again.

Aventurine hadn't played at that since Shep had been lost at sea. She shuddered and blinked her eyes.

Two small girls in matching jackets and hats shrieked as they ran past on the cold beach, chasing a dog trailing a leash. Purple pails swung from their chubby fists. A handful of gulls leapt into the air at their gleeful approach, squawking in disapproval. Mick and Avi had had matching swimsuits at that age—matching everything, except in blue and green—the swimsuits had been a turquoise compromise, with bejeweled fish swimming across the front. Avi had a sudden flash of memory of them at some beach, with Mick digging determinedly in the sand with a plastic shovel.

Had they been looking for treasure? Had either of them found it?

In her pocket, the copy of *Dracula* seemed a lead weight. Whitby, it had told her, and she'd now been here for the better part of twenty-four hours, waiting. For a sign. For something. Anything. She had seen nothing, heard nothing, further of Mick—or Nicola—since last night.

She thought of Genevieve and her conflicting advice. Go. Stay. Act. React. Aventurine looked out beyond the tideline to where the stubborn red lifeboat bobbed its way resolutely along. There was the rhythmic sound of the pounding of hooves on the sand, and as she watched, a horse and rider passed between her and the water, looking like something out of a movie. Well, she had gone; she had acted. Genevieve was ignoring her. She had come to Whitby, and found either Micheline or Nicola here before her.

As for the book? It was agony, not knowing: somewhere out there—here?—was a person who was leading them all on some kind of treasure hunt. Clue here, clue there. Aventurine hoped desperately that it was a treasure hunt, hoped that there would be a pot of gold: the solutions to all the mysteries, perhaps leading back to Shep. The place where she'd be reunited with her sister, physically, emotionally, mentally. She also hoped, bitterly, that she'd find the person who'd done this to them: attempted to split them up, to tear them apart.

And had, so far, been effective.

She tossed her head against the wind, and returned to sifting the sand, for lack of something else to do. Perhaps someone up on West Cliff would see the swirl of her yellow hair, and recognize her, just as she'd recognized it from her hotel room yesterday.

"Here, miss," a voice called against the growing wind, and at first Aventurine didn't notice the words were directed at her. "Miss?"

An elderly man was approaching across the sand, his gait dragging slightly; he wore a scally cap and had an eyepatch over his left eye, and a neatly trimmed silver beard valanced his chin. He held out a cell phone.

"This yours?" he called over the sound of the wind and waves.

Aventurine's first instinct was to pat her pockets, then unzip her purse and root about inside. Nothing. She scrambled to her feet and took the iPhone the stranger held out to her. It looked like her case, but just to be sure, she touched the power button with her index finger. The screen bloomed into life.

"Guess it is," he said.

"Thanks! Wherever did you find it? I didn't even know it was missing." There was another new crack across the face of the screen protector; she'd really have to get herself another one, and soon.

The man gestured over his shoulder to the walkway and steps to the promenade. "Just over there. Must have fallen out of your pocket or something." He rocked slightly in the sand; he was obviously favoring his left leg.

Aventurine instinctively took his arm. It felt thin and bony, even through the blue windcheater. That looked a bit the worse for wear. OAP, she wondered. The only others she knew were Genevieve and Henry Hallsey; and Genevieve would not thank her for the label.

"Thanks," he said, drawing himself up. "I'm fine. Don't come down here to the sand very often. Hard to walk in it."

His accent was hard to place, but definitely not local. Probably not even English. To her untrained ear there was something of Portuguese, or perhaps Spanish, to it.

He said something else, his one good eye—hazel, she saw—trained on her face; but the wind picked up his words and whirled them away.

"Come on," she said "Let me show my thanks by buying you a cup of coffee. I'd have been lost without this." Aventurine didn't dare think *how* lost.

For a moment, he looked indecisive, but apparently the idea of a coffee was too difficult to resist.

"Help me back to the stairs," he suggested. Aventurine tucked his arm through hers and shortened her gait. The man did drag his left leg slightly, and the walk across the sand seemed to require careful concentration on his part.

They reached the road at last and turned left. The first coffee shop kiosk they passed was buttoned up tightly against the encroaching low season. At his direction, they turned right and found one open along the cliff top. Inside, her companion took a seat, leaning back and rubbing his shin while grimacing slightly; Aventurine went to the counter and ordered, at his direction, a couple of café Americanos.

They were the only patrons in the shop. Aventurine handed him his coffee, then drew out a chair for herself.

"There. Thanks again for bringing me my phone. Though you shouldn't have come down to the beach if it causes you this much trouble." She took a sip. The coffee was too hot. "I don't even know your name."

The eyebrow over his one good eye lifted sardonically. He had removed his cap, and now brushed his thin white hair away from his forehead. "Swales," he said. "Ernest Swales."

They shook hands.

"Aventurine Morrow," she introduced herself.

He frowned, tilting his head. "Have I heard of you?"

Aventurine flushed as she always did. "I write books."

Swales nodded. "Ah. I read books. I must have come across your name at the lending library." He lifted his coffee cup to his lips, full against his beard, which was nearly as white as his hair in this light.

"Do you live here in Whitby? Or are you just visiting, as I am?"

The accent, an amalgam, was proving impossible for her to place.

"Lived here for several years. Retirement," he said. "Over in the Old Town. Get out and walk most days. Not when the weather's bad, though—makes my bad leg ache." The coffee, apparently, was not too hot for him, and he drank it appreciatively.

For a moment, she studied him. He was like Genevieve Smithson, then, a person driven to walk his route every day. What demons did he keep pace with, or attempt to outrun? A limp, an eyepatch; he held his coffee cup in his right hand, but his left hand, lying on the table before him, was criss-crossed with scars. He obviously had his own variety of demons. But he was not as old as Genevieve, so his scars were not engendered by the Second World War, as hers were. And his were obvious and physical, while Genevieve's were hidden from view.

"Visiting, you say?" The raised eyebrow again. "Friends?"

"Just to look," Aventurine dodged.

"Most people," he countered, "come to look at Whitby when the weather's nicer. Summer, and all that."

She looked away. "I'm not most people."

"No. You write books." For the briefest of moments, Swales smiled, and the expression spooked something in her.

Forty-two

Aventurine looked toward the east, where the full moon was rising behind the ruins of St. Hilda's. It didn't align perfectly behind the stone gable, but hung slightly off to the side. She decided she liked the off-center positioning, as she liked the curls of ground fog that shimmered around the base of the abbey, obscuring and then revealing the ruins. It was no wonder at all that Bram Stoker had envisioned Dracula here: she wrapped her arms around herself against the oddly delicious chill, imagining the creator imagining that particular undead wandering the headland as the moon rose, calling Lucy Westenra to him. It was damp, but not too cold, though the occasional gust of wind off the sea moved the ghostly fog all the more, blurring all the edges. Everything was in greyscale from the moon's eerie light.

Her hands were cold, though. Aventurine shoved them into her jacket pockets, and felt again the copy of *Dracula*. The book with the cover bearing a picture similar to the one she was now a part of.

Mourning moon, Ernest Swales had called it. He hadn't explained.

But her internet research had called her to this particular place, and this time. Aventurine was used to the North American traditional Indigenous moon names; to find what she thought of as the Beaver Moon was actually the Mourning Moon around here—and the other traditional name, the Darkest Depths Moon, was just as bad—had shaken her in ways she hadn't expected. Who was she mourning? Was it Shep? Then he'd have to be dead; there would be no way around that. But what if the mourning was for something more ephemeral, like trust? Like life as she had grown accustomed to it?

She drew out the book now and opened it to look at her name. The invitation, as it were, to Whitby. Where she might have seen Micheline, where Nicola might have arrived before her. It was difficult to make out the handwriting, but she had stared at it so long and so often that she could see it in her mind's eye. Whose writing? Not her sister's. Not Shep's. Nicola's? Someone else's entirely?

The sound of laughter made her jump, but it was only a group of three emerging from the fog and passing toward the brewery, where the wall was low enough to climb. After a moment they were swallowed up again. She wondered momentarily whether they had seen her; even if they had, however, she was only another clandestine night visitor to the Abbey, just another thrill-seeker who had scaled the wall. Easily discounted.

Aventurine shivered. It had been foolish and pointless to come up here after dark. After the Abbey was closed to visitors. Just as it had been foolish to wile away the afternoon on the beach. But she had no idea where to look for Micheline here. Nicola here. She had texted both, and as a last resort, had called them both as well. Neither of them had answered. If one or the other were here, she had no idea how to flush her quarry out.

But. The book. She turned it over in her hands, the skin of which felt cold and clammy, whether from the atmosphere, or from uneasiness. Someone had enticed her to Whitby, just as someone had enticed them to Llanthony. It struck her then. There had been two kinds of books, two kinds of clues: the ones that pointed to Shep and hinted at suicide, and the ones that gave direction. Why those kinds? What was the difference?

When she had followed directions and gone to Llanthony, in the Black Mountains, someone had tampered with the car. *Who wants you dead?* Burroughs had asked. Any way they had driven away from the Priory had put them on narrow lanes with steep hills, blind corners, hedgerows knitted over the top of them. The detective's take on the crash was beginning to feel like the right one. So, who had wanted to ambush them at Llanthony?

And who wanted her in Whitby now?

She glanced around the ruins, but the stones were a chiaroscuro of shadow. Anyone could be up here, watching her. But again, why would they want to do that? What did this mysterious messenger want with her?

They didn't know she was up here. Alone. She reminded herself of that, fiercely. *They didn't know she was up here alone.*

Or did they?

She was being paranoid. She pushed the feeling down, but the one that bubbled up in its place was not much better. Aventurine was nearly knocked down by a wave of preemptive grief. *Mourning Moon.* She should be up here in the Abbey, trying to unravel this latest clue, place this latest puzzle piece, with Paul and Lance—but they had fallen away, just as everyone was falling away. She wished for a seat, feeling the weakness of sadness course through her bones. There were benches over in the cemetery at St. Mary's, but they were too reminiscent of *Dracula* itself; and she had no need to have her neck snapped like the hundred-year-old sailor in the story, nor did she fancy herself as Lucy, trysting with the Count. Shivering again, she touched her neck.

A hand fell on her shoulder.

"Holy Mary, Mother of God," she spat out when she had regained her breath. "You scared the living hell out of me."

Burroughs smiled, apparently amused at her response. The moon took this opportunity to break through the mist and bathe their surroundings in an unearthly glow. Aventurine could see nothing of him against the light save his teeth. This was not, on the whole, comforting.

She drew away sharply. "What are you doing here?"

Burroughs shrugged. The clouds swirled again, and the momentary blaze of moonlight was lost. He was just a man. He was just Dominic Burroughs. "I followed you," he said. "You're trespassing."

He'd come over the wall, too. Aventurine took another step back. The ground below her feet was uneven, and she caught herself in mid-stumble. "Followed me," she repeated. Something did not feel right in her gut.

Again the shrug, as though it were all the most natural thing in the world. "Of course. My choice, when you lot all split up, was to either follow your nephew, or you." He paused, and she thought there was the slightest hint of a frown between his eyes, before it flitted away again. "Overall, I thought you were my better prospect."

Prospect?

He had appeared on the platform in York. *Her* platform in York.

And she had fallen right into it. He'd texted, and she'd told him she was in Whitby.

The sound of conversation drifted to them from back near the pond, though the mist was thickening, and they could see no one. Aventurine inched in that direction.

"I'm certainly the better kisser," she said. Against her better judgment. She felt her cheeks flush in the cold night air. Were the voices coming closer? The mist made it impossible to tell.

"Are you offering?" he asked. He stood very still, hands in coat pockets, mirroring her, the mist swirling around his knees. He could have been floating. *She* could have been floating.

Everyone was gone, fallen away. But Dominic Burroughs had followed her. For whatever reason, he had come to Whitby to find her. She tried to read his face, but it was impossible.

"I've offered before," she said, huskily.

"No, you didn't offer," he corrected. "You just did it."

For a long moment, they were still, staring at each other in the eerie night.

Then Aventurine stepped forward, and, without taking her own hands from her pockets, leaned in and pressed her mouth to his.

Forty-three

Despite the cold and damp, Burroughs lay on his back in the dead grass, his hands behind his head. Aventurine leaned her own head on her hand and gazed at him, but he steadfastly looked away toward the moon. All around them, the fitful sounds of the moving air, across the headland from the North Sea. That wind made Aventurine shiver, but she didn't want to give up this moment. Far away, the tide encroached and withdrew with a mournful hush. All that was missing was the sound of the Whitby Hawkser Bull.

"I really don't know anything about it," he said lightly, as though it didn't matter. "I was an orphan. Raised in care, as they say." His tone wasn't bitter, but matter-of-fact.

"No aunts? Uncles? Grandparents? No one who could take you in?"

"No one who cared enough."

Despite the evenness of his voice, as though he were discussing the weather, the words made Aventurine feel bereft. She wondered what he had been like as a child—as taciturn and watchful as now?

"I don't know what it's like," he continued, "to have a sister, let alone a twin. I envy you that. I don't know what it's like to have a nephew. Or even parents, for that matter."

"We lost ours when we were in college," Avi said.

"But you had them up to then. And when you lost them, you still had your sister."

225

Aventurine fell back in the long grass. Above them a nightbird wheeled and cried out its complaint against the starless sky. She watched it until it disappeared among the ruins.

"I don't know what I have anymore," she said slowly. "This whole thing with Shep. I thought we could get through anything, Mick and I. I thought we knew each other better than anyone else could possibly know us. I thought we understood each other. But now I'm seeing all the cracks in our relationship. Shep's shipwreck has destroyed us all. I hate him for that." She laughed bitterly, and the sound was higher, sharper than she intended, sounding like the nightbird which had flown away. "Isn't that an awful thing to say? I hate my brother-in-law. A dead man."

"You don't know he's dead."

"Don't you start, too."

"My colleague checked into the BARD records of Shep Genthner's shipwreck. Other than the perfectly clear weather, and no radio distress call, there was nothing else in the incident reports. Clear bill of health, as your sister claimed." He took a deep breath. "The investigators have left the case open, but with no new information forthcoming, they've pretty much concluded that a rogue wave took the boat down. But—"

"No body."

"Which means no certainty. For anyone. Let alone someone so emotionally invested as your sister. And your nephew."

Burroughs was right. She didn't know; no one knew. In fact, Aventurine didn't know anything anymore; everything was uncertain, and all that uncertainty led all the way back to Shep, and the foundering of *La Máquina de los Vientos*. And because of that, she was without Micheline, and without Paul. Without Lance, too, because those two had, in the midst of everything, managed to form some sort of relationship. Aventurine sighed deeply and wiped her hands over her cold face. At least Paul had someone; at least he wasn't alone. But somewhere out there, Micheline was searching on, trying to discover what had happened to her husband, and was alone. That was the part that hurt Aventurine, and frightened her the most. Mick was all alone.

"Come on." Burroughs clambered to his feet. He reached down to her, and after a moment, she took his hand and allowed him to help her up. "It's getting colder. Windier. And darker. It's time for the vampires to come out."

"Are you one?"

"Not that I know of. You?"

"I don't think so." A stronger breeze from the ocean was blowing across East Cliff now, and the wisps of fog were breaking apart and drifting away, to find some other spot to haunt. "But Lucy Westenra didn't realize she was one, either, until it was far too late."

Burroughs laughed. The sound bounced back from the worn stone of the Abbey; as the mists cleared, Aventurine realized they were on their own in the grounds. When they scrambled back over the wall, she could see why; the brewery was closed and tucked in for the night.

"I suppose I should be warned, then," he said, as he gave her a hand to jump down.

Aventurine shook her head as they turned along Church Lane in the direction of the 199 Steps. "Oh, I'm quite sure, Dominic, that you can take care of yourself well enough."

He fell into step beside her. "You know—"

"What?" she demanded when he broke off.

"You've never called me by my first name before."

Quickly Aventurine cast her thoughts back and realized it was true, she hadn't. Not even when they'd crashed the car into the hedgerow. Not even when he'd kissed her, or she'd kissed him. She felt the familiar flush now, and was grateful that the moon, climbing overhead, bleached all color out of everything. "Sorry," she said. "Does it bother you? I won't do it again, then."

They reached the steps and started down. A woman with a small dog, who seemed inclined to sniff at everything on the way by, including them, passed with a quiet greeting.

"It's not that it bothers me," Burroughs said. His voice, and his expression when she glanced over at him, were inscrutable. They passed under a lamp that turned his face to planes and shadows.

They turned to their right, as if by some silent agreement, toward the East Pier. Aventurine shoved her hands into her pockets again, though the narrow stone houses along Henrietta Street protected them from the wind. All too soon, they'd come to the turnaround—*strictly no parking*—and the wind from the sea blasted them with its full force again. It probably would have been a better choice, upon reflection, to have returned to the hotel to hunker down near the fire in the pub; a pub of any kind, at this point, would be preferable. To most people, she amended. The sense of futility had returned, stronger than ever, and the anxiety. She was wasting time. She could be searching for Micheline. But where? She felt the Dover Thrift paperback in her pocket, and wrapped her icy hand around the spine. Someone had wanted her to come to Whitby, and here she was. Who, she demanded again, and for what reason? The barrenness of East Pier, with the waves moving against it with a sibilant hush and the single red glow from the lighthouse made her feel like an outcast.

But Dominic Burroughs had shown up when she was at her wits' end. Had followed her. Those were his words. A tiny knot of something warmed deep inside her. *Dominic.* She tried out his name in her mind, experimentally. He had cared enough to come after her when she had fled. She cast a look at him, beside her, as they moved down the hill toward the pier.

How had he known?

A niggling thought, and the tiny know of warmth cooled suddenly. How had Burroughs known she'd left London? Was changing trains in York?

Quickly followed by Genevieve's unwelcome voice. *Don't sleep with the policeman.*

Aventurine shivered and stiffened when he moved too close in their walk. They were all in danger from the police, she reminded herself: she, Micheline—wherever she was—and Paul and Lance. Who had left her as well. Genevieve: well, she could take care of herself.

They were out on the pier now, the stones glistening underfoot, the tide moving restlessly under the moon. Aventurine leaned against a brick wall, which cut the wind, looking across to the West Pier, which was lit cheerfully along its length, unlike East Pier. In *Dracula*, this was the way, between the two piers, that the Russian ship had run into the River Esk and up onto Tate Hill Pier, a dead man lashed to the wheel. She shivered again.

"Cold?" Burroughs asked. He didn't seem affected by the wind. He never seemed affected by anything.

She nodded. It was freezing cold out here and getting colder, with the spray from the waves against the stonework of the pier; but it was clear—there would probably be no rain overnight. A cloud scudded over the moon and they were in shadow, but then the cloud moved on again.

"What did you mean?" she asked. He leaned against the wall as well, their shoulders nearly touching; despite her anxiety, and Genevieve's commanding voice in her head, she did not pull away. "When you said that it wasn't my using your name that bothered you? What is it that bothers you, then?"

Burroughs did not look at her, but instead seemed intent upon the West Pier and the lighthouse midway along it. Aventurine surreptitiously studied his profile: the slightly long nose with the bump where it had been broken at some time; the hair that tumbled at his forehead in the wind.

When he spoke, it was as though he were thinking in circles, or tangents. "You've got your puzzles, and I've got mine," he said slowly. For a long moment, he looked down at his hands, fingers spread, then clenched them into fists and looked again to the west.

"What are yours?" Aventurine's hackles rose. It always came back to the thing which separated them. She felt defensive.

A gust of wind made her blink as she studied his profile. She put up a hand to brush her own hair out of her eyes.

"Dafydd Davies," he said. "Magnus Etheridge. Alyona Morozova Davies. And—" he took a deep breath here, as though shoring himself up—"Neil Barrett."

Aventurine froze, her eyes still locked on his face. She could feel her heart rate climb, could feel the cold sweat of panic, prickling at her hairline. Despite Genevieve's constant warning, she still forgot—perhaps willfully forgot—that Dominic Burroughs, before all, was a police detective.

"No?" he prodded, still looking away to the lighthouse on West Pier. "Nothing to say, Aventurine?"

"No," she answered, despairing. "Nothing." She so wanted to touch him, be held by him, feel his mouth on hers again. She settled for placing a shaking hand on his sleeve.

Now he looked down at her fingers for the longest minute, and then slowly, slowly stepped away. Her hand dropped to her side.

"The common denominator, Aventurine, is you." Burroughs stuffed his fists into his coat pocket. His face was now in shadow, and all she could see was the glint of his eyes. "I have four bodies. Four dead people. And what they all have in common is you."

"You've said that before."

"And you didn't tell me anything then, either. So I don't know, Aventurine. *I don't know.*"

It was obviously an invitation—or a plea—for her to explain herself, to explain everything. But—he'd included Neil in the list, and to explain Neil was to implicate Paul. And that she simply could not do. She closed her eyes tightly for a moment. She had to protect Paul at all costs. She had promised her sister. She had promised herself.

"Tell me," he urged, his voice nearly drowned out by the wind and the sudden surge of waves between the piers. More clouds scudded fitfully overhead. The tide, and the wind, was changing.

"Can't you just trust me when I tell you I'm not a killer?"

The words, when she spoke them aloud, were ludicrous.

But neither of them laughed.

In a sudden rogue flash of moonlight, his expression was almost anguished.

"No," he said at last. "No, Aventurine. I can't trust you. And that's all the problem."

She opened her mouth to speak, but it was too late. Far too late, she realized. For Dominic Burroughs had turned on his heel and walked away.

Aventurine didn't know how long she stood there, watching his retreating back, until the night on Henrietta Street swallowed him whole. The pier had grown colder, the sea louder, the world more cruel and dangerous. She dropped her face into her hands, but fought the urge to break down. Burroughs was gone, she told herself. Just one more person who, in the past few days, had abandoned her.

How had it come to this? *How had it come to this?*

All she wanted—all she had ever wanted—was to explore the world and write about it, knowing that her personal life was comfortable, always in the background, with her sister and her sister's family. The occasional meeting with Gio Constantine to keep her in practice. She had been satisfied with that, would have been nearly content to grow old in the midst of all that. But how quickly it had all unraveled

Because of Shep, and the wreck of *La Máquina de los Vientos*. Because of Shep.

Aventurine didn't have the courage to wrest herself from the furious circle of blame. It was easier to curse Shep, a man she had not seen in over a year, someone who had removed himself from her life, from their lives. Dead or alive, accident or intent, he was gone, and she cursed him. Cursed him to hell with every fiber in her being.

A cloud covered the moon yet again, leaving only the glow of red from the lighthouse down the pier. She stumbled slightly as she pushed away from the windbreak, and dropped her purse. When she stooped to retrieve it, she felt the blow against her shoulder, and the shove. She tumbled sideways toward the edge, and scrabbled, but there was no purchase for her fingers, and with a scream, she fell.

Forty-four

The water was paralyzingly cold, and she swallowed a mouthful with the shock of it. She surfaced momentarily and took another mouthful when she gasped for air. A wave hit her in the face. Her clothes—her shoes—were heavy, and she panicked, trying to fight the weight to stay above water. She went down again. Her chest was burning. Is this how it ended, then?

Some smidgen of thought told her, as she surfaced once more and was pushed by the waves, to turn with the water. The blood was pounding in her ears, and she could see nothing. Another wave pushed her toward the shore.

Stay afloat, she told herself. *Go with the waves.*

And then her knees hit the shingle. She fell forward.

"Here!"

She wasn't certain she'd heard a voice until the shout came again. "Grab onto me! Here!"

Aventurine dragged herself forward on her hands and knees, and then vomited. She felt a hand at her shoulder, pulling her upwards onto the beach. Again she vomited up sea water, feeling it burn in her throat, her mouth, her nose.

"Dominic?" she managed at last.

There was a shift of sand and rocks beside her ear. "Aventurine—Miss Morrow—are you all right?"

She pressed her eyes closed, feeling the shingle beneath her cheek.

It was still hard to breathe.

"What happened?"

What happened? She felt the impact again, the shove toward the edge of the pier. Again the panic: she struggled to her knees, coughing.

It wasn't Burroughs. It was Ernest Swales.

No. With his limp, he wouldn't have been able to push her off the pier and then make it around to the shingle in time to drag her to safety. That made no sense anyway.

"Did you fall?"

"Pushed," she gasped.

To his credit, the old man did not question her. Instead, he looked around, and then upward, scanning the pier. There was no one there, unless that person was hiding behind the windbreak.

"We'd better get out of here," he said.

Aventurine coughed up some more sea water. "My bag—"

Swales shook his head. He got to his feet unsteadily, and then reached down to her with his right hand. "Gone now, in the water."

"No," she said, shaking her head. Once on her feet, she leaned forward, hands on knees. Her clothing soaked, the wind cut through them like a knife. "I dropped it. Up there. Somebody kicked it in after me." Neil had taken her things, she thought disjointedly. But this wasn't Neil. Still, she needed her bag. Passport, cards, money, *Dracula*. Phone. "Please."

Swales looked around uncertainly. "Stay here," he growled at last. "Don't move." The old man seemed unwilling to leave her, but something in her urgency decided him. "You washed up—maybe it did, too." He glanced around, and his eyes lighted on a length of wood—a branch, a spar—hard to tell on the darkened beach. He picked it up in his good hand and moved away, becoming little more than a shadow.

Aventurine had retched again by the time he reappeared, dragging his bad leg along the shingle. He threw his makeshift weapon to the side. "Here," he said, holding out the leather strap. When she lifted the flap, she found the bag was still zipped closed; a quick rifling told her that her wallet, her passport, her phone, and even the book were still there. Wet, but there. Swales had gone still; she thought he was watching her. She zipped the bag up again quickly. "I found it like that. So either they closed it back up after going through it, or—" and he took her by the arm— "the purse wasn't their target to begin with."

Henrietta Street was deserted, lights on behind the curtains of only a few cottages. From up on the cliff overhead, Avi thought she heard the cry of a bird, cut off quickly.

"We should go to the police. Make a report," Swales offered.

"No," Aventurine said quickly. "No police."

In the light of a passing window, his expression might have been relieved. "Okay. They probably wouldn't believe you anyway."

"Thanks."

He shrugged, not letting go of her arm. "Lots of drunks have fallen off the piers over the years."

"I'm not drunk," she shot back.

"I know that, but they don't." His steps dragged against the stones, loud between the cottages looming on either side. At least they were protected from the wind.

Swales was right, of course. She shivered.

"I could have drowned," she said as they neared the 199 steps. *Who wants you dead?*

"But you didn't. You dragged your way out."

"With your help."

They turned the corner. It was better lit here. She saw Swales grimace. "Whatever help I was." A pub was open across the road; a couple let themselves out and turned in the direction of Tate Hill Pier, holding hands. "Come on, then," he said. "You need a drink. We both do."

The publican looked up warily as they entered. "I've got this one," Swales said. He indicated a table near the fire. Aventurine sat, her arms and legs weak. She coughed again, but this time it did not wrack her. Then Swales was back. "Here." He placed a shot glass on the worn table before her. "Drink this." He set a glass in front of his own chair, and sank into the seat awkwardly.

Aventurine did not, for a moment, touch her drink. "Someone pushed me off the pier." She felt disembodied, and listened to the shock and confusion in her own voice. "Somebody *pushed* me."

"If the tide had been out further, you might have just hit the shingle," Swales said. "Broken your arms or legs."

"Or neck," she agreed grimly. "And lain there until the tide came in again and drowned me."

"Thank God I saw you in the water." He brushed a hand across his beard, adjusted his eyepatch. "Thank God. I don't have any depth perception with this damned thing."

Aventurine wondered whether he needed it. Still, there was a thin line along his temple, white against the sunburn, which indicated he'd worn the patch for a long time. If it were a prop, his was a long-running show. She shook herself quickly, feeling like an ingrate: this man had just saved her life. She was borderline hysterical. Nonsensical. *Someone had pushed her off the pier.*

He shook his head. "Who wants you dead, Aventurine?"

She grabbed up the shot glass and threw the drink back. The contents burned on the way down her throat, and her eyes watered. She blinked back the tears as she slammed the glass down on the tabletop.

The words were so like Burroughs's that she glanced up at Swales's face. He was watching her intently with that one good eye. "I don't know what you're talking about."

"I think you might." He glanced around, and sipped his own whisky, but the pub was emptying, closing time nearly upon them. "But now we ought to think about how to get you back to your hotel." He drank and paused. "But no police? You're sure?"

"I'm sure." And she was certain, this time, that the flash of relief on his face was not imagined. Aventurine found she was shivering now, uncontrollably. Cold, or shock? Did it matter?

The barkeeper called time.

"Another?" Swales asked, leaning forward. The fire picked out golden lights in his silver beard.

"God, no." Aventurine covered her face with her hands.

"What were you doing out there on the pier so late? If you don't mind me asking." He coughed, drew out a handkerchief, and wiped his nose. "Don't know how safe it is, all alone, after dark."

"I wasn't alone." Well, not until those last minutes. "Anyway, it obviously wasn't safe, was it?"

Aventurine had been on the cliff, and then on the pier, with a police detective. No one had attempted to push her from a high place while Burroughs was there. No one had tried to harm her until he was gone. Coincidence? She wondered what he would think of someone pushing her off the pier: *did she fall or was she pushed?* He'd probably think the perp had ironically become the victim. Poetic justice. She resisted the urge to giggle hysterically.

Maybe it was all a coincidence. Maybe it *had* been a purse-snatching gone wrong. But that didn't explain the hard push at her shoulder—she touched her wet jacket now—and the fact that her purse had been thrown in after her. Maybe the mugger had panicked, run off?

Swales was watching her with his one hazel eye.

"No," he said, almost as though reading her mind. "Your bag didn't seem to be the target. Which means it was you. Which means it was intentional."

Play stupid, she told herself: wide-eyed and surprised, like Mary Wentworth. "That seems unlikely."

"It's highly unlikely that some stranger was just wandering along the pier and decided, 'Oh, there's somebody. It'd be really fun to throw her off and have her drown.'"

Target. Aventurine was having a hard time with it. She shivered, the warmth of the fire making no inroads. The whisky had been a mistake; now it was roiling in her stomach. *She had been standing on the pier with a policeman. Then she wasn't standing with a policeman. And then someone pushed her off.*

"A warning of some kind, do you suppose?" Swales mused, rubbing his good hand along his beard. His eye narrowed. Standing, he gathered the shot glasses, then seemed to notice her shivering. "We've got to get you back to the hotel," he said again, his gravelly voice softening with concern. "I'll walk you there."

She shook her head. "You told me you lived in Old Town. I can't make you walk all the way to West Cliff and back."

"Someone tonight tried to drown you," he shot back, as though reminder of his lack of mobility insulted him. "I can't make you walk all that way to your hotel by yourself."

Aventurine didn't feel like arguing. They brought their shot glasses back up. Outside, she let Swales take her arm again, and they made their way along the uneven pavement of Church Street.

At the swing bridge, however, she put her foot down. Below them, the river sparked with reflected light. A car crossed, its headlights picking them out and then moving past.

"All right," he said at last. He squeezed her arm gently before taking a few steps back. "Look. If I were you, I'd get the hell out of Dodge in the morning. Someone is warning you off—something." He looked around swiftly. "I don't know who it is, and I don't know what it is."

"I don't know what it is, either," Aventurine protested helplessly.

In the amber light from the traffic signal, Swales leaned forward. "Then you'd best find someone who does know. Only then can you avoid—whatever it is."

His warning, her soaked and freezing clothing, and the feeling of being watched or followed—there was no one there, no one—made her hurry. Pier Road was deserted; debating speed versus enclosed spaces, she finally opted for the stairs between the arcades, running up them as quickly as she could, glancing over her shoulder to be sure the footsteps she heard were echoes of her own. Her heart was pounding by the time she hit Khyber Pass; there was no traffic, and she bounded across to the steps upward to East Terrace. At the top she paused, a hand to her chest, a stitch in her side; she huddled in the shadow of a shrub as a car went by toward the cliff. Then she crossed the road and hurried to the front doors of the hotel.

Her keycard, still, thankfully, in her purse and not destroyed by the salt water, allowed her entrance to the lobby; she nodded to the night clerk, who looked taken aback by her appearance, and climbed aboard the elevator.

At her door, her fingers uncooperative from the cold, she fumbled with the card. At last, the tiny green light flashed, and she stumbled inward, reaching for the wall switch.

For a moment she blinked in the light, and then it registered.

The room was empty. All of her things were gone.

Part IV:

Trickster

Forty-five

You'd best find someone who does know.

Later, Aventurine would remember the water on the pond behind the Abbey like a skin, the eerie moonlight skimming off it and disorienting her. She had been blind, hadn't she? And she still was. Because the answer, finally, had been in Whitby. She had stood there, in the November wind off the ocean—that damned ocean—staring at the pond, trying to make sense of it. The shimmering night reflection. And in all that time, the pieces of the puzzle had been so close to hand, and she had not seen them; but had she seen them, she thought in disgust, she would, no doubt, have been unable to fit them together. Too blinded.

All she needed was one. The corner piece. The one that would lead her logically to the next, and the next, until the pattern became clear, and the entire picture could be constructed. Then she would understand—whatever this was.

And the corner piece, she knew now, was sitting in a darkened library in a row house in York, petting a foul-tempered cat and drinking tea, while waiting for Aventurine to find the fit.

Aventurine had had the piece the entire time, and had simply not recognized it.

She felt incredibly stupid.

She felt as though she had been taken in by the trickster's sleight of hand.

She felt the fury welling up inside her.

Slowly, trying to retain control, Aventurine pushed away from the window overlooking the town and its lights. She had nothing except for the forty pounds, the bank card, and her passport in her purse; the phone was beyond repair. Still, that would be enough to get the bus back to York.

And then she would confront the old woman, whom she had grown to love, and who had betrayed her in so many ways.

She checked both locks on her bedroom door and, for good measure, shoved the dresser in front of it as a precaution. *I thought you were leaving*, the desk clerk had protested, when she'd stumbled to the lobby to demand answers about her missing belongings. *That's what you said when you came down with your luggage earlier.* If the push from the pier had been a warning, the theft of her belongings had been doubly so. She was warned. If this was all more than a warning—if Burroughs and Swales were right, and someone wanted her dead—this was the best she could do until the 840 bus left Whitby station at eleven the next morning. All the same, she slept fitfully, tossing about in the double bed, throwing the blankets off, and then clawing them back again, dozing and then starting awake at the slightest sound.

In the morning, the street below her window glistened darkly from a sea roke she had slept through, but was otherwise empty. No one lurked beyond the Arch across the way; no one walked past the hotel purposely, pretending not to look. She had a sharp memory of Neil, and squeezed her head between her hands. Neil was dead. She had seen him die. She had lied and evaded for months, to protect Paul, to protect them all. Now it had come to this. Aventurine felt the cold glass against her forehead, but then straightened and let the curtain fall.

She dressed again in yesterday's clothes, grimacing at their clamminess, and hoping they didn't smell too bad; she'd have to pick up at least some more underwear once she got into York, as well as a replacement phone. She unzipped her purse and, stealing a hand towel to go inside, shoved in her money, passport, and cards. She touched them several times neurotically, feeling them as talismans, before she shoved the dresser back to make her way down to the breakfast room. Might as well kill as much time as possible over breakfast; it would only take her fifteen minutes to walk down to the bus. She turned over her wrist to check the time, but the watch was dead and, of course, the charger had been among the stuff that had been cleared out of her room. Of course it had been. She didn't even know the time, she thought bitterly. On her way out the door, she grabbed the copy of *Dracula* from the bedside table, the cover and pages curling as they dried out.

The breakfast room was deserted. Aventurine ordered tea with her full English, hold the beans and black pudding. The server, a young man with a black apron cinched around his waist, and with a touch of magenta in the hair at his temples, had set a rack of white and brown toast on the table, and Aventurine chewed on a piece distractedly, trying to think. Trying to come up with a working plan.

The 840 bus would deposit her at York station in the early afternoon. She had a hazy idea that if she left the station and followed Queen Street, she could find a hotel somewhere along the way to Scarcroft Road. Clothes could come later. Mostly, she just needed to get to Genevieve.

The clock over the door informed her that it was ten past nine. When the server returned with her plate, he was frowning.

"You're the lady in 34," he said.

Aventurine nodded and set down her teacup.

"I'm sorry about your things." He folded the cloth with which he had held the hot plate, and tucked it into the pocket of his apron. "I was covering the desk yesterday afternoon. If I'd known it wasn't you, I'd never have let her in. I told the manager that."

"It's all right," she said grimly.

"It's uncanny," he continued, throwing a glance over his shoulder. "I could have sworn it was you. I wanted to call the police—"

She shook her head quickly. "No police. It—it doesn't matter."

The server apologized again and disappeared back into the kitchen. Aventurine looked at her full English and felt decidedly queasy. Still, she would need sustenance. She took a forkful of the scrambled egg and a sliver of grilled tomato. It didn't taste as good as it had the previous day.

It wasn't Neil, she told herself in a sing-songy voice. He had stolen her story; he had stolen her relationship with Paul; he had stolen her peace of mind. But he had left her suitcase alone this time. And he was dead.

Still, it was someone who looked like her. Someone who knew which room she was in. Someone who had waited for her chance, manipulated the young man into letting her into the room, and cleared her out. Then disappeared.

If she'd drowned off the pier, no one would have been the wiser about her look-alike taking her things. Unless the push had been a warning only, and this was a warning, too.

To do what? To avoid what?

To the left of her plate was the ruined copy of *Dracula*. Someone had wanted her to come to Whitby. To stage her drowning? For some other reason?

Aventurine cut herself a sliver of the Cumberland sausage, then, chewing slowly, set the silver on the edge of the plate, and flicked through the water-damaged pages.

A name caught her eye.

Swales.

On the 840 bus at last. Off-season, so it wasn't crowded, and she was able to get a seat. Despite her disjointed state, Aventurine remembered to sit on the left, the better to look out the window at the passing Yorkshire countryside. Even so, she found herself with her head against the glass, her eyes unseeing—if later anyone asked her, she would not have been able to remember much of what she saw. If anyone asked her. Was there anyone left who would?

Except that she did make a note of a small churchyard, somewhere around the turnoff to Kirby Misperton. The church itself was of some pale brown stone, with a dark roof and a pointed bell tower; in the walled yard, old grave markers listed tiredly. Then it was gone again as the bus ate up the road to York. Aventurine closed her eyes, thinking to doze off, but instead, in her mind's eye, the English churchyard metamorphosed into the one down the road from the house where she and Micheline grew up: the one with the tall monument which pinpointed the memory of a ship captain lost at sea. Funny how those things came full-circle, she mused bitterly. She and Mick playing at the foot of this obelisk, like the ghoulish children they were, a stone sacred to the memory of a man whose body was never found. And Micheline, later, refusing to set a monument to Shep, another man whose body was never found. Aventurine grimaced now, feeling the bus slow to a stop, but refused to open her eyes. Shep. Everything came back to Shep.

It had been a happy childhood, really, she thought. There had been no aunts or uncles, no grandparents, either; but, never having known them, Aventurine and Micheline had never missed them. They had had each other, with their shared imaginations, their shared games, their shared experiences at school, and later, at college—they had chosen different colleges, but both in New York, and had eventually ended up sharing a tiny walk-up apartment. They had the long-standing knowledge of each other, which had had its genesis even before birth.

They had shared the grief when their parents had died in the car accident on the Rodovia Regis Bittencourt outside of Curitiba; it had been Shep, at that time engaged to Mick but already making a name—and plenty of money—in finance, who had been able to bring Michele and Daniel Morrow back home to their burial. Thinking of that, Aventurine opened her eyes, but the scenery outside the coach window was a blur now. At least, she thought with a pang low in her gut, she and Micheline knew where their parents were. At least Shep had been able to make sure of that for them.

The irony, though. If only they had been able to find Shep's body with the flotsam of *La Máquina de los Vientos*. If only they had been able to close this chapter with some certainty. If only.

Aventurine checked her watch, but it was still dead. All she knew was that it was sometime between eleven, when they'd pulled out of Whitby, and one twenty-five, when they were due in York station. She dared not doze off again.

Forty-six

By the time the coach reached York, the sky had darkened even more, as though thunderstorms might be coming through; she'd just begun to dry out, and now she'd get soaked again. With the dark clouds building as quickly as they were, it was unlikely there'd be an amelioration in the gloominess of the afternoon before sunset. Aventurine quickly found herself a room at a hotel not far from the station, and paused only long enough to give her face a quick scrub before heading out for Scarcroft Road.

It seemed eerily familiar.

And somehow hostile.

Her footsteps echoed along the pavement. Aventurine shivered, remembering her trepidation of the summer, when she had first approached the door of the old spy she was to interview for her latest book. One of the Badass Bitches of Britain, though Avi had not known that at the time. This afternoon Aventurine's trepidation was of a different flavor.

She took the steps up to the door and raised the knocker. It made a hollow sound when it fell.

Aventurine was prepared to wait a few moments for Genevieve to get to the door, and was surprised at an almost immediate response. A small blonde woman in a cleaning smock frowned at her from the entryway. "*Ja*? Yes?"

"Aventurine Morrow, for Mrs. Smithson. Is she in?"

The cleaning lady—for that was what she most likely was—looked uncertainly over her shoulder. "*Ich verstehe nicht? Entschuldigung?*"

"*Lass sie rein*, Else," the voice commanded from somewhere along the dim hallway. "*Dann kannst du gehen, bitte.*"

Else pulled the door open, and, letting Aventurine inside, dipped her head with a nervous smile, then slipped into the street. Aventurine closed the door after her.

"Lock it, please, Aventurine," Genevieve ordered.

Deadbolts, a Yale with a key. Carefully, Aventurine locked each one, and then tugged at the door for good measure. Nothing moved. The fortress was secure. Only then did she make her way along the hallway, her footsteps muffled by the Oriental runner. She purposely avoided looking at the umbrella stand at the foot of the staircase. As she passed the longcase clock, it rang three times.

Rather than at her accustomed seat beside the open hearth, Genevieve was ensconced in a wing chair before the French windows looking out on the bedraggled November garden. The cat was in the chair facing hers, and looked up with a slow blink at Aventurine, making no move whatsoever to relinquish its seat. Its gaze, like the usual one of its mistress, was one of challenge. This afternoon, however, when Genevieve looked up, her eyes were hooded, her expression unreadable.

"You might have called ahead," she said mildly. "I might not have been in. I might have had an appointment."

"With your contacts?"

She tilted her head in that sardonic way she had. "With my GP. I'm an old woman, Aventurine."

"So you keep telling me." Aventurine took a couple of steps into the room, which felt cold. The fire was not alight.

A strange little half-smile played around Genevieve's lips. "And it's true. At some point, I will die. And let's face the facts: that point will happen relatively soon for me. Old women die, Aventurine."

It was a diversion, but one Aventurine allowed herself to follow, if only momentarily. "Does that frighten you?"

"Not particularly."

"The idea of an afterlife?"

Genevieve shook her head. "No. I think once I'm done, I'm done. I'll let them cremate me and throw my ashes to the wind."

"Like you did for Honoré?"

"Exactly like that. You might make that your mission, Aventurine. To see that those wishes are carried out."

"Me?"

"Why not you?" The old woman's tone was reasonable. "You are the closest I have to any sort of relation. I think I might be able to trust you as much or more than I trust any other person I know."

"You don't trust *anyone*."

Genevieve's laugh was more of a bark. "You're right on that account," she agreed. She shifted in her chair, and then turned away to look out into the garden. The rain had started again. "Let's just say, then, that you might know me best of anyone."

"Because no one knows you at all." This conversation was quicksand.

Was that a smile? With her head turned, it was impossible to tell.

"But you didn't ring before you came. That, I don't think, is like you." Trust Genevieve to pick up when someone was acting out of character. When Aventurine was acting out of character. "Were you trying to surprise me?"

"Nothing surprises you."

"I have my lapses." But Genevieve tapped her foot on the carpet, obviously waiting for the answer to her question.

"My phone was ruined by the North Sea. Last night. And my suitcase was stolen from my hotel room in Whitby. Along with my computer. In fact, everything except my passport, my cards, and the bit of cash I had on me."

Slowly Genevieve lifted a teacup to her lips with her right hand, still gazing out the French windows. "In Whitby?"

"Yes."

"I *told you* not to go there."

"And I was nearly killed."

Genevieve nodded. "I told you not to go there."

"Did you know this was going to happen?"

"I didn't *know* anything was going to happen. But I suspected something might. Because that was not one of my lapses." The old woman set the cup down, gently, but the tiny clink was jarring in the cold stillness of the room. "And did you file a police report?"

"Of course I didn't."

Genevieve nodded. "Good girl. But what about your friend? That Chief Inspector Burroughs?"

Aventurine wiped a hand across her brow. "He's not my friend. And he went back to Lincoln. I haven't told him."

"Good girl."

The cat leapt from the chair. Keeping its gleaming eyes on Aventurine, it arched its back and wound its way around Genevieve's ankles. Avi wondered fleetingly whether that cat viewed her as a threat, or as prey. And how did its owner view her?

The wayward thought startled Aventurine, and she narrowed her eyes in the gloom, studying the other woman. The pointed nose, the high forehead, the thin lips. An old woman. Yet one, even now, who gave off the sense of being a coiled spring, ready for any action.

The rain was picking up. A gust of wind shook the French windows. Genevieve seemed not to notice.

"It's just as well, Aventurine," she said now. "The policeman was too close. And you need always to think about protecting your flank."

"Paul."

"Of course."

Paul, who had become enraged at the suggestion that his father might have died by suicide. Aventurine breathed deeply, but the room felt stuffy, airless. "He doesn't believe I'm protecting him."

"His father has become iconic. People do that with death—whole religions have grown up because of that. And the rest of us suffer for it. He will come around."

"I wish he'd hurry up about it."

"Grief, Aventurine, takes different paths for different people. You need to allow for that. Grief doesn't just go away because the rest of us are impatient."

The rest of us meant Aventurine, obviously. She hated how Genevieve could make her feel chastised with an offhand phrase.

"What if he's not grieving, because he refuses to believe his father is dead?" she demanded. "What do we do then?"

"What if he's right?" The old woman stared out at the rain.

Here it was. "What do you know?" Aventurine's question was shrill.

The teacup set aside, Genevieve lifted her right hand and let it fall. "It's not what I do or do not know. But if Shep is not dead, then your Paul has a different kind of grieving to go through. You should have thought of that."

Avi had. She wouldn't have ever thought Shep to be this cruel, but if he was, that might be worse than death for his family.

"What do you know?" she pressed.

"You can live for yourself, Aventurine," Genevieve continued, "or you can live for those you love. You can live for your son."

"Paul is Micheline's son."

The faint half-smile. "Play it your way, then. But know that I am not stupid, though I am old."

"And Micheline is still missing." Aventurine's voice broke. *I am all alone, except for you*, she thought. The idea mortified her—it made her sound as though she were looking for protection, looking for a mother; and of all the things she was, Genevieve was definitely not a mother figure.

"Micheline, like Paul, needs to find a truth about her husband that she can accept," Genevieve said mildly. "She loves you as a sister, but she loves him as her life."

"You say *loves* as though he's still alive."

"I say *loves* because you can still love a person who is dead. You can love that person until *you* are dead."

The pain that gripped Aventurine at Genevieve's words was unbearable, filled with horrible possibilities as it was. She caught her breath, and saw that the old woman was watching her intently.

Micheline dead.

Then, *Paul dead.*

She pressed the balls of her hands into her eyes.

She couldn't bear to think of these things. Is this what Micheline had been feeling, every moment since the phone call came in the middle of the night? Aventurine felt the terror of loss, the terror of being lost. Of having nothing, no one. Of being unmoored for the rest of her life.

She took a long shuddering breath. Then she lifted her eyes to Genevieve's.

"Is he here?" she asked. The one thing she had come for. "Is Paul here?"

Since he had met her, Paul had looked to Genevieve as some sort of safety. He had lashed out at her, Avi, and fled, so it made sense that he had come here. To Lance's *great-grandmother.*

"He is not."

Genevieve sounded disappointed in her.

"You're the only one he trusts," Avi protested. "He'd come to you."

The old woman held out her hands and lifted her chin. "Have a look around, if you like."

Aventurine spun on her heel and pounded through the empty dining room to the kitchen door, which she thrust open with such force that pans and glassware rattled. "Paul?" she shouted, but the kitchen was empty as well.

Upstairs. Aventurine threw open door after door, looking for some sign of habitation from Paul and Lance. Nothing.

At last she found herself in the room where Genevieve had shown her the SOE uniform, back when this was merely a job of research. Aventurine paused, with her hand on the doorframe, and looked in on the spartan guest room, the bed neatly made with a chenille coverlet pulled so tight she could bounce a pound coin off it: Else's doing, no doubt. There were no signs of occupancy here, either. Aventurine took a breath, and, hand on her ribs, lowered herself to the bed.

She had been so sure that the answer—all the answers—were here. All she had found were more questions.

It was obvious that, even had Paul and Lance come to Scarcroft Road, they were not here now. She had either missed them—or she had been wrong entirely.

Aventurine leaned her head back on her aching neck and took a deep breath. She had to rethink. Recalculate. Try to figure out where to go next, search next. The possibilities were enormous. They could be anywhere in the world. Anywhere.

Or she could simply take Genevieve's advice and find somewhere to light. To stay. None of them were her responsibility. If Shep were dead, he was dead; if not, he was not her husband, and it was not down to her to find him. If Micheline wanted to expend her energy following strange clues in the search for her possibly-alive husband, that was her business. If Paul wanted to follow after his mother, with Lance in tow, or simply be done with all of them, that was his business. They were adults. They could make decisions for their own lives. Aventurine lifted her head and looked into the mirror on the opposite wall at a tired, distressed, frantic woman with mussed hair and a worn face.

It would be safer, she assumed. If she just took the next flight out to her little apartment in the Back Bay. No one would attempt to cause her car to crash. No one would hurl her from a pier. She could just go on, living her life, writing her books, being left alone. It would be easier. She stared into the shadowed eyes of her reflection. *What do you want to do?*

Then she saw the door of the closet, behind her reflection to the left. Slightly open: a black sliver of shadow.

She stood quickly and yanked open the door.

The garment bag containing the uniform took her by surprise; but that's all it was. There was no one hiding in the closet. There were no suitcases, no trace of her nephew or Lance. On the shelf above the rod was the hatbox containing, she knew, the uniform cap. She took the box down, opened it, took the cap out.

At her feet was another box. One that she'd hadn't seen before, one that had not been there when she'd looked in this closet with Genevieve. She bent down.

"There's a box," Aventurine said. "Upstairs. In the bedroom where you keep your uniform."

Back in the front room, Genevieve's face was half-shadowed. "There are many boxes in this house." She sat gazing out into the November garden, wrapped and mulched and prepared for winter, but still looking forlorn. The orange cat now sat on the arm of her chair, a sphinx, while she stroked its back. They both were inscrutable. "There are many boxes in that room."

Aventurine lay the uniform hat on the table near the door, and once again, felt a reluctance to advance into the room. It had grown colder, the hearth holding only cold ash. She wondered why Else had not swept it clear. "On the floor, in the closet," she pressed.

Only stillness from the old woman. Suddenly a gust of wind rattled the French doors and spattered rain against the glass. Genevieve didn't even turn her head.

"It was addressed to Micheline."

Genevieve sighed. "Did you open it?"

The question was not accusatory, but curious. No doubt Genevieve, in the same situation, would have opened it; of course she would have. She leaned forward now to the teapot and topped off her cup; steam rose up gently into the dimness and disappeared.

She was not Genevieve.

"I did not," Avi said.

Setting aside the fact that Aventurine had opened far too much of what was addressed to Micheline in the past week.

"Come sit down and have tea." Always commanding. Aventurine's hackles rose.

"I will not be fobbed off with tea."

"Suit yourself."

Genevieve picked up her cup and continued to sip her tea, continued to gaze out at the rain.

"I didn't open the box," Aventurine repeated. "It wasn't addressed to me. Did you address it?"

"I did."

The coldness and stillness were beginning to get to Aventurine. She leaned to pull the chain on the table lamp next to the door. It cast surprisingly little light, making next to no headway against the gloom of the dying afternoon: only a small island of illumination picked out the grain of the wooden table.

"*In Lisbon?*"

"Information received."

"And you didn't bother to pass it on to me? Information, you said, flows both ways."

"I lied."

Genevieve sipped her tea, as though she had not just dropped a bomb.

"What is she doing in Lisbon?"

"She didn't say."

"Does it have to do with Shep?"

The sigh that escaped Genevieve was one of exasperation. "Can you think of any other reason she'd rush off to Lisbon right now?"

A rhetorical question if ever there was one. Aventurine put a shaking hand to her brow, which felt hot. Obviously she'd have to go to Lisbon.

"What are you sending to my sister?"

Genevieve did not answer, only lifting her teacup to her lips with one hand. Aventurine resisted the urge to cross the room to the other armchair. To wrest the old woman's attention from the garden beyond the window. The cat looked up and blinked lazily at her with its unfriendly yellow eyes.

"What are you sending to Micheline?" she demanded again.

This time Genevieve turned her head ever so slightly, her gaze measured, but somehow pained. "There are some things," she said slowly, "that are best left unsaid. Some stories that should be allowed to die and be swept away."

"I don't think this is one of them."

"You've always been very circumspect where your sister Micheline is concerned," Genevieve continued, as though she had not spoken.

Aventurine did not think that worthy of an answer.

"Except of course for that one time. The letter."

The flush warmed Aventurine's skin even more. Mortification. "You *ordered* me to do it."

Another sip of tea. The rain was growing more forceful against the French windows. The cat stood, and leapt to the high back of Genevieve's chair, arching its back before settling and beginning to groom a paw. Claws extended.

"I did. You see, I would argue that you've been far too circumspect altogether. That your sister has kept secrets from you—possibly dangerous secrets—and the best way to help her is to gather all the information you can, by whatever means you can."

"I'm not you."

"You're Mary Wentworth."

"No. I'm not."

"We're all Mary Wentworth."

Mary Wentworth is a state of mind.

It was the old woman's tone that infuriated her. Advancing to the tea table, Aventurine grabbed a butter knife. She felt the ornate metalwork in her palm, and examined the rounded blade, with its ineffectual serrations. This would do.

She spun on her heel.

At the door, she heard Genevieve's cold humorless laugh. "Good girl."

Forty-seven

The air in the bedroom was cold, and smelled more stale than she remembered. Aventurine didn't bother to close the door behind her. Genevieve knew exactly what she was doing. There were no secrets from that woman.

That thought frightened her, as it hadn't before. Aventurine swallowed.

She opened the closet door again, and bent to lift the box out onto the bed. She lowered herself once again onto the chenille bedspread, and examined the address, printed in block letters in a strong impatient hand: Micheline Genthner, at an address on Rua Vasco da Gama. In Lisbon. *Lisbon?* The label made no sense to her. Aventurine desperately wished for her phone, to snap a photo, perhaps to send it to Paul and Lance. Instead, she repeated the address over and over to herself, trying to commit it to memory.

The box itself was securely taped shut, but the butter knife made quick work of that when she slipped it under the top flap. She flung the knife to the Oriental carpet. Inside the box, she found crumpled newspaper, which she also tossed aside; but then she thought of all the books, the underlines. Biting her lip, she forced herself to retrieve each page to smooth it and examine both sides before folding it in half and setting it in a neat pile.

Nothing.

She took a deep breath. All right, then—the contents of the box.

A book.

Another book.

Of course.

Aventurine lifted it out and turned it over to look at the lurid cover: reds, greens, blues—the ocean, some white villas in the distance, a shirtless man, a woman with long tousled blonde hair and smoky eyes, leaning back with a lot of throat exposed.

Passage to Portugal.

By N. B. Hallsey.

Aventurine rocked back on her heels. She dropped the book as though poisoned, and convulsively wiped her hands on her jeans. One of Nicola's bodice-rippers, in a box, in Genevieve's upstairs closet, addressed to Micheline at an address in Lisbon.

And downstairs, Genevieve, the old spy, sat gazing out the French windows into the rainy November garden. Surprisingly still, as though her batteries were running down.

Yes. No. Aventurine slid down onto the floor and slumped against the bed, her head in her hands. She tried and failed to gather her thoughts. Genevieve was an old woman. How many times had she repeated that line since they two had met? That, in fact, had been the impetus for their meeting: an old woman with a checkered past had to be sure that her story was told before her death. Even then Genevieve had surprised Avi, with her vigor, her determination, her sense of—yes—adventure and secrecy. But she was still an old woman.

And old women died.

Aventurine wouldn't think of that now. She wouldn't. She had lived nearly all her life without the abrasiveness that was Genevieve in it; but now she couldn't imagine a world without the old spy. Wouldn't imagine it.

Get a grip, she ordered herself, pressing the balls of her hands into her eyes. *Stop this.* Genevieve was right downstairs, drinking tea, communing with that foul-tempered cat. And right now, there was something far more immediate to think about: this book. Of

Nicola's, that Genevieve had been intending, at some point, to mail to Micheline in Lisbon.

A bodice-ripper.

Avi turned to the cover again, to the illustration hinting at passion, at wild abandoned sex.

The thoughts whirled about like frantic things, and she tried to reach for them, grasp them.

Something to do with Shep.

Oh, no. *Oh, no.*

Aventurine flipped to the author photo, the one she'd come to know so well: Nicola, in the hat.

Nicola, their half-sister.

Oh, no.

She clattered down the staircase, nearly tumbling in her haste, and grasping the railing to keep from breaking her neck. She dropped the book, and it turned end over end on its way to the landing. It came to rest near the umbrella stand next to the front door.

Breathless, Aventurine put a hand to the stitch in her side, and retrieved the book. Then she turned to the parlor.

"Tell me," she said as she entered, "that this doesn't mean what I think it means."

She was stopped by a gust of wind from the open French window.

The chair before it was empty.

She took a few steps forward, numbly. On the high back, the orange cat took one look at her and hissed.

Acknowledgments

To Dido, for the theme song to *Aventurine on the Border*: "My Lover's Gone" from the album *No Angel*.

To Duolingo, for the nearly four years of Welsh lessons, and for character names. *Fodd bynnag, gall Owen gadw'r pannas.*

To Bram Stoker, who wasn't the reason why I went to Whitby, but who did prepare the way, with *Dracula*. He wasn't the reason I blew out my knee there, either.

To the members of the Writers' Workshop class at CHS, who listened to scenes from this story, five minutes at a time.

To my eldest daughter Molly, and granddaughter Cecilia, who tended to Toast when I had to go look at things.

To John Ford, who answered all the mundane questions without laughing at me very much at all. And introduced me to espresso martinis in Seven Dials.

To Bar Torelli, for my very first pastel de nata. I'd been waiting for that all my life.

To the Sussex Arms and its purple Concorde splendor, to which I keep returning. For more research, don't you know?

To Julia Hawkes-Moore and Roger O'Neill, for first taking me to The Kingdom of Hay and the Honesty Book Shop. *Diolch i chi'ch dau, mwy nag y gallaf ei ddweud, fy ffrindiau.*

To the Swan Hotel in Hay, and its proprietor, for taking good care of me, and bringing me a pancake for Pancake Day, when I was worried I would miss it.

To Ian Blake, again, for talking process, and for all the research help. All of it. Including the tax deductible stuff.

And as always, to Brenda Prescott and Rebecca Bearden Welsh, for being my best friends and strongest supporters. What would I do without the Simply Not Done Monday night Zoom meetings?

About the Author

Anne Britting Oleson lives and writes in a small town in Central Maine. A frequent traveler to the U.K., she has published seven previous novels, including *The Springs* (Encircle Publications, March 2023), and the Aventurine Morrow Thrillers, *Aventurine and the Reckoning* (Encircle Publications, January 2022), *Aventurine on the Bailgate* (Encircle Publications, September 2023), and *Aventurine on the Border* (Encircle Publications, June 2024), as well as four poetry chapbooks. She has three children, five grandchildren, and two cats. Anne is currently working on her next Aventurine Morrow novel. Follow Books by Anne Britting Oleson on Facebook and @ annebrittingoleson on Instagram for the latest news.

If you enjoyed this book,
please consider writing a review
and sharing it with other readers.

Many of our authors are happy to participate in
Book Club and Reader Group discussions.
For more information, contact us at info@encirclepub.com.

Thank you,
Encircle Publications

For news about more exciting new fiction, join us at:

Facebook: www.facebook.com/encirclepub

Instagram: www.instagram.com/encirclepublications

Sign up for the Encircle Publications newsletter:
eepurl.com/cs8taP

www.ingramcontent.com/pod-product-compliance
Lightning Source LLC
Chambersburg PA
CBHW050152120726
47903CB00002B/597